The Humans

MATT HAIG

SIMON & SCHUSTER
New York   London   Toronto   Sydney   New Delhi

Simon & Schuster
1230 Avenue of the Americas
New York, NY 10020

First Simon & Schuster hardcover edition July 2013
Originally published in Great Britain in 2013 by Canongate Books.

SIMON & SCHUSTER and colophon are registered trademarks
of Simon & Schuster, Inc.

For information about special discounts for bulk purchases,
please contact Simon & Schuster Special Sales at 1-866-506-1949
or business@simonandschuster.com.

The Simon & Schuster Speakers Bureau can bring authors
to your live event. For more information or to book an event
contact the Simon & Schuster Speakers Bureau at 1-866-248-3049
or visit our website at www.simonspeakers.com.

Manufactured in the United States of America

10 9 8 7 6 5 4 3 2 1

Library of Congress Cataloging-in-Publication Data
Haig, Matt, 1975–
  The humans : a novel / Matt Haig. — First Simon & Schuster
hardcover edition.
  pages   cm
1. Aliens — Fiction. 2. Science fiction. I. Title.
  PR6108.A39H86 2013
  823'.92 — dc23
                                    2013003203

ISBN 978-1-4767-2791-2
ISBN 978-1-4767-2792-9 (ebook)

To Andrea, Lucas, and Pearl

I have just got a new theory of eternity.
　　　　　　　　　　　　—ALBERT EINSTEIN

Contents

The Humans

Preface: An Illogical Hope in the Face of Overwhelming Adversity

I know that some of you reading this are convinced humans are a myth, but I am here to state that they do actually exist. For those that don't know, a human is a real bipedal life form of midrange intelligence, living a largely deluded existence on a small, waterlogged planet in a very lonely corner of the universe.

For the rest of you, and those who sent me, humans are in many respects exactly as strange as you would expect them to be. Certainly it is true that on a first sighting you would be appalled by their physical appearance.

Their faces alone contain all manner of hideous curiosities. A protuberant central nose, thin-skinned lips, primitive external auditory organs known as "ears," tiny eyes, and unfathomably pointless eyebrows. All of which take a long time to mentally absorb and accept.

The manners and social customs too are a baffling enigma at first. Their conversation topics are very rarely the things they want to be talking about, and I could write ninety-seven books on body shame and clothing etiquette before you would get even close to understanding them.

Oh, and let's not forget the Things They Do to Make Themselves Happy That Actually Make Them Miserable. This is an infinite list. It includes shopping, watching TV, taking the better job, getting the bigger house, writing a semiautobiographical novel, educating their young, making their skin look mildly less old, and harboring a vague desire to believe there might be a meaning to it all.

Yes, it is all very amusing, in a painful kind of way. But I have discovered human poetry while on Earth. One of these poets, the very best one (her name was Emily Dickinson), said this: "I dwell in possibility." So let us humor ourselves and do the same. Let us open our minds entirely, for what you are about to read will need every prejudice you may have to stand aside in the name of understanding.

And let us consider this: what if there actually *is* a meaning to human life? And what if—humor me—life on Earth is something not just to fear and ridicule but also to cherish? What then?

Some of you may know what I have done by now, but none of you know the reason. This document, this guide, this account—call it what you will—will make everything clear. I plead with you to read this book with an open mind, and to work out for yourself the true value of human life.

Let there be peace.

PART ONE

I Took My Power in My Hand

The Man I Was Not

So, what is this?

You ready?

Okay. Inhale. I will tell you.

This book, this actual book, is set right *here,* on Earth. It is about the meaning of life and nothing at all. It is about what it takes to kill somebody, and save them. It is about love and dead poets and wholenut peanut butter. It's about matter and antimatter, everything and nothing, hope and hate. It's about a forty-one-year-old female historian called Isobel and her fifteen-year-old son called Gulliver and the cleverest mathematician in the world. It is, in short, about how to become a human.

But let me state the obvious. I was not one. That first night, in the cold and the dark and the wind, I was nowhere near. Before I read *Cosmopolitan,* in the garage, I had never even seen this written language. I realize that this could be your first time too. To give you an idea of the way people here consume stories, I have put this book together as a human would. The words I use are human words, typed in a human font, laid out consecutively in the human style. With your almost instantaneous ability to translate even the most exotic and primitive linguistic forms, I trust comprehension should not be a problem.

Now, to reiterate, I was not Professor Andrew Martin. I was like you.

Professor Andrew Martin was merely a role. A disguise. Someone I needed to be in order to complete a task. A task that had begun with his abduction and death. (I am conscious this is setting a grim tone; I will resolve not to mention death again for at least the rest of this page.)

The point is that I was not a forty-three-year-old mathematician—husband, father—who taught at Cambridge University and who had devoted the last eight years of his life to solving a mathematical problem that had so far proved insolvable. Prior to arriving on Earth I did not have midbrown hair that fell in a natural side parting. Equally, I did not have an opinion on *The Planets* by Holtz or Talking Heads' second album, because I did not agree with the concept of music. Or I shouldn't have, anyway. And how could I believe that Australian wine was automatically inferior to wine sourced from other regions on the planet when I had never drunk anything other than liquid nitrogen?

Belonging as I did to a postmarital species, I need hardly say that I hadn't been a neglectful husband with an eye for one of my students any more than I had been a man who walked his English springer spaniel—a category of hairy domestic deity otherwise known as "dog"—as an excuse to leave the house. Nor had I had written books on mathematics or insisted that my publishers use an author photograph that was now nearing its fifteenth anniversary.

No, I wasn't that man.

I had no feeling for that man whatsoever. And yet he had been real, as real as you and I, a real mammalian life-form, a diploid eukaryotic primate who, five minutes before midnight, had been sitting at his desk, staring at his computer screen and drinking black coffee (don't worry, I shall explain coffee and my misadventures with it a little later). A life-form who may or may not have jumped out of his chair as the breakthrough came, as his mind arrived at a place no human mind had ever reached before, the very edge of knowledge.

And at some point shortly after his breakthrough he had been taken by the hosts. My employers. I had even met him, for the very briefest of moments. Enough for the—wholly incomplete—reading to be made. It was complete physically, just not mentally. You see, you can clone human brains but not what is stored inside them, not much of it anyway, so I had to learn a lot of things for myself. I was a forty-three-year-old newborn on planet Earth. It would become annoying to me, later on, that I had never met him *properly,* as meeting him properly would have been extremely useful. He could have told me about Maggie, for one thing. (Oh, how I wish he had told me about Maggie!)

However, any knowledge I gained was not going to alter the simple fact that I had to halt progress. That is what I was there for. To destroy evidence of the breakthrough Professor Andrew Martin had made. Evidence that lived not only in computers but in living human beings.

Now, where should we start?

I suppose there is only one place. We should start with when I was hit by the car.

Detached Nouns and Other Early Trials for the Language Learner

Yes, like I said, we should start with when I was hit by the car.

We have to, really. Because for quite a while before that there was nothing. There was nothing and nothing and nothing and—

Something.

Me, standing there, on the road.

Once there, I had several immediate reactions. First, what was with the weather? I was not really used to weather you had to think about. But this was England, a part of Earth where thinking about the weather was the chief human activity. And for good reason. Second, where was the computer? There was meant to be a computer. Not that I actually knew what Professor Martin's computer would look like. Maybe it looked like a road. Third, what was that noise? A kind of muted roaring noise. And fourth, it was night. Being something of a homebird, I was not really accustomed to night. And even if I had been, this wasn't just any night. It was the kind of night I had never known. This was night to the power of night to the power of night. This was night cubed. A sky full of uncompromising darkness, with no stars and no moon. Where were the suns? Were there even suns? The cold suggested there might not have been. The cold was a shock. The cold hurt my lungs, and the harsh wind beating against my skin caused me to shake. I wondered if humans ever went outside. They must have been insane if they did.

Inhaling was difficult, at first. And this was a concern. After all, inhaling really was one of the most important requirements of being a human. But I eventually got the knack.

And then another worry. I was not where I was meant to be, that was increasingly clear. I was meant to be where he had been. I was meant to be in an office, but this wasn't an office. I knew that, even then. Not unless it was an office that contained an entire sky, complete with those dark, congregating clouds and that unseen moon.

It took a while—too long—to understand the situation. I did not know at that time what a road was, but I can now tell you that a road is something that connects points of departure with points of arrival. This is important. On Earth, you see, you can't just move from one place to another place instantaneously. The technology isn't there yet. It is nowhere near there yet. No. On Earth you have to spend a lot of time traveling in between places, be it on roads or on rail tracks or in careers or relationships.

This particular type of road was a motorway. A motorway is the most advanced type of road there is, which as with most forms of human advancement essentially means accidental death is considerably more probable than formerly. My naked feet were standing on something called tarmac, feeling its strange and brutal texture. I looked at my left hand. It seemed so crude and unfamiliar, almost hilariously so, and yet my laughter halted when I realized this fingered freaky thing was a part of me. I was a stranger to myself. Oh and by the way, the muted roaring was still there, minus the muted part.

It was then I noticed what was approaching me at considerable speed.

The lights.

White, wide, and low, they may as well have been the bright eyes of a fast-moving plain-sweeper, silver-backed, and now screaming. It was trying to slow and swerve.

There was no time for me to move out of the way. There had been, but not now. I had waited too long.

And so it hit me with great, uncompromising force. A force which hurled me off the ground and sent me flying. Only not real flying, because humans can't fly, no matter how much they flap their limbs. The only real option was pain, which I felt right until I landed, after which I returned to nothing again.

Nothing and nothing and—

Something.

A man wearing clothes stood over me. The proximity of his face troubled me.

No. A few degrees more than troubled.

I was repulsed, terrified. I had never seen anything like this man. The face seemed so alien, full of unfathomable openings and protrusions. The nose, in particular, bothered me. It seemed to my innocent eyes as if there was something else inside him, pushing through. I looked lower. Noticed his clothes. He was wearing what I would later realize was a shirt and a tie, trousers, and shoes. The exact clothes he should have been wearing, and yet they seemed so exotic I didn't know whether to laugh or scream. He was looking at my injuries. Or rather, *for them.*

I checked my left hand. It hadn't been touched. The car had collided with my legs, then my torso, but my hand was fine.

"It's a miracle," he said quietly, as though it were a secret.

But the words were meaningless.

He stared into my face and raised his voice, to compete with the sound of cars. "What are you doing out here?"

Again, nothing. It was just a mouth moving, making noise.

I could tell it was a simple language, but I needed to hear at least a hundred words of a new language before I could piece the whole grammatical jigsaw together. Don't judge me on this. I know some of you only need ten or so, or just a single adjectival clause somewhere. But languages were never my thing. Part of my aversion to travel, I suppose. I must reiterate this. I did not want to be sent here. It was a job that someone had to do and—following my blasphemous talk at the Museum of Quadratic Equations, my so-called crime against mathematical purity—the hosts believed it to be a suitable punishment. They knew it was a job no one in their right mind would choose to do and, though my task was important, they knew I (like you) belonged to the most advanced race in the known universe and so would be up to the job.

"I know you from somewhere. I recognize your face. Who are you?"

I felt tired. That was the trouble with teleportation and matter shifting and bio-setting. It really took it out of you. And even though it put it back into you, energy was always the price.

I slipped into darkness and enjoyed dreams tinged with violet and indigo and home. I dreamt of cracked eggs and prime numbers and ever-shifting skylines.

And then I awoke.

I was inside a strange vehicle, strapped to primitive heart-reading equipment. Two humans, male and female (the female's appearance confirmed my worst fears: within this species, ugliness does not discriminate between genders), dressed in green. They seemed to be asking me something in quite an agitated fashion. Maybe it was because I was using my new upper limbs to rip off the crudely de-signed electrocardiographic equipment. They tried to restrain me, but they apparently had very little understanding of the mathematics involved, and so with relative ease I managed to leave the two green-clothed humans on the floor, writhing around in pain.

I rose to my feet, noticing just how much gravity there was on this planet, as the driver turned to ask me an even more urgent ques-tion. The vehicle was moving fast, and the undulating sound waves of the siren were an undeniable distraction, but I opened the door and leapt toward the soft vegetation at the side of the road. My body rolled. I hid. And then, once it was safe to appear, I got to my feet. Compared to a human hand, a human foot is relatively untrou-bling, toes aside.

I stood there for a while, just staring at all those odd cars, confined to the ground, evidently reliant on fossil fuel and each making more noise than it took to power a polygon generator. And the even odder sight of the humans—all clothed, inside, holding on to circular steer-control equipment and, sometimes, extrabiological telecommunications devices.

I have come to a planet where the most intelligent life-form still has to drive its own cars . . .

Never before had I so appreciated the simple splendors you and

I have grown up with. The eternal light. The smooth, floating traffic. The advanced plant life. The sweetened air. The nonweather. Oh, gentle readers, you really have no idea.

Cars blared high-frequency horns as they passed me. Wide-eyed, gape-mouthed faces stared out of windows. I didn't understand it: I looked as ugly as any of them. Why wasn't I blending in? What was I doing wrong? Maybe it was because I wasn't in a car. Maybe that's how humans lived, permanenetly contained in cars. Or maybe it was because I wasn't wearing any clothes. It was a cold night, but could it really have been something so trivial as a lack of artificial body covering? *No. It couldn't be that.*

I looked up at the sky.

There was evidence of the moon now, veiled by thin cloud. It too seemed to be gawping down at me with the same sense of shock. But the stars were still blanketed, out of sight. I wanted to see them. I wanted to feel their comfort.

On top of all this, rain was a distinct possibility. I hated rain. To me, as to most of you dome dwellers, rain was a terror of almost mythological proportions. I needed to find what I was looking for before the clouds opened.

There was a rectangular aluminum sign ahead of me. Nouns minus context were always tricky for the language learner, but the arrow was pointing only one way, so I followed it.

Humans kept on lowering their windows and shouting things at me, above the sound of their engines. Sometimes this action seemed good-humored, as they were spitting oral fluid, in my direction, orminurk-style. So I spat back, in a friendly fashion, trying to hit their fast-moving faces. This seemed to encourage more shouting, but I tried not to mind.

Soon, I told myself, I would understand what the heavily articulated greeting "get off the fucking road you fucking wanker" actually meant. In the meantime I kept walking, got past the sign, and saw an illuminated but disconcertingly unmoving building by the side of the road.

I will go to it, I told myself. *I will go to it and find some answers.*

Texaco

The building was called "Texaco." It stood there shining in the night with a terrible stillness, like it was waiting to come alive.

As I walked toward it, I noticed it was some kind of refill station. Cars were parked there, under a horizontal canopy, and stationed next to simple-looking fuel-delivery systems. It was confirmed: the cars did absolutely nothing for themselves. They were practically brain-dead, if they even had brains.

The humans who were refueling their vehicles stared at me as they went inside. Trying to be as polite as possible, given my verbal limitations, I spat an ample amount of saliva toward them.

I entered the building. There was a clothed human behind the counter. Instead of his hair being on the top of his head, it covered the bottom half of his face. His body was more spherical than those of other humans, so he was marginally better-looking. From the scent of hexanoic acid and androsterone I could tell personal hygiene wasn't one of his top priorities. He stared at my (admittedly distressing) genitalia and then pressed something behind the counter. I spat, but the greeting was unreciprocated. Maybe I had gotten it wrong about the spitting.

All this salivary off-loading was making me thirsty, so I went over to a humming refrigerated unit full of brightly colored cylindrical objects. I picked one of them up and opened it, a can of liquid called "Diet Coke." It tasted extremely sweet, with a trace of phosphoric acid. It was disgusting. It burst out of my mouth almost the moment it entered. Then I consumed something else. A foodstuff wrapped in synthetic packaging. This was, I would later realize, a planet of things wrapped inside things. Food inside clothing. Bodies inside wrappers. Contempt inside smiles. Everything was hidden away. The foodstuff was called "Mars." That got a little bit further down my throat, but only far enough for me to discover I had a gag reflex. I closed the door and saw a container with the words "Pringles" and "Barbecue" on it. I opened it up and started to eat. They tasted okay—a bit like sorp-cake—and I crammed as many as I could into my mouth. I wondered when I had last actually fed myself with no droid assistance. I seriously couldn't remember. Not since infancy, that was for sure.

"You can't do that. You can't just eat stuff. You've got to pay for it."

The man behind the counter was talking to me. I still had little idea of what he was saying, but from the volume and frequency I sensed it wasn't good. Also, I observed that his skin—in the places on his face where it was visible—was changing color.

I noticed the lighting above my head, and I blinked.

I placed my hand over my mouth and made a noise. Then I held it at arm's length and made the same noise, noting the difference.

It was comforting to know that even in the most remote corner of the universe the laws of sound and light obeyed themselves, although it has to be said they seemed a little more lackluster here.

There were shelves full of what I would shortly know as "magazines," nearly all of which had faces with near-identical smiles on the front of them. Twenty-six noses. Fifty-two eyes. It was an intimidating sight.

I picked up one of these magazines as the man picked up the phone.

On Earth, the media is still locked in a precapsule age, and most of it has to be read via an electronic device or via a printed media made of a thin, chemically pulped tree derivative known as paper. Magazines are very popular, despite no human's ever feeling better for having read them. Indeed, their chief purpose is to generate a sense of inferiority in the reader that consequently leads to a feeling of needing to buy something, which the humans then do, and then feel even worse, and so need to buy another magazine to see what they can buy next. It is an eternal and unhappy spiral that goes by the name of capitalism, and it is really quite popular. The particular publication I was holding was called *Cosmopolitan,* and I realized that if nothing else, it would help me grasp the language.

It didn't take long. Written human languages are preposterously simple, as they are made up almost entirely of words. I had interpolated the entire written language by the end of the first article, in addition to the touch that can boost your mood—as well as your relationship. Also, orgasms, I realized, were an incredibly big deal. It seemed orgasms were the central tenet of life here. Maybe this was the only meaning humans had on this planet. Their purpose was simply to pursue the enlightenment of orgasm. A few seconds of relief from the surrounding dark.

But reading wasn't speaking, and my new vocal equipment was still sitting there, in my mouth and throat, like yet more food I didn't know how to swallow.

I placed the magazine back on the shelf. There was a thin vertical piece of reflective metal beside the stand, allowing me a partial glimpse of myself. I too had a protruding nose. And lips. Hair. Ears. So much *externality.* It was a very inside-out kind of look. Plus a large lump in the center of my neck. Very thick eyebrows.

A piece of information came to me, something I remembered from what the hosts had told me. *Professor Andrew Martin.*

My heart raced. A surge of panic. This was what I was now. This was who I had become. I tried to comfort myself by remembering that it was just temporary.

At the bottom of the magazine stand were some newspapers. There were photographs of more smiling faces, and some of dead bodies too, lying beside demolished buildings. Next to the newspapers was a small collection of maps. A *Road Map of the British Isles* was among them. Perhaps I was on the British Isles. I picked up the map and tried to leave the building.

The man hung up the phone.

The door was locked.

Information arrived, unprompted: *Fitzwilliam College, Cambridge University.*

"You're not bloody leaving," said the man, in words I was

beginning to comprehend. "The police are on their way. I've locked the door."

To his bafflement, I then proceeded to open the door. I stepped out and heard a distant siren. I listened and realized the noise was only three hundred meters away and getting rapidly closer. I began to move, running as fast as I could away from the road and up a grass embankment toward another flat area.

There were lots of stationary haulage vehicles, parked in an ordered geometric fashion.

This was such a strange world. Of course, when viewed afresh, all worlds are strange, but this one must have been strangest of all. I tried to see the similarity. I told myself that here all things were still made of atoms, and that those atoms would work precisely as atoms always do. They would move toward each other if there was distance between them. If there was no distance between them, they would repel each other. That was the most basic law of the universe, and it applied to all things, even here. There was comfort in that. The knowledge that wherever you were in the universe, the small things were always exactly the same. Attracting and repelling. It was only by not looking closely enough that you saw difference.

But still, right then, difference was all I saw.

The car with the siren was now pulling into the fueling station, flashing blue light, so I hid among the parked lorries for a few minutes. I was freezing and crouched into myself, my whole body shaking and my testicles shrinking. (A male human's testicles were the most attractive thing about him, I realized, and vastly unappreciated by humans themselves, who would very often rather look at almost anything else, including smiling faces.) Before the police car left, I heard a voice behind me. Not a police officer but the driver of the vehicle I was crouched behind.

"Hey, what are you doing? Fuck off away from my lorry."

I ran away, my bare feet hitting hard ground scattered with random pieces of grit. And then I was on grass, running across a field, and I kept on in the same direction until I reached another road. This one was much narrower and had no traffic at all.

I opened the map, found the line which matched the curve of this other road and saw that word: "Cambridge."

I headed there.

As I walked and breathed in that nitrogen-rich air, the idea of myself was forming. Professor Andrew Martin. With the name came facts, sent to me across space by those who had sent me.

I was to be a married man. I was forty-three years old, the exact midpoint in a human life. I had a son. I was the professor who had just solved the most significant mathematical puzzle the humans had ever faced. I had, only three short hours ago, advanced the human race beyond anyone's imagining. The facts made me queasy, but I kept on heading in the direction of Cambridge to see what else these humans had in store for me.

Corpus Christi

I was not told to provide this document of human life. That was not in my brief. Yet I feel obliged to do so to explain some remarkable features of human existence. I hope you will thereby understand why I chose to do what, by now, some of you must know I did.

Anyhow, I had always known Earth was a real place. I knew that, of course I did. I had consumed, in capsule form, the famous travelogue *The Fighting Idiots: My Time with the Humans of Water Planet 7,081.* I knew Earth was a real event in a dull and distant solar system, where not a great deal happened and where travel options for the locals were severely limited. I'd also heard that humans were a life-form of, at best, middling intelligence and prone to violence, deep sexual embarrassment, bad poetry, and walking around in circles.

But I was starting to realize that no preparation could have been enough.

By morning I was in this Cambridge place.

It was horrendously fascinating. The buildings were what I noticed first, and it was quite startling to realize that the garage hadn't been a one-off. All such structures—whether built for consumerist, habitative, or other purposes—were *static* and *stuck to the ground.*

Of course, this was meant to be my town. This was where I had lived, on and off, for over twenty years. And I would have to act like that was true, even though it was the most alien place I had ever seen in my life.

The lack of geometric imagination was startling, as there was not so much as a decagon in sight. Though I did notice that some of the buildings were larger and—relatively speaking—more ornately designed than others.

Temples to the orgasm, I imagined.

Shops were beginning to open. In human towns, I would soon learn, everywhere is a shop. Shops are to Earth dwellers what equation booths are to Vonnadorians. In one I saw lots of books in the window. I was reminded that humans have to *read* books. And that takes time. Lots of time. A human can't just swallow every book going, can't chew different tomes simultaneously, or gulp down near-infinite knowledge in a matter of seconds. They can't just pop a word capsule in their mouth like we can. Imagine! Being not only mortal but also forced to take some of that precious and limited time and read. No wonder they were a species of primitives. By the time they have read enough books to actually reach a state of knowledge where they can do anything with it, they are dead. They need to sit down and look at each word consecutively.

Later, I too would read books. And I'd find that long books—things like *War and Peace* or *The History of Western Philosophy* or *Don Quixote*—would take me a full twenty minutes. Altogether, that was an hour I was never getting back. An hour!

Understandably, humans need to know what kind of book they are about to read, because time is money and money costs time and there's no time like the present and all of that. They need to know if it is a love story. Or a murder story. Or a story about aliens. Perhaps the book they have in their hands is a war story. It wouldn't be a surprise.

There are other questions too that humans have in bookstores. Such as, is it one of those books they read to feel clever, or one of those they will pretend they never read in order to stay *looking* clever? Will it make them laugh or cry? Or will it simply force them to stare out of the window watching the tracks of raindrops? Is it a true story? Or is it a false one? Is it the kind of story that will work on their brain or one which aims for lower organs? Is it one of those books that ends up acquiring religious followers or getting burned by them? Is it a book about mathematics or—like everything else in the universe—simply *because of it*? And also, of course, there is the ultimate, all-important question: does it have a dog in it? (*This* book, by the way, does indeed have a dog in it, and this fact would very much excite a human but unfortunately does nothing for you.)

Yes, there are lots of questions. And even more books. So, so many. Humans in their typical human way have written far too many to get through. Reading is added to that great pile of things—work, love, sexual prowess, the words they didn't say when they really needed to say them—that they are bound to feel a bit dissatisfied about.

So, humans need to know about a book. Just as they need to know, when they apply for a job, if it will cause them to lose their mind at the age of fifty-nine and lead them to jump out of the office window. Or if, when they go on a first date, the person who is now making witticisms about his year in Cambodia will one day leave her for a younger woman called Francesca who runs her own public relations firm and says "Kafkaesque" without having ever read Kafka.

Anyway, there I was walking into this bookshop and having a look at some of the books out on the tables. I noticed two of the females who worked there were laughing and pointing toward my midsection. Again, I was confused. Weren't men meant to go in bookshops? Was there some kind of war of ridicule going on between the genders? Did booksellers spend all their time mocking their customers? Or was it that I wasn't wearing any clothes? Who knew? Anyway, it was a little distracting, especially as the only laughter I had ever heard had been the fur-muffled chuckle of an ipsoid. I tried to focus on the books themselves and decided to look at those stacked on the shelves.

I soon noticed that the system they were using was alphabetical and related to the initial letter in the last name of each author. As the human alphabet only has 26 letters, it was an incredibly simple system, and I soon found the *M*s.

One of these *M* books was called *The Dark Ages* and it was by Isobel Martin. I pulled it off the shelf. It had a little sign on it saying "Local Author." There was only one of them in stock, which was considerably fewer than the number of books by Andrew Martin.

For example, there were thirteen copies of an Andrew Martin book called *The Square Circle* and eleven of another one called *American Pi*. They were both about mathematics.

I picked up these books and realized they both said "£8.99" on the back. The interpolation of the entire language I had done with the aid of *Cosmopolitan* meant I knew this was the price of the books, but I did not have any money. So I waited until no one was looking (a *long* time) and then I ran very fast out of the shop.

I eventually settled into a walk, as running without clothes is not entirely compatible with external testicles, and then I started to read.

I searched both the books for the Riemann hypothesis, but I couldn't find anything except unrelated references to the long-dead German mathematician Bernhard Riemann himself.

I let the books drop to the ground.

People were really beginning to stop and stare. All around me there were things I didn't yet quite comprehend: litter, advertisements, bicycles. Uniquely human things.

I passed a large man with a long coat and a hairy face who, judging from his asymmetrical gait, seemed to be injured.

Of course, we may know brief pain but this did not seem of that type. It reminded me that this was a place of death. Things deteriorated, degenerated, and died here. The life of a human was surrounded on all sides by darkness. How on Earth did they cope?

Idiocy, from slow reading. It could only be idiocy.

This man, though, didn't seem to be coping. His eyes were full of sorrow and suffering.

"Jesus," the man mumbled. I think he was mistaking me for someone. "I've seen it all now." He smelled of bacterial infection and several other repugnant things I couldn't identify.

I thought about asking him for directions, as the map was rendered in only two dimensions and a little vague, but I wasn't up to it yet. I might have been able to say the words, but I didn't have the confidence to direct them toward such a close face, with its bulbous nose and sad pink eyes. (How did I know his eyes were sad? That is an interesting question, especially as we Vonnadorians never really feel sadness. The answer is I don't know. It was a feeling I had. A ghost inside me, maybe the ghost of the human I had become. I didn't have all his memories, but did I have other things? Was empathy part biological? All I know is it unsettled me, more than the sight of pain. Sadness seemed to me like a disease, and I worried it was contagious.) So I walked past him and, for the first time in as long as I could remember, I tried to find my own way to somewhere.

Now, I knew Professor Martin worked at the university but I had no idea what a university looked like. I guessed they wouldn't be zirconium-clad space stations hovering just beyond the atmosphere, but other than that I didn't really know. The ability to view two different buildings and say, oh this was that type of building, and that was this, well, that was simply beyond me. So I kept walking, ignoring the gasps and the laughter and feeling whichever brick or glass façade I was passing by, as though touch held more answers than sight.

And then the very worst possible thing happened. (Brace yourself, Vonnadorians.) It began to rain.

The sensation of rain on my skin and my hair was horrific, and I needed it to end. I felt so exposed. I began to jog, looking for an entry into somewhere. Anywhere. I passed a vast building with a large gate and sign outside. The sign said "The College of Corpus Christi and the Blessed Virgin Mary." Having read *Cosmopolitan,* I knew what "virgin" meant in full detail but I had a problem with some of the other words. There were smaller words too, and a different sign. These words said "Cambridge University." I used my left hand to open the gate and walked through, onto grass, heading toward the building that still had lights on.

Signs of life and warmth.

The grass was wet. The soft dampness of it repulsed me and I seriously considered screaming.

It was very neatly trimmed, this grass. I was later to realize that a neatly trimmed lawn was a powerful signifier and should have commanded in me a slight sense of fear and respect, especially in conjunction (as this was) with "grand" architecture. But right then, I was oblivious to the significance of both tidy grass and architectural grandeur and so I kept walking toward the main building.

A car stopped somewhere behind me. Again, there were blue lights flashing, sliding across the stone façade of Corpus Christi.

(Flashing blue lights on Earth = trouble.)

A man ran toward me. There was a whole crowd of other humans behind him. Where had they come from? They all seemed so sinister, in a pack, with their odd-looking clothed forms. They were aliens to me. That was the obvious part. What was less obvious was the way I seemed like an alien to them. After all, I *looked* like them. Maybe this was another human trait. Their ability to turn on themselves, to ostracize their own kind. If that was the case, it added weight to my mission. It made me understand it better.

Anyway, there I was, on the wet grass, with the man running toward me and the crowd further away. I could have run or fought, but there were too many of them—some with archaic-looking recording equipment. The man grabbed me. "Come with me, sir." I thought of my purpose. But right then I had to comply. Indeed, I just wanted to get out of the rain.

"I am Professor Andrew Martin," I said, having complete confidence that I knew how to say this phrase. And that is when I discovered the truly terrifying power of other people's laughter.

"I have a wife and a son," I said, and I gave their names. "I need to see them. Can you take me to see them?'"

"No. Not right now. No, we can't."

He held my arm tightly. I wanted, more than anything, for his hideous hand to let go. To be touched by one of them, let alone gripped, was too much. And yet I did not attempt to resist as he led me toward a vehicle.

I was supposed to draw as little attention to myself as possible while doing my task. In that, I was failing already.

You must strive to be normal.

    Yes.

You must try to be like them.

    I know.

Do not escape prematurely.

    I won't. But I don't want to be here. I want to go home.

You know you can't do that. Not yet.

    But I will run out of time. I must get to the professor's office, and to his home.

You are right. You must. But first you need to stay calm and do what they tell you. Go where they want you to go. Do what they want you to do. They must never know who sent you. Do not panic. Professor Andrew Martin is not among them now. You are. There will be time. They die, and so they have impatience. Their lives are short. Yours is not. Do not become like them. Use your gifts wisely.

    I will. But I am scared.

You have every right to be. You are among the humans.

◻ ◻ ◻

Human Clothes

They made me put on clothes.

What humans didn't know about architecture or nonradioactive isotopic helium-based fuels, they more than made up for with their knowledge of clothes. They were geniuses in the area and knew all the subtleties. And there were, I promise you, *thousands* of them.

The way clothes worked was this: there was an under layer and an outer layer. The under layer consisted of "pants" and "socks," which covered the heavily scented regions of the genitals, bottom, and feet. There was also the option of a "vest," which covered the marginally less shameful chest area. This area included the sensitive skin protrusions known as "nipples." I had no idea what purpose nipples served, though I did notice a pleasurable sensation when I tenderly stroked my fingers over them.

The outer layer of clothing seemed even more important than the under layer. This layer covered ninety-five percent of the body, leaving only the face, head hair, and hands on show. This outer layer of clothing seemed to be the key to the power structures on this planet. For instance, the two men who took me away in the car with the blue flashing lights were both wearing identical outer layers, consisting of black shoes over their socks, black trousers over their pants, and then, over their upper bodies, there was a white "shirt" and a dark, deep-space blue "jumper." On this jumper, directly over the region of their left nipple, was a rectangular badge made of a slightly finer fabric which had the words "Cambridgeshire POLICE" written on it. Their jackets were the same color and had the same badge. These were clearly the clothes to wear.

However, I soon realized what the word "police" meant. It meant police.

I couldn't believe it. I had broken the law simply by *not wearing clothes.* I was pretty sure that most humans must have known what a naked human looked like. It wasn't as though I had done something wrong while *not wearing clothes.* At least, not yet.

They placed me inside a small room that was, in perfect accord with all human rooms, a shrine to the rectangle. The funny thing was that although this room looked precisely no better or worse than anything else in that police station, or indeed that planet, the officers seemed to think it was a particular punishment to be placed in this place—a "cell"—more than any other room. *They are in a body that dies,* I chuckled to myself, *and they worry more about being locked in a room!*

This was where they told me to get dressed. To "cover myself up." So I picked up those clothes and did my best, and then, once I had worked out which limb went through which opening, they said I had to wait for an hour. Which I did. Of course, I could have escaped. But I realized it was more likely that I would find what I needed by staying there, with the police and their computers. Plus, I remembered what I had been told. *Use your gifts wisely. You must try and be like them. You must strive to be normal.*

Then the door opened.

Questions

There were two men.

These were different men. These men weren't wearing the same clothes, but they did have pretty much the same face. Not just the eyes, protruding nose, and mouth but also a shared look of complacent misery. In the stark light I felt not a little afraid. They took me to another room for questioning. This was interesting knowledge: you could only ask questions in certain rooms. There were rooms for sitting and thinking and rooms for inquisition.

They sat down.

Anxiety prickled my skin. The kind of anxiety you could only feel on this planet. The anxiety that came from the fact that the only ones who knew who I was were a long way away. They were as far away as it was possible to be.

"Professor Andrew Martin," said one of the men, leaning back in his chair. "We've done a bit of research. We googled you. You're quite a big fish in academic circles."

The man stuck out his bottom lip and displayed the palms of his hands. He wanted me to say something. What would they plan on doing to me if I didn't? What could they have done?

I had little idea what "googling" me meant, but whatever it was, I couldn't say I had felt it. I didn't really understand what being a "big fish in academic circles" meant either, though I must say it was a kind of relief—given the dimensions of the room—to realize they knew what a circle was.

I nodded my head, still a little uneasy about speaking. It involved too much concentration and coordination.

Then the other one spoke. I switched my gaze to his face. The key difference between them, I suppose, was in the lines of hair above their eyes. This one kept his eyebrows permanently raised, causing the skin of his forehead to wrinkle.

"What have you got to tell us?"

I thought long and hard. It was time to speak. "I am the most intelligent human on the planet. I am a mathematical genius. I have made important contributions to many branches of mathematics, such as group theory, number theory, and geometry. My name is Professor Andrew Martin."

They gave each other a look and released a brief air chuckle out of their noses.

"Are you thinking this is funny?" the first one said, aggressively. "Committing a public order offense? Does that amuse you? Yeah?"

"No. I was just telling you who I am."

"We've established that," the officer said, who kept his eyebrows low and close, like doona-birds in mating season. "The last bit anyway. What we haven't established is: what were you doing walking around without your clothes on at half past eight in the morning?"

"I am a professor at Cambridge University. I am married to Isobel Martin. I have a son, Gulliver. I would very much like to see them, please. Just let me see them."

They looked at their papers. "Yes," the first one said. "We see you are a teaching fellow at Fitzwilliam College. But that doesn't explain why you were walking naked around the grounds of Corpus Christi College. You are either off your head or a danger to society or both."

"I do not like wearing clothes," I said, with quite delicate precision. "They chafe. They are uncomfortable around my genitals." And then, remembering all I had learned from *Cosmopolitan* magazine, I leaned in toward them and added what I thought would be the clincher. "They may seriously hinder my chances of achieving a tantric full-body orgasm."

It was then they made a decision, and the decision was to submit me to a psychiatric test. This essentially meant going to *another* rectilinear room to have to face looking at *another* human with *another* protruding nose. This human was female. She was called Priti, which was pronounced "pretty" and means pretty. Unfortunate, given that she was human and, by her very nature, vomit-provoking.

"Now," she said, "I would like to start by asking you something very simple. I'm wondering if you've been under any pressure recently?"

I was confused. What kind of pressure was she talking about? Atmospheric? Gravitational? "Yes," I said. "A lot. Everywhere, there is some kind of pressure."

It seemed like the right answer.

Coffee

She told me she had been talking to the university. This, alone, made little sense. How, for instance, was that done? But then she told me this: "They tell me you've been working long hours, even by the standards of your peers. They seem very upset about the whole thing. But they are worried about you. As is your wife."

"My wife?"

I knew I had one, and I knew her name, but I didn't really understand what it actually meant to have a wife. Marriage was a truly alien concept. There probably weren't enough editions of *Cosmopolitan* on the planet for me to ever understand it. She explained. I was even more confused. Marriage was a "loving union," which meant two people who loved each other stayed together forever. But that seemed to suggest that love was quite a weak force and needed marriage to bolster it. Also, the union could be broken with something called "divorce," which meant there was—as far as I could see—very little point to it, in logical terms. But then, I had no real idea what "love" was, even though it had been one of the most frequently used words in the magazine I'd read. It remained a mystery. And so I asked her to explain that too, and by this point I was bewildered, overdosing on all this bad logic. It sounded like delusion.

"Do you want a coffee?"

"Yes," I said.

So the coffee came and I tasted it—a hot, foul, acidic, dual-carbon compound liquid—and I spat it out all over her. A major breach of human etiquette: apparently, I was meant to *swallow* it.

"What the—" She stood up and patted herself dry, showing intense concern for her shirt. After that there were more questions. Impossible stuff, like what was my address? What did I do in my spare time, to relax?

Of course, I could have fooled her. Her mind was so soft and malleable and its neural oscillations were obviously so weak that even with my as then still-limited command of the language, I could have told her I was perfectly fine and that it was none of her business and could she please leave me alone. I had already worked out the rhythm and the optimal frequency I would have needed. But I didn't.

Do not escape prematurely. Do not panic. There will be time.

The truth is, I was quite terrified. My heart had begun racing for no obvious reason. My palms were sweating. Something about the room, and its proportions, coupled with so much contact with this irrational species, was setting me off. Everything here was a test.

If you failed one test, there was a test to see why. It was a planet full of tests and meta-tests. I suppose they loved tests so much because they believed in free will. Ha! Humans, I was discovering, believed they were in control of their own lives, and so they were in awe of questions and tests, as these made them feel like they had a certain mastery over other people, who had failed in their choices and who had not worked hard enough on the right answers. And by the end of the last failed test many were sat, as I was soon sat, in a mental hospital, swallowing a mind-blanking pill called diazepam and placed in another empty room full of right angles. Only this time, I was also inhaling the distressing scent of the hydrogen chloride they used to annihilate bacteria.

My task was going to be easy, I decided in that room. The meat of it, I mean. And the reason it was going to be easy was that I had the same sense of indifference toward them as they had toward single-celled organisms. *I could wipe a few of them out, no problem, and for a greater cause than hygiene.* But what I didn't realize was that when it came to that sneaking, camouflaged, untouchable giant known as the Future, I was as vulnerable as anyone.

Mad People

Humans, as a rule, don't like mad people unless they are good at painting, and only then once they are dead. But the definition of mad, on Earth, seems to be very unclear and inconsistent. What is perfectly sane in one era turns out to be insane in another. The earliest humans walked around naked with no problem. Certain humans, in humid rain forests mainly, still do so. So, we must conclude that madness is a question sometimes of time and sometimes of postcode.

Basically, the key rule is, if you want to appear sane on Earth, you have to be in the right place, wearing the right clothes, saying the right things, and only stepping on the right kind of grass.

The Cubic Root of 912,673

After a while, my wife came to visit. Isobel Martin, in person. Author of *The Dark Ages*. I wanted to be repulsed by her, as that would make everything easier. I wanted to be horrified and, of course, I was, because the whole species was horrific to me. On that first encounter I thought she was hideous. I was frightened of her. I was frightened of everything here, now. It was an undeniable truth. To be on Earth was to be frightened. I was even frightened by the sight of my own hands.

But anyway, Isobel. When I first saw her, I saw nothing but a few trillion poorly arranged, mediocre cells. She had a pale face and tired eyes and a narrow but still protruding *nose*. There was something very poised and upright about her, something very contained. She seemed, even more than most, to be holding something back. My mouth dried just from my looking at her. I suppose if there was a challenge with this particular human it was that I was meant to know her very well, and also that I was going to be spending more time with her, to glean the information I needed, before doing what I had to do.

She came to see me in my room, while a nurse watched. It was, of course, another test. Everything in human life was a test. That was why they all looked so stressed out.

I was dreading her hugging me or kissing me or blowing air into my ear or any of those other human things the magazine had told me about, but she didn't. She didn't even seem to *want* to do that. What she wanted to do was sit there and stare at me, as if I were the cubic root of 912,673 and she was trying to work me out. And indeed, I tried very hard to act as harmoniously as that. The indestructible 97. My favorite prime.

Isobel smiled and nodded at the nurse, but when she sat down and faced me, I realized she was exhibiting a few universal signs of fear—tight facial muscles, dilated pupils, fast breathing. I paid special attention to her hair now. She had dark hair growing out of the top and rear of her head that extended to just above her shoulders, where it halted abruptly to form a straight horizontal line. This style was known as a "bob." She sat tall in her chair with a straight back, and her neck was long, as if her head had fallen out with her body and wanted nothing more to do with it. I would later discover that she was forty-one and had an appearance that passed for beautiful, or at least *plainly* beautiful, on this planet. But right then she had just another human face. And human faces were the last of the human codes that I would learn.

She inhaled. "How are you feeling?"

"I don't know. I don't remember a lot of things. My mind is a little bit scrambled, especially about this morning. Listen, has anyone been to my office? Since yesterday?"

This confused her. "I don't know. How would I know that? I doubt very much they'll be in over the weekend. And anyway you're the only one who has the keys. Please, Andrew, what happened? Have you suffered an accident? Have they tested you for amnesia? Why were you out of the house at that time? Tell me what you were doing. I woke up and you weren't there."

"I just needed to get out. That is all. I needed to be outside."

She was agitated now. "I was thinking all sorts of things. I checked the whole house, but there was no sign of you. And the car was still there, and your bike, and you weren't picking up your phone, and it was three in the morning, Andrew. Three in the morning."

I nodded. She wanted answers, but I had only questions. "Where is our son? Gulliver? Why is he not with you?"

This answer confused her even more. "He's at my mother's," she said. "I could hardly bring him here. He's very upset. After everything else this is, you know, hard for him."

Nothing she was telling me was information I needed. So I decided to be more direct. "Do you know what I did yesterday? Do you know what I achieved while I was at work?"

I knew that however she answered this, the truth remained the same. I would have to kill her. Not then. Not there. But somewhere, and soon. Still I had to know what she knew. Or what she might have said to others.

The nurse wrote something down at this point.

Isobel ignored my question and leaned in closer toward me, lowering her voice. "They think you have suffered a mental breakdown. They don't call it that, of course. But that is what they think. I've been asked lots of questions. It was like facing the Grand Inquisitor."

"That's all there is around here, isn't it? Questions."

I braved another glance at her face and gave her more questions. "Why did we get married? What is the point of it? What are the rules involved?"

Certain inquiries, even on a planet designed for questions, go unheard.

"Andrew, I've been telling you for weeks—*months*—that you need to slow down. You've been overdoing it. Your hours have been ridiculous. You've been truly burning the candle. Something had to give. But even so, this was so sudden. There were no warning signs. I just want to know what triggered it all. Was it me? What was it? I'm worried about you."

I tried to come up with a valid explanation. "I suppose I just must have forgotten the importance of wearing clothes. That is, the importance of acting the way I was supposed to act. I don't know. I must have just forgotten how to be a human. It can happen, can't it? Things can be forgotten sometimes?"

Isobel held my hand. The glabrous underportion of her thumb stroked my skin. This unnerved me even more. I wondered why she was touching me. A policeman grips an arm to take you somewhere, but why does a wife stroke your hand? What was the purpose? It wasn't the touch *Cosmopolitan* had talked about, and it certainly didn't boost my mood. Did it have something to do with love? I stared at the small glistening diamond on her ring.

"It's going to be all right, Andrew. This is just a blip. I promise you. You'll be right as rain soon."

"As rain?" I asked, the worry adding a quiver to my voice.

I tried to read her facial expressions, but it was difficult. She wasn't terrified anymore, but what was she? Was she sad? Confused? Angry? Disappointed? I wanted to understand, but I couldn't. She left me, after a hundred more words of the conversation. Words, words, words. There was a brief kiss on my cheek, and a hug, and I tried not to flinch or tighten up, hard as that was for me. And then she turned away and wiped something from her eye, which had leaked. I felt like I was expected to do something, say something, feel something, but I didn't know what. "I saw your book," I said. "In the shop. Next to mine."

"Some of you still remains then," she said. The tone was soft but slightly scornful, or I think it was. "Andrew, just be careful. Do everything they say and it will be all right. Everything will be all right."

And then she was gone.

Dead Cows

I was told to go to the dining hall to eat. This was a terrible experience. For one thing, it was the first time I had been confronted with so many of their species in an enclosed area. Second, the smell. Of boiled carrot. Of pea. Of dead cow.

A cow is an Earth-dwelling animal, a domesticated and multipurpose ungulate, which humans treat as a one-stop shop for food, liquid refreshment, fertilizer, and designer footwear. The humans farm it and cut its throat and then cut it up and package it and refrigerate it and sell it and cook it. By doing this, apparently they have earned the right to change its name to "beef," which is the monosyllable furthest away from "cow," because the last thing a human wants to think about when eating cow is an actual cow.

I didn't care about cows. If it had been my assignment to kill a cow, then I would have happily done so. But there was a leap to be made from not caring about someone to wanting to eat them. So I ate the vegetables. Or rather, I ate a single slice of boiled carrot. Nothing, I realized, could make you feel quite so homesick as eating disgusting, unfamiliar food. One slice was enough. More than enough. It was, in fact, far too much, and it took me all my strength and concentration to battle that gag reflex and not throw up.

I sat on my own, at a table in the corner, beside a tall potted plant. The plant had broad, shining, rich-green flat vascular organs known as leaves, which evidently served a photosynthetic function. It looked exotic to me, but not appallingly so. Indeed, the plant looked rather pretty. For the first time I was looking at something here and not being troubled. But then I looked away from the plant, toward the noise, and all the humans classified as crazy. The ones for whom the ways of this world were beyond them. If I was ever going to relate to any people on this planet, they were surely going to be in this room. And just as I was thinking this, one of them came up to me. A girl with short pink hair and a circular piece of silver through her nose (as if that region of the face needed more attention given to it), thin orange-pink scars on her arms, and a quiet, low voice that seemed to imply that every thought in her brain was a deadly secret. She was wearing a T-shirt. On the T-shirt were the words "Everything was beautiful (and nothing hurt)." Her name was Zoë. She told me that straightaway.

The World as Will and Representation

And then she said, "New?"

"Yes," I said.

"Day?"

"Yes," I said. "It is. We do appear to be angled toward the sun."

She laughed, and her laughter was the opposite of her voice. It was a kind of laugh that made me wish there was no air for those manic waves to travel on and reach my ears.

Once she had calmed down, she explained herself. "No, I mean, are you here permanently or do you just come in for the day? Like me? A 'voluntary commitment' job."

"I don't know," I said. "I think I will be leaving soon. I am not mad, you see. I have just been a little confused about things. I have a lot to get on with. Things to do. Things to finish off."

"I recognize you from somewhere," said Zoë.

"Do you? From where?"

I scanned the room. I was starting to feel uncomfortable. There were seventy-six patients and eighteen members of staff. I needed privacy. I needed, really, to get out of there.

"Have you been on the telly?"

"I don't know."

She laughed. "We might be Facebook friends."

"Yeah."

She scratched her horrible face. I wondered what was underneath. It couldn't have been any worse. And then her eyes widened with a realization. "No. I know. I've seen you at uni. You're Professor Martin, aren't you? You're something of a legend. I'm at Fitzwilliam. I've seen you around the place. Better food in Hall than here, isn't there?"

"Are you one of my students?"

She laughed again. "No. No. GCSE maths was enough for me. I hated it."

This angered me. "Hated it? How can you hate mathematics? Mathematics is everything."

"Well, I didn't see it like that. I mean, Pythagoras sounded like a bit of a dude, but no, I'm not really über-big on numbers. I'm philosophy. That's probably why I'm in here. OD'd on Schopenhauer."

"Schopenhauer?"

"He wrote a book called *The World as Will and Representation*. I'm meant to be doing an essay on it. Basically it says that the world is what we recognize in our own will. Humans are ruled by their basic desires and this leads to suffering and pain, because our desires make us crave things from the world but the world is nothing but representation. Because those same cravings shape what we see. We end up feeding from ourselves, until we go mad. And end up in here."

"Do you like it in here?"

She laughed again, but I noticed her kind of laughing somehow made her look sadder. "No. This place is a whirlpool. It sucks you deeper. You want out of this place, man. Everyone in here is *off the charts,* I tell you." She pointed at various people in the room and told me what was wrong with them. She started with an oversized, red-faced female at the nearest table to us. "That's Fat Anna. She steals everything. Look at her with the fork. Straight up her sleeve . . . Oh, and that's Scott. He thinks he's the third in line to the throne . . . And Sarah, who is totally normal for most of the day and then at a quarter past four starts screaming for no reason. Got to have a screamer . . . And that's Crying Chris . . . and there's Bridget the Fidget, who's always moving around at the speed of thought . . ."

"The speed of thought," I said. "That slow?"

"And Lying Lisa . . . and Rocking Rajesh. Oh, oh yeah, and you see that guy over there, with the sideburns? The tall one, mumbling to his tray?"

"Yes."

"Well, he's gone the full K-Pax."

"What?"

"He's so cracked he thinks he's from another planet."

"*No,*" I said. "*Really?*"

"Yeah. Trust me. In this canteen we're just one mute Native American away from a full cuckoo's nest."

I had no idea what she was talking about.

She looked at my plate. "Are you not eating that?"

"No," I said. "I don't think I could." And then, thinking I might get some information out of her, I asked, "If I had done something, achieved something remarkable, do you think I would have told a lot of people? I mean, we humans are proud, aren't we? We like to show off about things."

"Yes, I suppose."

I nodded. Felt panic rising as I wondered how many people knew about Professor Andrew Martin's discovery. Then I decided to broaden my inquiry. To act like a human, I would after all need to understand them, so I asked her the biggest question I could think of. "What do you think the meaning of life is, then? Did you discover it?"

"Ha! The meaning of life. *The meaning of life.* There is none. People search for external values and meaning in a world which not only can't provide it but is also indifferent to their quest. That's not really Schopenhauer. That's more Kierkegaard via Camus. I'm with them. Trouble is, if you study philosophy and stop believing in a meaning, you start to need medical help."

"What about love? What is love all about? I read about it. In *Cosmopolitan.*"

Another laugh. "*Cosmopolitan?* Are you joking?"

"No. Not at all. I want to understand these things."

"You're definitely asking the wrong person here. See, that's one of my problems." She lowered her voice by at least two octaves, stared darkly. "I like violent men. I don't know why. It's a kind of self-harm thing. I go to pubs a lot. Rich pickings."

"Oh," I said, realizing it was right I had been sent here. The humans were as weird as I had been told, and as in love with violence. "So love is about finding the right person to hurt you?"

"Pretty much."

"That doesn't make sense."

"There is always some madness in love. But there is also always some reason in madness. That was . . . someone."

There was a silence. I wanted to leave. Not knowing the etiquette, I just stood up and left.

She released a little whine. And then laughed again. Laughter, along with madness, seemed to be the only way out, the emergency exit for humans.

I went over optimistically to the man mumbling to his tray. The apparent extraterrestrial. I spoke to him for a while. I asked him, with considerable hope, where he was from. He said Tatooine. A place I had never heard of. He said he lived near the Great Pit of Carkoon, a short drive from Jabba's Palace. He used to live with the Skywalkers, on their farm, but it burned down.

"How far away is your planet? From Earth, I mean."

"Very far."

"*How* far?"

"Fifty thousand miles," he said, crushing my hope and making me wish I'd never diverted my attention away from the plant with the lush green leaves.

I looked at him. For a moment, I had thought I wasn't alone among them, but now I knew I was.

So, I thought to myself as I walked away, *this is what happens when you live on Earth. You crack. You hold reality in your hands until it burns and then you have to drop the plate.* (Someone somewhere else in the room, just as I was thinking this, actually did drop a plate.) Yes, I could see it now—being a human drove you insane. I looked out of a large glass *rectangular* window and saw trees and buildings, cars and people. Clearly, this was a species not capable of handling the new plate Andrew Martin had just handed them. I really needed to get out of there and do my duty. I thought of Isobel, my wife. She had knowledge, the kind of knowledge I needed. I should have left with her.

What am I doing?

I walked toward the window, expecting it to be like windows on my planet, Vonnadoria, but it wasn't. It was made of glass. Which was made of rock. And instead of walking through it, I banged my nose into it, prompting a few yelps of laughter from other patients. I left the room, quite desperate to escape all the people and the smell of cow and carrots.

Amnesia

Acting human was one thing, but if Andrew Martin had told people, then I really could not afford to waste any more time in this place. Looking at my left hand and the gifts it contained, I knew what I had to do.

After lunch, I visited the nurse who had sat watching me talk to Isobel. I lowered my voice to just the right frequency. I slowed the words to just the right speed. To hypnotize humans was easy because, out of any species in the universe, they seemed the one most desperate to *believe*. "I am perfectly sane. I would like to see the doctor who can discharge me. I really need to get back home, to see my wife and child, and to continue my work at Fitzwilliam College, Cambridge University. Plus, I really don't like the food here. I don't know what happened this morning, I really don't. It was an embarrassing public display, but I wholeheartedly assure you that whatever it was I suffered, it was temporary. I am sane now, and I am happy. I feel very well indeed."

He nodded. "Follow me," he said.

The doctor wanted me to have some medical tests. A brain scan. They were worried about possible damage to my cerebral cortex, which could have prompted amnesia. I realized whatever else was to occur, the one thing that couldn't possibly happen to me was to have my brain looked at, not while the gifts were active. So I convinced him I was not suffering from amnesia. I made up a lot of memories. I made up a whole life.

I told him that I had been under a lot of pressure at work and he understood. He then asked me some more questions. But as with all human questions, the answers were always there, inside them like protons inside an atom, for me to locate and give as my own independent thoughts.

After half an hour the diagnosis was clear. I hadn't lost my memory. I had simply suffered a period of temporary insanity. Although he disapproved of the term "breakdown," he said I had suffered a "mental collapse" due to sleep deprivation and work pressures and a diet which, as Isobel had already informed the doctor, consisted largely of strong black coffee—a drink, of course, I already knew I hated.

The doctor then gave me some prompts, wondering if I'd suffered from panic attacks, low moods, nervous jolts, sudden behavioral swings, or feelings of unreality.

"Unreality?" I could ponder with conviction. "Oh yes, I have definitely been feeling that one. But not anymore. I feel fine. I feel very real. I feel as real as the sun."

The doctor smiled. He told me he had read one of my books on mathematics—an apparently "really funny" memoir of Andrew Martin's time teaching at Princeton University. The book I had seen already. The one called *American Pi*. He wrote me a prescription for more diazepam and advised I take things "one day at a time," as if there were another way for days to be experienced. And then he picked up the most primitive piece of telecommunications technology I had ever seen and told Isobel to come and take me home.

Remember, during your mission, never to become influenced or corrupted.

The humans are an arrogant species, defined by violence and greed. They have taken their home planet, the only one they currently have access to, and placed it on the road to destruction. They have created a world of divisions and categories and have continually failed to see the similarities among themselves. They have developed technology at a rate too fast for human psychology to keep up with, and yet they still pursue advancement for advancement's sake, and for the pursuit of the money and fame they all crave so much.

You must never fall into the humans' trap. You must never look at particular individuals and fail to see their relation to the crimes of the whole. Every smiling human face hides the terrors they are all capable of and are all responsible for, however indirectly.

You must never soften, or shirk your task.

Stay pure.

Retain your logic.

Do not let anyone interfere with the mathematical certainty of what needs to be done.

4 Campion Row

It was a warm room.

There was a window, but the curtains were drawn. They were thin enough for electromagnetic radiation from the only sun to filter through and I could see everything clear enough. The walls were painted sky blue, and there was an incandescent "lightbulb" hanging down from the ceiling with a cylindrical shade made of paper. I was lying in bed. It was a large, square bed, made for two people. I had been lying asleep in this same bed for over three hours, and now I was awake.

It was Professor Andrew Martin's bed, on the second floor of his house. His house was at 4 Campion Row. It was large, compared to the exteriors of other houses I had seen. Inside, all the walls were white. Downstairs, in the hallway and the kitchen, the floor was made of limestone, which was made of calcite, and so provided something familiar for me to look at. The kitchen, where I had gone to drink some water, was especially warm owing to the presence of something called an "oven." This particular type of oven was made of iron and powered by gas, with two continually hot disks on its top surface. It was called an AGA. It was cream-colored. There were lots of doors in the kitchen and also here in the bedroom. Oven doors and cupboard doors and wardrobe doors. Whole worlds shut away.

The bedroom had a beige carpet, made of wool. Animal hair. There was a poster on the wall which had a picture of two human heads, one male and one female, very close together. It had the words "Roman Holiday" on it. Other words too. Words like "Gregory Peck" and "Audrey Hepburn" and "Paramount Pictures."

There was a photograph on top of a wooden, cuboid piece of

furniture. A photograph is basically a two-dimensional nonmoving holograph catering only to the sense of sight. This photograph was inside a rectangle of steel. It was a photograph of Andrew and Isobel. They were younger, their skins more radiant and unwithered. Isobel looked happy to me because she was smiling and a smile is a signifier of human happiness. In the photograph Andrew and Isobel were standing on grass. She was wearing a long white dress. It seemed to be the dress to wear if you wanted to be happy.

There was another photo. They were standing somewhere hot. Neither of them had dresses on. They were among giant, crumbling stone columns under a perfectly blue sky. An important building from a former human civilization. On Earth, incidentally, civilization is the result of a group of humans coming together and suppressing their instincts. This civilization, I guessed, was one that must have been neglected or destroyed. They were smiling, but this was a different kind of smile and one which was confined to their mouths and not their eyes. They looked uncomfortable, though I attributed this to the heat on their thin skin. Then there was a later photograph, taken indoors somewhere. They had a child with them. Young. Male. He had hair as dark as his mother's, maybe darker, with paler skin. He was wearing an item of clothing that said "Cowboy."

Isobel was there in the room a lot of the time, either sleeping beside me or standing nearby, watching. Mostly I tried not to look at her.

I didn't want to connect to her in any way. It would not serve my mission well if any kind of sympathy or even empathy toward her were to form. Admittedly, this was unlikely. Her very otherness troubled me. She was so alien. But the universe was unlikely before it happened and it had almost indisputably happened.

Though I did brave her eyes for one question.

"When did you last see me? I mean, before. Yesterday?"

"At breakfast. And then you were at work. You came home at eleven. In bed by half past."

The War and Money Show

I watched the television she had brought in for me. She had struggled with it. It was heavy for her. I think she expected me to help her. It seemed so wrong, watching a biological life-form putting herself through such effort. I was confused and wondered why she would do it for me. I attempted, out of sheer telekinetic curiosity, to lighten it for her with my mind.

"That was easier than I was expecting," she said.

"Oh," I said, catching her gaze face-on. "Well, expectation is a funny thing."

"You still like to watch the news, don't you?"

Watch the news. That was a very good idea. The news might have something for me.

"Yes," I said, "I like to watch the news."

I watched it, and Isobel watched me, both of us equally troubled by what we saw. The news was full of human faces, but generally smaller ones, and often at a great distance away.

Within my first hour of watching, I discovered three interesting details.

1. The term "news" on Earth generally meant "news that directly affects humans." There was, quite literally, nothing about the antelope or the sea horse or the red-eared slider turtle or the other nine million species on the planet.

2. The news was prioritized in a way I could not understand. For instance, there was nothing on new mathematical observations or still-undiscovered polygons, but quite a bit about politics, which on this planet was essentially all about war and money. Indeed, war and money seemed to be so popular on the news, it should more accurately have been

"Did I say anything to you? Did I tell you anything?"

"You said my name, but I pretended to be sleeping. And that was it. Until I woke up, and you were gone."

I smiled. Relieved, I suppose, but back then I didn't quite understand why.

titled *The War and Money Show*. I had been told right. This was a planet characterized by violence and greed. A bomb had exploded in a country called Afghanistan. Elsewhere, people were worrying about the nuclear capability of North Korea. So-called stock markets were falling. This worried a lot of humans, who gazed up at screens full of numbers, studying them as if they displayed the only mathematics that mattered. Oh, and I waited for the stuff on the Riemann hypothesis but nothing came. This was either because no one knew or no one cared. Both possibilities were, in theory, comforting and yet I did not feel comforted.

3. Humans cared more about things if they were happening closer to them. South Korea worried about North Korea. People in London were worried chiefly about the cost of houses in London. It seemed people didn't mind someone's being naked in a rain forest so long as it was nowhere near their lawn. And they didn't care at all about what was happening beyond their solar system, and very little about what was happening inside it, except what was happening right here on Earth. (Admittedly, not a great deal *was* happening in their solar system, which might have gone some way to explain where human arrogance came from. A lack of competition.) Mostly, humans just wanted to know about what was going on within their country, preferably within that bit of the country which was their bit, the more local the better. Given this view, the absolutely ideal human news program would only concern what was going on inside the house where the human watching it actually lived. The coverage could then be divided up and prioritized on the basis of the specific rooms within that house, with the lead story always being about the room where the television was, and typically concerning the most important fact that it was being watched by a human. But until a human follows the logic of news to this inevitable conclusion, the best they had

was local news. So, in Cambridge, the most important thing on the news was the story about the human called Professor Andrew Martin who was discovered walking unclothed around the grounds of the New Court at Corpus Christi College, Cambridge University, during the early hours of that morning.

The repeated coverage of this last detail also explained why the telephone had been ringing almost continuously since I had arrived, and why my wife had been talking about emails arriving into the computer all the time.

"I've been fielding them," she told me. "I've told them you aren't up to talking right now and that you are too ill."

"Oh."

She sat on the bed, stroked my hand some more. My skin crawled. A part of me wished I could just end her, right there. But there was a sequence, and it had to be followed.

"Everyone is very worried about you."

"Who?" I said.

"Well, your son, for a start. Gulliver's got even worse since this."

"We only have one child?"

Her eyelids descended slowly; her face was a tableau of forced calm. "You know we do. And I really don't understand how you left without a brain scan."

"They decided I didn't need one. It was quite easy."

I tried to eat a bit of the food she had placed by the side of the bed. Something called a cheese sandwich. Another thing humans had to thank cows for. It was bad, but edible.

"Why did you make me this?" I asked.

"I'm looking after you," she said.

A moment's confusion. The idea was slow to compute. But then I realized, where we were used to service technology, humans had each other.

"But what is in it for you?"

She laughed. "That question's been a constant our whole marriage."

"Why?" I said. "Has our marriage been a bad one?"

She took a deep breath, as if the question were something she had to swim under. "Just eat your sandwich, Andrew."

A Stranger

I ate my sandwich. Then I thought of something else.

"Is that normal? To have just one. Child, I mean."

"It's about the only thing that is, right now."

She scratched a little bit at her hand. Just a tiny bit, but it still made me think of that woman, Zoë, at the mental hospital, with the scars on her arms and the violent boyfriends and the head full of philosophy.

There was a long silence. I was accustomed to silence, having lived alone most of my life, but somehow this silence was a different kind. It was the kind you needed to break.

"Thank you," I said. "For the sandwich. I liked it. The bread, anyway."

I didn't honestly know why I said this, as I hadn't enjoyed the sandwich. And yet, it was the first time in my life I had thanked anyone for anything.

She smiled. "Don't get used to it, Emperor."

And then she patted her hand on my chest and rested it there. I noticed a shift in her eyebrows, and an extra crease arrive in her forehead.

"That's odd," she said.

"What?"

"Your heart. It feels irregular. And like it's hardly beating."

She took her hand away. Stared at her husband for a moment as if he was a stranger. Which of course he was. *I* was. Stranger, indeed, than she could ever know. She looked worried too, and there was a part of me that resented it, even as I knew fear—of all the emotions— was precisely what she should have been feeling at that moment.

"I have to go to the supermarket," she told me. "We've got nothing in. Everything has gone off."

"Right," I said, wondering if I should allow this to happen. I supposed I had to. There was a special sequence to follow and the start of that sequence was at Fitzwilliam College, in Professor Andrew Martin's office. If Isobel left the house, then I could leave the house too, without prompting any suspicion.

"All right," I said.

"But remember, you've got to stay in bed. Okay? Just stay in bed and watch television."

"Yes," I said. "That is what I will do. I will stay in bed and watch television."

She nodded, but her forehead remained creased. She left the room, and then she left the house. I got out of bed and stubbed my toe on the door frame. It hurt. That wasn't weird in itself, I suppose. The weird thing was, it stayed hurting. Not a severe pain—I had only stubbed my toe, after all—but it was a pain which wasn't being fixed. Or not until I walked out of the room and onto the landing; then it faded and disappeared with suspicious speed. Puzzled, I walked back into the bedroom. The pain increased the closer I got to the television, where a woman was talking about the weather, making predictions. I switched the television off and the ache in the toe immediately disappeared. Strange. The signals must have interfered with the gifts, the technology I had inside my left hand.

I left the room, vowing in times of crisis never to be anywhere near a television.

I went downstairs. There were lots of rooms here. In the kitchen, there was a creature sleeping in a basket. It had four legs and its body was entirely covered with brown-and-white hair. This was a dog. A male. He stayed lying there with his eyes closed but growled when I entered the room.

I was looking for a computer but there was no computer in the kitchen. I went into another room, a square room at the back of the house which I would soon learn was the "sitting room," though most human rooms were sitting rooms if the truth be told. There was a computer here, and a radio. I switched the radio on first. A man was talking about the films of another man called Werner

Herzog. I punched the wall and my fist hurt, but when I switched off the radio, it stopped hurting. *Not just televisions, then.*

The computer was primitive. It had the words "MacBook Pro" on it, and a keypad full of letters and numbers, and a lot of arrows pointing in every possible direction. It seemed like a metaphor for human existence.

A minute or so later and I was accessing it, searching emails and documents, finding nothing on the Riemann hypothesis. I accessed the Internet—the prime source for information here. News of what Professor Andrew Martin had proved was nowhere to be found, though details of how to get to Fitzwilliam College were easy to access.

Memorizing them, I took the largest batch of keys on the chest in the hallway and then left the house.

Starting the Sequence

Most mathematicians would trade their soul
with Mephistopheles for a proof of the Riemann
hypothesis.

—MARCUS DU SAUTOY

The woman on the television had told me there would be no rain, so I rode Professor Andrew Martin's bicycle to Fitzwilliam College. It was evening now. Isobel would be at the supermarket already, so I knew I didn't have long.

It was a Sunday. Apparently this meant the college would be quiet, but I knew I had to be careful. I knew where to go, and although riding a bicycle was a relatively easy thing to do, I was still a bit confused by the laws of the roads and narrowly escaped accidents a couple of times.

Eventually, I made it to a long, quiet tree-lined street called Storey's Way, and the college itself. I leaned my bike against a wall and walked toward the main entrance of this, the largest of the three buildings. This was a wide, relatively modern example of Earth's architecture, three stories high. As I was entering the building, I passed a woman with a bucket and a mop, cleaning the wooden floor.

"Hello," she said. She seemed to recognize me, though it wasn't a recognition that made her happy.

I smiled. (I had discovered, at the hospital, that smiling was the appropriate first response on greeting someone. Saliva had little to do with it.) "Hello. I'm a professor here. Professor Andrew Martin. I know this sounds terribly strange, but I have suffered a little accident—nothing major, but enough to cause me some short-term memory loss. Anyway, the point is I am off work for a little while but

I really need something in the office. My office. Something of purely personal value. Is there any chance you know where my office is?"

She studied me for a couple of seconds. "I hope it wasn't anything serious," she said, though it didn't sound like the sincerest of hopes.

"No. No, it wasn't. I fell off my bike. Anyway, I'm sorry, but I am a little bit pressed for time."

"Upstairs, along the corridor. Second door on the left."

"Thank you."

I passed someone on the stairs. A gray-haired woman, astute-looking by human standards, and with glasses hanging around her neck.

"Andrew!" she said. "My goodness. How are you? And what are you doing? I heard you were unwell."

I studied her closely. I wondered how much she knew.

"Yes, I had a little bump on the head. But I am all right now. Honestly. Don't worry. I've been checked out, and I should be fine. As right as the rain."

"Oh," she said, unconvinced. "I see, I see, I see."

And then I asked, with a slight and inexplicable dread, an essential question: "When did you last see me?"

"I haven't seen you all week. Must have been a week ago Thursday."

"And we've had no other contact since then? Phone calls? Emails? Any other?"

"No. No, why would there have been? You've got me intrigued."

"Oh, it's nothing. It's just, this bump on my head. I am all over the place."

"Dear, that's terrible. Are you sure you should be here? Shouldn't you be at home in bed?"

"Yes, probably I should. After this, I am going home."

"Good. Well, I hope you feel better soon."

"Oh. Thank you."

"Bye."

She continued downstairs, not realizing she had just saved her own life.

I had a key, so I used it. There was no point in doing anything overtly suspicious in case anyone else should have seen me.

And then I was inside his—*my*—office. I didn't know what I had been expecting. That was a problem, now: expectation. There were no reference points; everything was new.

So, an office.

A static chair behind a static desk. A window with the blinds down. Books filling nearly three of the walls. There was a brown-leaved potted plant on the windowsill, smaller and thirstier than the one I had seen at the hospital. On the desk there were photos in frames amid a chaos of papers and unfathomable stationery, and there in the center of it all was the computer.

I didn't have long, so I sat down and switched it on. This one seemed only fractionally more advanced than the one I had used back at the house. Earth computers were still very much at the pre-sentient phase of their evolution, just sitting there and letting you reach in and grab whatever you wanted without even the slightest complaint.

I quickly found what I was looking for. A document called "Zeta."

I opened it up and saw it was twenty-six pages of mathematical symbols. Or most of it was. At the beginning there was a little introduction written in words, which said:

PROOF OF THE RIEMANN HYPOTHESIS

As you know, the proof of the Riemann hypothesis is the most important unsolved problem in mathematics. To solve it would revolutionize applications of mathematical analysis in a myriad of unknowable ways that would transform our lives and those of future generations. Indeed, it is mathematics itself that is the bedrock of civilization, as first evidenced by architectural achievements such as the Egyptian pyramids, and by astronomical observations essential to architecture. Since then our mathematical understanding has advanced, but never at a constant rate.

As with evolution itself, there have been rapid advances and crippling setbacks along the way. If the Library of Alexandria had never been burned to the ground, it is possible to imagine that we would have built upon the achievements of the ancient Greeks to greater and earlier effect, and therefore it could have been in the time of a Cardano or a Newton or a Pascal that we first put a man on the moon. And we can only wonder where we would be. And what planets we would have terraformed and colonized by the twenty-first century. Which medical advances we would have made. Maybe if there had been no Dark Ages, no switching off of the light, we would have found a way to never grow old, to never die.

People joke, in our field, about Pythagoras and his religious cult based on perfect geometry and other abstract mathematical forms, but if we are going to have religion at all, then a religion of mathematics seems ideal, because if God exists, then what is He but a mathematician?

And so today we may be able to say, we have risen a little closer toward our deity. Indeed, potentially we have a chance to turn back the clock and rebuild that ancient library so we can stand on the shoulders of giants that never were.

Primes

The document carried on in this excited way for a bit longer. I learned a little bit more about Bernhard Riemann, a painfully shy, nineteenth-century German child prodigy who displayed exceptional skill with numbers from an early age, before succumbing to a mathematical career and a series of nervous breakdowns, which plagued his adulthood. I would later discover this was one of the key problems humans had with numerical understanding—their nervous systems simply weren't up to it.

Primes, quite literally, drove people insane, particularly as so many puzzles remained. They knew a prime was a whole number that could only be divided by one or itself, but after that they hit all kinds of problems.

For instance, they knew that the total of all primes was precisely the same as the total of all numbers, as both were infinite. This was, for a human, a very puzzling fact, as surely there must be more numbers than prime numbers. So impossible was this to come to terms with that some people, on contemplating it, placed a gun into their mouth, pulled the trigger, and blew their brains out.

Humans also understood that primes were very much like the atoms of the Earth's air. The higher you went, the fewer of them there were. For instance, there were twenty-five primes below 100, but only twenty-one between 100 and 200, and only sixteen between 1,000 and 1,100. However, unlike with the Earth's air, it didn't matter how high you went with prime numbers as there were always some around. For instance, 2,097,593 was a prime, and there were millions more between it and, say, 4,314,398,832,739,895,727,932,419, 750,374,600,193. So, the atmosphere of prime numbers covered the numerical universe.

However, people had struggled to explain the apparently random pattern of primes. They thinned out, but not in any way that humans could fathom. This frustrated the humans very much. They knew that if they could solve this puzzle, they could advance in all kinds of ways, because prime numbers were the heart of mathematics and mathematics was the heart of knowledge.

Humans understood other things. Atoms, for instance. They had a machine called a spectrometer which allowed them to see the atoms a molecule was made from. But they didn't understand primes the way they understood atoms, sensing that they would do so only if they could work out why prime numbers were spread out the way they were.

And then in 1859, at the Berlin Academy, the increasingly ill Bernhard Riemann announced what would become the most studied and celebrated hypothesis in all mathematics. It stated that there *was* a pattern, or at least there was one for the first hundred thousand or so primes. And it was beautiful and clean, and it involved something called a "zeta function"—a kind of mental machine in itself, a complex-looking curve that was useful for investigating properties of primes. You put numbers into it and they would form an order that no one had noticed before. A pattern. The distribution of prime numbers was not random.

There were gasps when Riemann—mid panic attack—announced this to his smartly dressed and bearded peers. They truly believed the end was in sight and that in their lifetimes there would be a proof that worked for *all* prime numbers. But Riemann had only located the lock, he hadn't actually found the key, and shortly afterward he died of tuberculosis.

And as time went on, the quest became more desperate. Other mathematical riddles were solved in due course—things like Fermat's Last Theorem and the Poincaré Conjecture—which left proof of the long-buried German's hypothesis as the last and largest problem to solve. The one that would be the equivalent of seeing atoms in molecules or identifying the chemical elements of the periodic table. The one that would ultimately give humans supercomputers, explanations of quantum physics, and interstellar transportation.

After getting to grips with all this, I then trawled through all the pages full of numbers, graphs, and mathematical symbols. This was another language for me to learn, but it was an easier and more truthful one than the one I had learned with the help of *Cosmopolitan*.

And by the end of it, after a few moments of sheer terror, I was in quite a state. After that very last and conclusive ∞, I was left in no doubt that the proof had been found, and the key had turned that all-important lock.

So, without so much as a second's thought, I deleted the document, feeling a small rush of pride as I did so.

There, I told myself, *you may have just managed to save the universe.*

But of course, things are never that simple, not even on Earth.

A Moment of Sheer Terror

$$\xi(1/2+it)=[e^{\Re\log(r(s/2))}\pi^{-1/4}(-t^2-1/4)/2]\times[e^{i\Im\log(r(s/2))}\pi^{-it/2}\zeta(1/2+it)]$$

The Distribution of Prime Numbers

I looked at Andrew Martin's emails, specifically the very last one in his sent folder. It had the subject heading "153 years later . . . ," and it had a little red exclamation mark beside it. The message itself was a simple one: "I have proved the Riemann hypothesis, haven't I? Need to tell you first. Please, Daniel, cast your eyes over this. Oh, and needless to say, this is for those eyes only at the moment. Until it goes public. What do you reckon? Humans will never be the same again? Biggest news anywhere since 1905? See attachment."

The attachment was the document I had deleted elsewhere and had just been reading, so I didn't waste much time on that. Instead, I looked at the recipient: daniel.russell@cambridge.ac.uk.

Daniel Russell, I swiftly discovered, was the Lucasian Professor of Mathematics at Cambridge University. He was sixty-three years old. He had written fourteen books, most of which had been international best sellers. The Internet told me he had taught at every English-language university with an intimidating enough reputation—Cambridge (where he was now), Oxford, Harvard, Princeton, and Yale among others—and had received numerous awards and titles. He had worked on quite a few academic papers with Andrew Martin, but as far as I could tell from my brief research, they were colleagues more than friends.

I looked at the time. In about twenty minutes my "wife" would be coming home and wondering where I was. The less suspicion there was at this stage, the better. There was a sequence of doing things, after all. I had to follow the sequence.

And the first part of the sequence needed to be done right now, so I trashed the email, and the attachment. Then, to be on the safe side, I quickly designed a virus—yes, with the help of primes—which would ensure that nothing could be accessed intact from this computer again.

Before I left, I checked the papers on the desk. There was nothing there to be worried about. Insignificant letters, timetables, blank pages, but then, on one of them, a telephone number, 0-786-554-2187. I put it in my pocket and noticed, as I did so, one of the photographs on the desk. Isobel, Andrew, and the boy I assumed to be Gulliver. He was the only one of the three who wasn't smiling. He had wide eyes, peeping out from below dark bangs. He carried the ugliness of his species better than most. At least he wasn't looking happy about what he was, and that was something.

Another minute had gone by. It was time to go.

□ □ □

We are pleased with your progress. But now the real work must begin.
    Yes.

Deleting documents from computers is not the same as deleting lives. Even human lives.
    I understand that.

A prime number is strong. It does not depend on others. It is pure and complete and never weakens. You must be like a prime. You must not weaken, you must distance yourself, and you must not change after interaction. You must be indivisible.
    Yes. I will be.

Good. Now, continue.

□ □ □

Glory

Isobel was still not back, on my return to the house, so I did a little more research. She was not a mathematician. She was a historian.

On Earth, this was an important distinction, as here history was not yet viewed as a subdivision of mathematics, which of course it was. I also discovered that Isobel, like her husband, was considered to be very clever by the standards of her species. I knew this because one of the books on the shelf in the bedroom was *The Dark Ages*, the one I had seen in the bookshop. And now I could see it had a quote from a publication called the *New York Times* which read "very clever." The book was 1,253 pages long. A door opened downstairs. I heard the soft sound of metal keys being rested on a wooden chest. She came up to see me. That was the first thing she did.

"How are you?" she asked.

"I've been looking at your book. About the Dark Ages."

She laughed.

"What are you laughing at?"

"Oh, it's that or crying."

"Listen," I said, "do you know where Daniel Russell lives?"

"Of course I do. We've been to his house for dinner."

"Where does he live?"

"In Babraham. He's got a whopping place. Can you seriously not remember? It's like not remembering a visit to Nero's palace."

"Yes. I can, I can. It's just that there are things which are still a bit hazy. I think it's the pills. That was a blank, so that's why I asked. That's all. So, I'm good friends with him?"

"No. You hate him. You can't stand him. Though deep hostility is your default setting with other academics these days, Ari excepted."

"Ari?"

She sighed. "Your best friend."

"Oh, Ari. Yes. Of course. Ari. My ears are a bit blocked. I didn't hear you properly."

"But with Daniel," she said, speaking a little louder, "if I dare say it, the hatred is just the manifestation of an inferiority complex on your part. But superficially, you get on with him. You've even sought his guidance a few times, with your prime number stuff."

"Right. Okay. My prime number stuff. Yes. And where am I with that? Where was I? When I last spoke to you, before?" I felt the urge to ask it outright. "Had I proved the Riemann hypothesis?"

"No. You hadn't. At least, not that I knew. But you should probably check that out, because if you have, we'll be a million pounds richer."

"What?"

"Dollars, actually, isn't it?"

"I—"

"The Millennium Prize, or whatever it is. Proof of the Riemann hypothesis is the biggest remaining puzzle that hasn't been solved. There is an institute in Massachusetts, the other Cambridge, the Clay Institute . . . You know this stuff backward, Andrew. You mumble this stuff in your sleep."

"Absolutely. Backward and forward. All the ways. I just need a little reminding, that is all."

"Well, it's a very wealthy institute. They obviously have a lot of money because they've already given about ten million dollars away to other mathematicians. Apart from that last guy."

"Last guy?"

"The Russian. Grigori something. The one who turned it down for solving the Whatever-it-was Conjecture."

"But a million dollars is a lot of money, isn't it?"

"It is. It's a nice amount."

"So why did he turn it down?"

"How do I know? I don't know. You told me he was a recluse who lives with his mother. There are people in this world who have motives that extend beyond the financial, Andrew."

This was genuinely news to me. "Are there?"

"Yes. There are. Because, you know, there's this new ground-breaking and controversial theory that money can't buy you happiness."

"Oh," I said.

She laughed again. She was trying to be funny, I think, so I laughed too.

"So, no one has solved the Riemann hypothesis?"

"What? Since yesterday?"

"Since, well, ever?"

"No. No one has solved it. There was a false alarm, a few years back. Someone from France. But no. The money is still there."

"So, that is why he . . . why I . . . this is what motivates me, money?"

She was now arranging socks on the bed, in pairs. It was a terrible system she had developed. But I didn't think this was the time to confront her on her sock-arranging abilities. "Not just that," she went on. "Glory is what motivates you. Ego. You want your name everywhere. Andrew Martin. Andrew Martin. Andrew Martin. You want to be on every Wikipedia page going. You want to be an Einstein. The trouble is, Andrew, you're still two years old."

This confused me. "I am? How is that possible?"

"Your mother never gave you the love you needed. You will forever be sucking at a nipple that offers no milk. You want the world to know you. You want to be a great man."

She said this in quite a cool tone. I wondered if this was how people always talked to each other or if it was just unique to spouses. I heard a key enter a lock.

Isobel looked at me with wide, astonished eyes. *"Gulliver."*

Dark Matter

Gulliver's room was at the top of the house. The "attic." The last stop before the thermosphere. He went straight there, his feet passing the bedroom I was in, with only the slightest pause before climbing the final set of stairs.

While Isobel went out to walk the dog, I decided to phone the number on the piece of paper in my pocket. Maybe it was Daniel Russell's number.

"Hello," came a voice. Female. "Who's this?"

"This is Professor Andrew Martin," I said.

The female laughed. "Well hello, Professor Andrew Martin."

"Who are you? Do you know me?"

"You're on YouTube. Everyone knows you now. You've gone viral. The Naked Professor."

"Oh."

"Hey, don't worry about it. Everyone loves an exhibitionist." She spoke slowly, lingering on words as if each one had a taste she didn't want to lose.

"Please, how do I know you?"

The question was never answered, because at that precise moment Gulliver walked into the room and I switched off the phone.

Gulliver. My "son." The dark-haired boy I had seen in the photographs. He looked as I had expected but maybe taller. He was nearly as tall as myself. His eyes were shaded by his hair. (Hair, by the way, is very important here. Not as important as clothes obviously, but getting there. To humans, hair is more than just a filamentous biomaterial that happens to grow out of their heads. It carries all kinds of social signifiers, most of which I couldn't translate.) His clothes were as black as space and his T-shirt had the words "Dark Matter" on them. Maybe this was how certain people communicated, via the slogans on their T-shirts. He wore "wrist-bands." His hands were in his pockets and he seemed uncomfortable looking at my face. (The feeling, then, was mutual.) His voice was low. Or at least low by human standards. About the same depth as a Vonnadorian humming plant. He came and sat on the bed and tried to be nice, at the start, but then at one point he switched to a higher frequency.

"Dad, why did you do it?"

"I don't know."

"School is going to be hell now."

"Oh."

"Is that all you can say? *Oh?* Are you serious? Is that fucking *it?*"

"No. Yes. I, I fucking don't fucking know, Gulliver."

"Well, you've destroyed my life. I'm a joke. It was bad before. Ever since I started there. But now—"

I wasn't listening. I was thinking about Daniel Russell and how I desperately needed to phone him. Gulliver noticed I wasn't paying attention.

"It doesn't even matter. You never want to talk to me, apart from last night."

Gulliver left the room. He slammed the door and let out a kind of growl. He was fifteen years old. This meant he belonged to a special subcategory of human called a "teenager," the chief characteristics of which were a weakened resistance to gravity, a vocabulary of grunts, a lack of spatial awareness, copious amounts of masturbation, and an unending appetite for cereal.

Last night.

I got out of bed and headed upstairs to the attic. I knocked on his door. There was no reply but I opened it anyway.

Inside, the environment was one of prevailing dark. There were posters for musicians. Thermostatic, Skrillex, The Fetid, Mother Night, and the Dark Matter his T-shirt referenced. There was a window sloped in line with the ceiling, but the blind was drawn. There was a book on the bed. It was called *Ham on Rye,* by Charles Bukowski. There were clothes on the floor. Together, the room was a data cloud of despair. I sensed he wanted to be put out of his misery, one way or another. That would come, of course, but first there would be a few more questions.

He didn't hear me enter owing to the audio transmitter he had plugged into his ears. Nor did he see me, as he was too busy staring at his computer. On the screen, there was a still-motion image of myself naked, walking past one of the university buildings. There was also some writing on the screen. At the top were the words "Gulliver Martin, You Must Be So Proud."

Underneath, there were lots of comments. A typical example read, "HA! HA! HA! HA! HA! HA! HA! HA! HA! HA! HA! HA! HA! HA! HA! HA! HA! HA! HA! HA! HA! HA! Oh almost forgot—HA!" I read the name next to that particular post.

"Who is Theo 'The Fucking Business' Clarke?" Gulliver jumped at my voice and turned around. I asked my question again but didn't receive an answer.

"What are you doing?" I asked, purely for research purposes.

"Just go away."

"I want to talk to you. I want to talk about last night."

He turned his back to me. His torso stiffened. "Go away, Dad."

"No. I want to know what I said to you."

He sprang out of his chair and, as the humans say, *stormed* over to me. "Just leave me alone, okay? You've never been interested in a single thing about my life, so don't start now. Why fucking start now?"

I watched the back of him in the small, circular mirror staring out from the wall like a dull and unblinking eye.

After some aggressive pacing he sat back in his chair, turned to his computer again, and pressed his finger on an odd-looking command device.

"I need to know something," I said. "I need to know if you know what I was doing. Last week at work?"

"Dad, just—"

"Listen, this is important. Were you still up when I came home? You know, last night? Were you in the house? Were you awake?"

He mumbled something. I didn't hear what. Only an ipsoid would have heard it.

"Gulliver, how are you at mathematics?"

"You know how I fucking am at maths."

"Fucking no, I don't. Not now. That is why I am fucking asking. Tell me what you fucking know."

Nothing. I thought I was using his language, but Gulliver just sat there, staring away from me, with his right leg jerking up and down in slight but rapid movements. My words were having no effect. I thought of the audio transmitter he still had in one ear. Maybe it was sending radio signals. I waited a little while longer and sensed it was time to leave. But as I headed for the door, he said, "Yeah. I was up. You told me."

My heart raced. "What? What did I tell you?"

"About you being the savior of the human race or something."

"Anything more specific? Did I go into detail?"

"You proved your precious Rainman hypothesis."

"Riemann. Riemann. The Riemann hypothesis. I told you that, fucking did I?"

"Yeah," he said, in the same glum tone. "First time you'd spoken to me in a week."

"Who have you told?"

"What? Dad, I think people are more interested in the fact that you walked around the town center naked, to be honest. No one's going to care about some equation."

"But your mother? Have you told her? She must have asked you if I'd spoken to you, after I'd gone missing. Surely she asked you that?"

He shrugged. (A shrug, I realized, was one of the main modes of communication for teenagers.) "Yeah."

"*And?* What did you say? Come on, speak to me, Gulliver. What does she know about it?"

He turned and looked me straight in the eye. He was frowning. Angry. Confused. "I don't fucking believe you, Dad."

"Fucking believe?"

"You're the parent, I'm the kid. I'm the one who should be wrapped up in myself, not you. I'm fifteen and you're forty-three. If you are genuinely ill, Dad, then I want to be there for you, but aside from your newfound love of streaking and your weird fucking swearing, you are acting very, very, very much like yourself. But here's a news flash. You ready? We don't actually care about your prime numbers. We don't care about your precious fucking work or your stupid fucking books or your genius-like brain or your ability to solve the world's greatest outstanding mathematical whatever because, because, because all these things hurt us."

"Hurt you?" Maybe the boy was wiser than he looked. "What do you mean by that?"

His eyes stayed on me. His chest rose and fell with visible intensity.

"Nothing," he said at last. "But, the answer is no, I didn't tell Mum. I said you said something about work. That's all. I didn't think it was relevant information right then to tell her about your fucking hypothesis."

"But the money. You know about that?"

"Yeah, 'course I do."

"And you still didn't think it was a big deal?"

"Dad, we have quite a lot of money in the bank. We have one of the biggest houses in Cambridge. I'm probably the richest kid in my school now. But it doesn't amount to shit. It isn't the Perse, remember?"

"The Perse?"

"That school you spent twenty grand a year on. You've forgotten that? Who the hell are you? Jason Bourne?"

"No. I am not."

"You probably forgot I was expelled too."

"No," I lied. "'Course I haven't."

"I don't think more money's going to save us."

I was genuinely confused. This went against everything we were meant to know about the humans.

"No," I said. "You're right. It won't. And besides, it was a mistake. I haven't proved the Riemann hypothesis. I think in fact it is unprovable. I thought I had, but I haven't. So there is nothing to tell anyone."

At which Gulliver pushed the audio-transmission device into his other ear and closed his eyes. He wanted no more of me.

"Fucking okay," I whispered and left the room.

Emily Dickinson

I went downstairs and found an "address book." Inside were addresses and telephone numbers for people, listed alphabetically. I found the telephone number I was looking for. A woman told me Daniel Russell was out but would be back in around an hour. He would phone me back. Meanwhile, I perused some more history books and learned things as I read between the lines.

As well as religion, human history is full of depressing things like colonization, disease, racism, sexism, homophobia, class snobbery, environmental destruction, slavery, totalitarianism, military dictatorships, inventions of things which they had no idea how to handle (the atomic bomb, the Internet, the semicolon), the victimization of clever people, the worshipping of idiotic people, boredom, despair, periodic collapses, and catastrophes within the psychic landscape. And through it all there has always been some truly awful food.

I found a book called *The Great American Poets*.

"I believe a leaf of grass is no less than the journey-work of the stars," wrote someone called Walt Whitman. It was an obvious point, but something about it was quite beautiful. In the same book, there were words written by another poet. The poet was Emily Dickinson. The words were these:

How happy is the little stone
That rambles in the road alone,
And doesn't care about careers,
And exigencies never fears;
Whose coat of elemental brown
A passing universe put on;
And independent as the sun,
Associates or glows alone,

Fulfilling absolute decree
In casual simplicity.

Fulfilling absolute decree, I thought. *Why do these words trouble me?* The dog growled at me. I turned the page and found more unlikely wisdom. I read the words aloud to myself: "The soul should always stand ajar, ready to welcome the ecstatic experience."

"You're out of bed," said Isobel.

"Yes," I said. To be a human is to state the obvious. Repeatedly, over and over, until the end of time.

"You need to eat," she added, after studying my face.

"Yes," I said.

She got out some ingredients.

Gulliver walked past the doorway.

"Gull, where are you going? I'm making dinner." The boy said nothing as he left. The slam of the door almost shook the house.

"I'm worried about him," said Isobel.

As she worried, I studied the ingredients on the worktop. Mainly green vegetation. But then something else. Chicken breast. I thought about this. And I kept thinking. *The breast of a chicken. The breast of a chicken. The breast of a chicken.*

"That looks like meat," I said.

"I'm going to make a stir-fry."

"With *that*?"

"Yes."

"The *breast* of a *chicken*?"

"Yes, Andrew. Or are you vegetarian now?"

The dog was in his basket. It was something by the name of Newton. It was still growling at me. "What about the dog's breasts? Are we going to eat those too?"

"No," she said, with resignation. I was testing her.

"Is a dog more intelligent than a chicken?"

"Yes," she said. She closed her eyes. "I don't know. No. I haven't got time for this. Anyway, you're the big meat eater."

I was uncomfortable. "I would rather not eat the chicken's breasts."

Isobel now clenched her eyes closed. She inhaled deeply. "Give me strength," she whispered.

I could have done so, of course. But I needed what strength I had right now.

Isobel handed me my diazepam. "Have you taken one lately?"

"No."

"You probably should."

So I humored her. I unscrewed the cap and placed a pill on my palm. These ones looked like word capsules. As green as knowledge. I popped a tablet in my mouth.

◻ ◻ ◻

Be careful.

◻ ◻ ◻

Dishwasher

I ate the vegetable stir-fry. It smelt like Bazadean body waste. I tried not to look at it, so I looked at Isobel instead. It was the first time that looking at a human face was the easier option. But I did need to eat. So I ate.

"When you spoke to Gulliver about me going missing, did he say anything to you?"

"Yes," she said.

"What was it that he said?"

"That you came in about eleven and that you'd gone into the living room where he was watching TV and that you'd told him that you were sorry you were late, but you'd been finishing something off at work."

"Was that it? There was nothing more specific?"

"No."

"What do you think he meant by that? I mean, what I meant by that?"

"I don't know. But I have to say, you coming home and being friendly to Gulliver—that's already out of character."

"Why, don't I like him?"

"Not since two years ago. No. Pains me to say it, but you don't act very much like you do."

"Two years ago?"

"Since he got expelled from Perse. For starting a fire."

"Oh yes. The fire incident."

"I want you to start making an effort with him."

So, afterward, I followed Isobel into the kitchen and put my plate and cutlery in the dishwasher. I was noticing more things about her. At first, I had just seen her as generically human, but now I was appreciating the details. Picking up things I hadn't noticed—differences between her and the others. She was wearing a cardigan and blue trousers known as jeans. Her long neck was decorated with a thin necklace made out of silver. Her eyes stared deep into things, as though she was continually searching for something that wasn't there. Or as if it was there but just out of sight. It was as though everything had a depth, an internal distance to it.

"How are you feeling?" she asked. She seemed worried about something.

"I feel fine."

"I only ask because you're loading the dishwasher."

"Because that's what you are doing."

"Andrew, you never load the dishwasher. You are, and I mean this in the least offensive way possible, something of a domestic primitive."

"Why? Don't mathematicians load dishwashers?"

"In this house," she said sadly, "no, actually. No, they don't."

"Oh yes. I know. Obviously. I just fancied helping today. I help sometimes."

"Now we're on to fractions."

She looked at my pullover. There was a bit of noodle resting on the blue wool. She picked it off and stroked the fabric where it had been. She smiled, quickly. She cared about me. She had her reservations, but she cared. I didn't want her to care about me. It wouldn't help things. She placed her hand through my hair, to tidy it a bit. To my surprise, I wasn't flinching.

"Einstein chic is one thing but this is ridiculous," she said, softly. I smiled like I understood. She smiled too, but it was a smile on top of something else. As if she were wearing a mask and there was a near-identical but less smiling face underneath.

"It's almost like an alien clone is in my kitchen."

"Almost," I said. "Yes."

It was then that the telephone rang. Isobel went to answer it and a moment later came back into the kitchen, holding out the receiver.

"It's for you," she said, in a suddenly serious voice. Her eyes were wide, trying to convey a silent message I didn't quite understand.

"Hello?" I said.

There was a long pause. The sound of breath, and then a voice on the next exhalation. A man, talking slowly and carefully. "Andrew? Is that you?"

"Yes. Who's this?"

"It's Daniel. Daniel Russell."

My heart tripped. I realized this was it, the moment things had to change.

"Oh hello, Daniel."

"How are you? I hear you might be unwell."

"Oh, I am fine, really. It was just a little bit of mental exhaustion. My mind had run its own marathon and it struggled. My brain is made for sprints. It doesn't have the stamina for long-distance running. But don't worry, honestly, I am back where I was. It wasn't anything too serious. Nothing that the right medication couldn't suppress, anyway."

"Well, that is good to hear. I was worried about you. Anyway, I was hoping to talk to you about that remarkable email you sent me."

"Yes," I said. "But let's not do this over the phone. Let's chat face-to-face. It would be good to see you."

Isobel frowned.

"What a good idea. Should I come to you?"

"No," I said, with a degree of firmness. "No. I'll come to you."

❑ ❑ ❑

We are waiting.

❑ ❑ ❑

A Large House

Isobel had offered to drive me and had tried to insist on it, saying I wasn't ready to leave the house. Of course, I had already left the house, to go to Fitzwilliam College, but she hadn't known about that. I said I felt like some exercise and Daniel needed to speak to me quite urgently about something, possibly some kind of job offer. I told her I'd have my phone on me and that she knew where I was. And so eventually I was able to take the address from Isobel's notebook, leave the house, and head to Babraham.

It was a large house, the largest I'd seen.

Daniel Russell's wife answered the door. She was a very tall, broad-shouldered woman, with quite long gray hair and aged skin.

"Oh, Andrew."

She held out her arms wide. I replicated the gesture. And she kissed me on the cheek. She smelt of soap and spices. It was clear she knew me. She couldn't stop saying my name.

"Andrew, Andrew, how *are* you?" she asked me. "I heard about your little misadventure."

"Well, I am all right. It was a, well, an episode. But I'm over it. The story continues."

She studied me a little more and then opened the door wide. She beckoned me inside, smiling broadly. I stepped into the hallway.

"Do you know why I am here?"

"To see Him Upstairs," she said, pointing to the ceiling.

"Yes, but do you know *why* I am here to see him?"

She was puzzled by my manner but she tried her best to hide it beneath a kind of energetic and chaotic politeness. "No, Andrew," she said, quickly. "As a matter of fact, he didn't say."

I nodded. I noticed a large ceramic vase on the floor. It had a yellow pattern of flowers on it, and I wondered why people bothered with such empty vessels. What was their significance? Maybe I would never know. We passed a room with a sofa and a television and bookcases and dark-red walls. Blood-colored.

"Do you want a coffee? Fruit juice? We've acquired a taste for pomegranate juice. Though Daniel believes antioxidants are a marketing ploy."

"I would like a water if that's okay."

We were in the kitchen now. It was about twice the size of Andrew Martin's kitchen, but it was so cluttered it felt no bigger. There were saucepans hanging above my head. There was an envelope on the counter addressed to "Daniel and Tabitha Russell."

Tabitha poured me water from a jug.

"I'd offer you a slice of lemon but I think we're out. There's one in the bowl but it must be blue by now. The cleaners never sort the fruit out. They won't touch it. And Daniel won't *eat* it. Even though the doctor has told him he's got to. But then the doctor has told him to relax and slow down too, and he doesn't do that either."

"Oh. Why?"

She looked baffled.

"His heart attack. You remember that? You aren't the only frazzled mathematician in the world."

"Oh," I said. "How is he?"

"Well, he's on beta-blockers. I'm trying to get him on muesli and skimmed milk and to take it easier."

"His heart," I said, thinking aloud.

"Yes. His heart."

"That is one of the reasons I came, in fact." She handed me a glass and I took a sip. As I did so, I thought of the startling capacity for belief inherent in this species. Even before I had fully discovered the concepts of astrology, homeopathy, organized religion, and probiotic yogurts, I was able to work out that what humans may have lacked in physical attractiveness, they made up for in gullibility. You could tell them anything in a convincing-enough voice and they would believe it. Anything, of course, except the truth. "Where is he?"

"In his study. Upstairs."

"His study?"

"You know where that is, don't you?"

"Of course. Of course. I know where that is."

Daniel Russell

Of course, I had been lying.

I had no idea where Daniel Russell's study was, and this was a very big house, but as I was walking along the first-floor landing, I heard a voice. The same dry voice I had heard on the phone.

"Is that the savior of mankind?"

I followed the voice all the way to the third doorway on the left, which was half-open. I could see framed pieces of paper lining a wall. I pushed open the door and saw a bald man with a sharp, angular face and a small—in human terms—mouth. He was smartly dressed. He was wearing a red bow tie and a checked shirt.

"Pleased to see you're wearing clothes," he said, suppressing a sly smile. "Our neighbors are people of delicate sensibilities."

"Yes. I am wearing the right amount of clothes. Don't worry about that."

He nodded and kept nodding, as he leaned back in his chair and scratched his chin. A computer screen glowed behind him, full of Andrew Martin's curves and formulas. I could smell coffee. I noticed an empty cup. Two of them, in fact.

"I have looked at it. And I have looked at it again. This must have taken you to the edge, I can see that. This is something. You must have been burning yourself with this, Andrew. I've been burning just reading through it."

"I worked very hard," I said. "I was lost in it. But that happens, doesn't it, with numbers?"

He listened with concern. "Did they prescribe anything?" he asked.

"Diazepam."

"Do you feel it's working?"

"I do. I do. I feel it is working. Everything feels a little bit *alien*

I would say, a tad *otherworldly,* as if the atmosphere is slightly different, and the gravity has slightly less pull, and even something as familiar as an empty coffee cup has a terrible difference to it. You know, from my perspective. Even you. You seem quite hideous to me. Almost terrifying."

Daniel Russell laughed. It wasn't a happy laugh.

"Well, there's always been a frisson between us, but I always put that down to academic rivalry. Par for the course. We're not geographers or biologists. We're numbers men. We mathematicians have always been like that. Look at that miserable bastard Isaac Newton."

"I named my dog after him."

"So you did. But listen, Andrew, this isn't a moment to nudge you to the curb. This is a moment to slap you on the back."

We were wasting time. "Have you told anyone about this?"

He shook his head. "No. Of course not. Andrew, this is yours. You can publicize this how you want. Though I would probably advise you, as a friend, to wait a little while. At least a week or so, until all this unwelcome stuff about your little Corpus incident has died down."

"Is mathematics less interesting for humans than nudity?"

"It tends to be, Andrew. Yes. Listen. Go home, take it easy this week. I'll put a word in with Diane at Fitz and explain that you'll be fine but you may need some time off. I'm sure she'll be flexible. The students are going to be tricky on your first day back. You need to build your strength up. Rest a while. Come on, Andrew, go home."

I could smell the foul scent of coffee getting stronger. I looked around at all the certificates on the wall and felt thankful to come from a place where personal success was meaningless.

"Home?" I said. "Do you know where that is?"

"'Course I do. Andrew, what are you talking about?"

"Actually, I am not called Andrew."

Another nervous chuckle. "Is Andrew Martin your stage name? If it is, I could have thought of better."

"I don't have a name. Names are a symptom of a species that values the individual self above the collective good."

This was the first time he stood up out of his chair. He was a tall man, taller than me. "This would be amusing, Andrew, if you weren't a friend. I really think you might need to get proper medical help for this. Listen, I know a very good psychiatrist who you—"

"Andrew Martin is someone else. He was taken."

"Taken?"

"After he proved what he proved, we were left with no choice."

"We? What are you talking about? Just have an objective ear, Andrew. You are sounding *out of your mind*. I think you ought to go home. I'll drive you back. I think it would be safer. Come on, let's go. I'll take you home. Back to your family."

He held out his right arm, gesturing toward the door.

But I wasn't going anywhere.

The Pain

"You said you wanted to slap my back."

He frowned. Above the frown, the skin covering the top of his skull shone. I stared at it. At the shine.

"What?"

"You wanted to slap my back. That is what you said. So, why not?"

"What?"

"Slap my back. Then I will go."

"Andrew—"

"Slap my back."

He exhaled slowly. His eyes were the midpoint between concern and fear. I turned, gave him my back. Waited for the hand, then waited some more. Then it came. He slapped my back. On that first contact, even with clothes between us, I made the reading. Then when I turned, for less than a second, my face wasn't Andrew Martin's. It was mine.

"What the—"

He lurched backward, bumping into his desk. I was, to his eyes, Andrew Martin again. But he had seen what he had seen. I only had a second, before he would begin screaming, so I paralyzed his jaw. Somewhere way below the panic of his bulging eyes, there was a question: how did he do that? To finish the job properly I would need another contact; my left hand on his shoulder was sufficient.

Then the pain began. The pain I had summoned.

He held his arm. His face became violet. The color of home.

I had pain too. Head pain. And fatigue.

But I walked past him, as he dropped to his knees, and deleted the email and the attachment. I checked his sent folder but there was nothing suspicious.

I stepped out onto the landing.

"Tabitha! Tabitha, call an ambulance! Quick! I think, I think Daniel is having a heart attack!"

Egypt

Less than a minute later she was upstairs, on the phone, her face full of panic as she knelt down, trying to push a pill—an aspirin—into her husband's mouth. "His mouth won't open! His mouth won't open! Daniel, open your mouth! Darling, oh my God, darling, open your mouth!" And then to the phone. "Yes! I told you! I told you! The name of our house is The Hollies! Yes! Chaucer Road! He's dying! He's dying!"

She managed to cram inside her husband's mouth a piece of the pill, which bubbled into foam and dribbled onto the carpet. "*Mnnnnnn*," her husband was saying desperately. "*Mnnnnnn*."

I stood there watching him. His eyes stayed wide, wide open, ipsoid-wide, as if staying in the world was a simple matter of forcing yourself to see.

"Daniel, it's all right," Tabitha was saying, right into his face. "An ambulance is on its way. You'll be okay, darling."

His eyes were now on me. He jerked in my direction. "*Mnnnnnn!*"

He was trying to warn his wife. "*Mnnnnnn.*"

She didn't understand.

Tabitha was stroking her husband's hair with a manic tenderness. "Daniel, we're going to Egypt. Come on, think of Egypt. We're going to see the Pyramids. It's only two weeks till we go. Come on, it's going to be beautiful. You've always wanted to go . . .

As I watched her I felt a strange sensation. A kind of longing for something, a craving, but for what I had no idea. I was mesmerized by the sight of this human female crouched over the man whose blood I had prevented from reaching his heart.

"You got through it last time and you'll get through it this time."

"No," I whispered, unheard. "No, no, no."

"*Mnnn*," he said, gripping his shoulder in infinite pain.

"I love you, Daniel."

His eyes clenched shut now, the pain too much.

"Stay with me, stay with me, I can't live all alone . . ."

His head was on her knee. She kept caressing his face. So this was love. Two life-forms in mutual reliance. I was meant to be thinking I was watching weakness, something to scorn, but I wasn't thinking that at all.

He stopped making noise, he seemed instantly heavier for her, and the deep, clenched creases around his eyes softened and relaxed. It was done.

Tabitha howled, as if something had been physically wrenched out of her. I have never heard anything like that sound. It troubled me greatly, I have to say.

A cat emerged from the doorway, startled by the noise maybe, but indifferent to the scene in general. It returned back from where it came. (A cat, I discovered, was very much like a dog. But smaller, and without the self-esteem issues.)

"No," said Tabitha, over and over, "no, no, no!"

Outside, the ambulance skidded to a halt on the gravel. Blue flashing lights appeared through the window.

"They're here," I told Tabitha, and went downstairs. It was a strange and overwhelming relief to tread my way down those soft, carpeted stairs, and for those desperate sobs and futile commands to fade away into nothing.

Where We Are From

Where we are from there are no comforting delusions, no religions, no impossible fiction.

Where we are from there is no love and no hate. There is the purity of reason.

Where we are from there are no crimes of passion because there is no passion.

Where we are from there is no remorse because action has a logical motive and always results in the best outcome for the given situation.

Where we are from there are no names, no families living together, no husbands and wives, no sulky teenagers, no madness.

Where we are from we have solved the problem of fear because we have solved the problem of death. We will not die. Which means we can't just let the universe do what it wants to do, because we will be inside it for eternity.

Where we are from we will never be lying on a luxurious carpet, clutching our chest as our faces turn purple and our eyes seek desperately to view our surroundings for one last time.

Where we are from our technology, created on the back of our supreme and comprehensive knowledge of mathematics, has meant not only that we can travel great distances, but also that we can rearrange our own biological ingredients, renew and replenish them. We are psychologically equipped for such advances. We have never been at war with ourselves. We never place the desires of the individual over the requirements of the collective.

Where we are from we understand that if the humans' rate of mathematical advancement exceeds their psychological maturity, then action needs to be taken. For instance, the death of Daniel

Russell, and the knowledge he held, could end up saving many more lives. And so he is a logical and justifiable sacrifice.

Where we are from there are no nightmares.

And yet, that night, for the very first time in my life I had a nightmare.

A world of dead humans with me and that indifferent cat walking through a giant carpeted street full of bodies. I was trying to get home. But I couldn't. I was stuck here. I had become one of them. Stuck in human form, unable to escape the inevitable fate awaiting all of them. And I was getting hungry and I needed to eat but I couldn't eat, because my mouth was clamped shut. The hunger became extreme. I was starving, wasting away at rapid speed. I went to the garage I had been in that first night and tried to shove food in my mouth, but it was no good. It was still locked from this inexplicable paralysis. I knew I was going to die.

Die.

How did humans ever stomach the idea?

I woke.

I was sweating and out of breath. Isobel touched my back. "It's all right," she said, as Tabitha had said. "It's all right, it's all right, it's all right."

The Dog and the Music

The next day I was alone.

Well no, actually, that's not quite true.

I wasn't alone. There was the dog. Newton. The dog named after a human who had come up with the ideas of gravity and inertia. Given the slow speed with which the dog left its basket, I realized the name was a fitting tribute to these discoveries. He was awake now. He was old and he hobbled, and he was half-blind.

He knew who I was. Or who I wasn't. And he growled whenever he was near me. I didn't quite understand his language just yet, but I sensed he was displeased. He showed his teeth, but I could tell years of subservience to his bipedal owners meant the very fact that I was standing up was enough for me to command a certain degree of respect.

I felt sick. I put this down to the new air I was breathing. But each time I closed my eyes, I saw Daniel Russell's anguished face as he lay on the carpet. I also had a headache, but that was the lingering aftereffect of the energy I had exerted yesterday.

I knew life was going to be easier during my short stay here if Newton was on my side. He might have information, have picked up on signals, heard things. And I knew there was one rule that held fast across the universe: if you wanted to get someone on your side, what you really had to do was *relieve their pain*. It seems ridiculous now, such logic. But the truth was even more ridiculous, and too dangerous to acknowledge to myself, that after the need to hurt I felt an urge to heal.

So I went over and gave him a biscuit. And then, after giving him the biscuit, I gave him sight. And then, as I stroked his hind leg, he whimpered words into my ear I couldn't quite translate. I healed him, giving myself not only an even more intense headache but also wave upon wave of fatigue in the process. Indeed, so exhausted was I that I fell asleep on the kitchen floor. When I woke up, I was coated in dog saliva. Newton's tongue was still at it, licking me with considerable enthusiasm. Licking, licking, licking, as though the meaning of canine existence was something just beneath my skin.

"Could you please stop that?" I said. But he couldn't. Not until I stood up. He was physically incapable of stopping.

And even once I had stood up, he tried to stand up with me, and on me, as if he wanted to be upright too. It was then I realized that the one thing worse than having a dog hate you is having a dog love you. Seriously, if there was a *needier* species in the universe, I have yet to meet it.

"Get away," I told him. "I don't want your love."

I went to the living room and sat down on the sofa. I needed to think. Would Daniel Russell's death be viewed by the humans as suspicious? A man on heart medication succumbing to a second and this time fatal heart attack? I had no poison and no weapon they would ever be able to identify.

The dog sat down next to me, placed his head on my lap, then lifted his head off my lap, and then put it on again, as if deciding whether or not to put his head on my lap was the biggest decision he had ever faced.

We spent hours together that day. Me and the dog. At first I was annoyed that he wouldn't leave me alone, as what I needed to do was to focus and work out when I was going to act next. To work out how much more information I needed to acquire before doing what would have to be my final acts here, eliminating Andrew Martin's wife and child. I shouted at the dog again to leave me alone, and he did so, but when I stood in the living room with nothing but my thoughts and plans, I realized I felt a terrible loneliness and so called him back. And he came and seemed happy to be wanted again.

I put something on that interested me. It was called *The Planets* by Gustav Holst. It was a piece of music all about the humans' puny solar system, so it was surprising to hear it had quite an epic feel. Another confusing thing was that it was divided into seven "movements," each named after "astrological characters." For instance, Mars was "the Bringer of War," Jupiter was "the Bringer of Jollity," and Saturn was "the Bringer of Old Age."

This primitivism struck me as funny. And so was the idea that the music had anything whatsoever to do with those dead planets. But it seemed to soothe Newton a little bit, and I must admit one or two parts of it had some kind of effect on me, a kind of electrochemical effect. Listening to music, I realized, was simply the pleasure of counting without realizing you were counting. As the electrical impulses were transported from the neurons in my ear through my body, I felt—I don't know—calm. It made that strange unease that had been with me since I had watched Daniel Russell die on his carpet settle a little.

As we listened I tried to work out why Newton and his species were so enamored of humans.

"Tell me," I said. "What is it about the humans?"

Newton laughed. Or as close as a dog can get to laughing, which is pretty close.

I persisted with my line of inquiry. "Go on," I said. "Spill the beans." He seemed a bit coy. I don't think he really had an answer. Maybe he hadn't reached his verdict, or he was too loyal to be truthful.

I put on some different music. I played the music of someone called Ennio Morricone. I played an album called *Space Oddity* by David Bowie, which, in its simple patterned measure of time, was actually quite enjoyable. As was *Moon Safari* by Air, though that shed little light on the moon itself. I played *A Love Supreme* by John Coltrane and *Blue Monk* by Thelonious Monk. This was jazz music. It was full of the complexity and contradictions that I would soon learn made humans human. I listened to "Rhapsody in Blue" by George Gershwin and "Moonlight Sonata" by Ludwig van Beethoven and Brahms's "Intermezzo op. 17." I listened to the Beatles, the Beach Boys, the Rolling Stones, Daft Punk, Prince, Talking Heads, Al Greene, Tom Waits, Mozart. I was intrigued to discover the sounds that could make it on to music—the strange talking radio voice on "I Am the Walrus" by the Beatles, the cough at the beginning of Prince's "Raspberry Beret" and at the end of Tom Waits's songs. Maybe that is what beauty was, for humans. Accidents, imperfections, placed inside a pretty pattern. Asymmetry. The defiance of mathematics. I thought about my speech at the Museum of Quadratic Equations. I listened to the Beach Boys and I got a strange feeling, behind my eyes and in my stomach. I had no idea what that feeling was, but it made me think of Isobel, and the way she had hugged me last night, after I had come home and told her Daniel Russell had suffered a fatal heart attack in front of me.

There'd been a slight moment of suspicion, a brief hardening of her stare, but it had softened into compassion. Whatever else she might have thought about her husband, he wasn't a killer. The last thing I listened to was a tune called "Clair de Lune" by Debussy. That was the closest representation of space I had ever heard, and I stood there, in the middle of the room, frozen with shock that a human could have made such a beautiful noise.

This beauty terrified me, like an alien creature appearing out of nowhere. An ipsoid, bursting out of the desert. I had to stay focused. I had to keep believing everything I had been told. That this was a species of ugliness and violence, beyond redemption.

Newton was scratching at the front door. The scratching was putting me off the music, so I went over and tried to decipher what he wanted. It turned out that what he wanted was to go outside. There was a "lead" I had seen Isobel use, and so I attached it to the collar.

As I walked the dog, I tried to think more negatively toward the humans.

And it certainly seemed ethically questionable, the relationship between humans and dogs, both of whom—on the scale of intelligence that covered every species in the universe—would have been somewhere in the middle, not too far apart. But I have to say that dogs didn't seem to mind it. In fact, they went along quite happily with the setup most of the time.

I let Newton lead the way.

We passed a man on the other side of the road. The man just

stopped and stared at me and smiled to himself. I smiled and waved my hand, understanding this was an appropriate human greeting. He didn't wave back. *Yes, humans are a troubling species.* We carried on walking, and we passed another man. A man in a wheelchair. He seemed to know me.

"Andrew," he said, "isn't it terrible—the news about Daniel Russell?"

"Yes," I said. "I was there. I saw it happen. It was horrible, just horrible."

"Oh my God, I had no idea."

"Mortality is a very tragic thing."

"Indeed, indeed it is."

"Anyway, I had better be going. The dog is in quite a hurry. I will see you."

"Yes, yes, absolutely. But may I ask: how are you? I heard you'd been a bit unwell yourself?"

"Oh, fine. I am over that. It was just a bit of a misunderstanding, really."

"Oh, I see."

The conversation dwindled further, and I made my excuses, Newton dragging me forward until we reached a large stretch of grass. This is what dogs liked to do, I discovered. They liked to run around on grass, pretending they were free, shouting, *"We're free, we're free, look, look, look how free we are!"* at each other. It really was a sorry sight. But, I had to admit, it worked for them, and for Newton in particular. It was a collective illusion they had chosen to swallow and they were submitting to it wholeheartedly, without any nostalgia for their former wolf selves.

That was the remarkable thing about humans—their ability to shape the path of other species, to change their fundamental nature. Maybe it could happen to me; maybe I could be changed; maybe I already was being changed? Who knew? I hoped not. I hoped I was staying as pure as I had been told, as strong and isolated as a prime, as a ninety-seven.

I sat on a bench and watched the traffic. No matter how long I stayed on this planet, I doubted I would ever get used to the sight of cars, bound by gravity and poor technology to the road, hardly moving on the roads because there were so many of them.

Was it wrong to thwart a species' technological advancement? That was a new question in my mind. I didn't want it there, so I was quite relieved when Newton started barking. I turned to look at him. He was standing still, his head steady in one direction, as he carried on making as loud a noise as he possibly could.

"*Look!*" he seemed to bark. "*Look! Look! Look!*" I was picking up his language.

There was another road, a different one to the one with all the traffic. A line of terraced houses facing the park.

I turned toward it, as Newton clearly wanted me to do. I saw Gulliver, on his own, walking along the pavement, trying his best to hide behind his hair. He was meant to be at school. And he wasn't, unless human school was walking along the street and thinking, which it really should have been. He saw me. He froze. And then he turned around and started walking in the other direction.

"Gulliver!" I called. "Gulliver!"

He ignored me. If anything, he started walking away faster than he had done before. His behavior concerned me. After all, inside his head was the knowledge that the world's biggest mathematical puzzle had been solved, and by his own father. I hadn't acted last night. I had told myself that I needed to find more information, check there was no one else Andrew Martin could have told. Also, I was probably too exhausted after my encounter with Daniel. I would wait another day, maybe even two. That had been the plan. Gulliver had told me he hadn't said anything, and that he wasn't going to, but how could he be totally trusted? His mother was convinced, right now, that he was at school. And yet he evidently wasn't. I got up from the bench and walked over the litter-strewn grass to where Newton was still barking.

"Come on," I said, realizing I should have probably acted already. "We have to go."

We arrived on the road just as Gulliver was turning off it, and so

I decided to follow him and see where he was going. At one point he stopped and took something from his pocket. A box. He took out a cylindrical object and put it in his mouth and lit it. He turned around, but I had sensed he would and was already hiding behind a tree. He began walking again. Soon he reached a larger road. Coleridge Road, this one was called. He didn't want to be on this road for long. Too many cars. Too many opportunities to be seen. He kept on walking, and after a while the buildings stopped and there were no cars or people anymore.

I was worried he was going to turn around, because there were no nearby trees—or anything else—to hide behind. Also, although I was physically near enough to be easily seen if he did turn to look, I was too far for any mind manipulation to work. Remarkably though, he didn't turn around again. Not once.

We passed a building with lots of empty cars outside, shining in the sun. The building had the word "Honda" on it. There was a man inside the glass in a shirt and tie, watching us. Gulliver then cut across a grass field.

Eventually, he reached four metal tracks in the ground: parallel lines, close together but stretching as far as the eye could see. He just stood there, absolutely still, waiting for something.

Newton looked at Gulliver and then up at me, with concern. He let out a deliberately loud whine. "Sh!" I said. "Keep quiet."

After a while, a train appeared in the distance, getting closer as it was carried along the tracks. I noticed Gulliver's fists clench and his whole body stiffen as he stood only a meter or so away from the train's path. As the train was about to pass where he was standing, Newton barked, but the train was too loud and too close to Gulliver for him to hear.

This was interesting. Maybe I wouldn't have to do anything. Maybe Gulliver was going to do it himself.

The train passed. Gulliver's hands stopped being fists and he seemed to relax again. Or maybe it was disappointment. But before he turned around and started walking away, I had dragged Newton back, and we were out of sight.

Grigori Perelman

So, I had left Gulliver.

Untouched, unharmed.

I had returned home with Newton while Gulliver had carried on walking. I had no idea where he was going, but it was pretty clear to me, from his lack of direction, that he hadn't been heading any- where specific. I concluded, therefore, that he wasn't going to meet someone. Indeed, he had seemed to want to avoid people.

Still, I knew it was dangerous.

I knew that it wasn't just proof of the Riemann hypothesis which was the problem. It was knowledge that it could be proved, and Gulliver had that knowledge, inside his skull, as he walked around the streets.

Yet I justified my delay because I had been told to be patient. I had been told to find out exactly who knew. If human progress was to be thwarted, then I needed to be thorough. To kill Gulliver now would have been premature, because his death and that of his mother would be the last acts I could commit before suspicions were aroused.

Yes, this is what I told myself, as I unclipped Newton's lead and reentered the house, and then accessed that sitting room computer, typing in the words "Poincaré Conjecture" into the search box.

Soon I found Isobel had been right. This conjecture—concerning a number of very basic topological laws about spheres and four- dimensional space—had been solved by a Russian mathematician called Grigori Perelman. On March 18, 2010—just over three years ago—it was announced that he had won a Clay Millennium Prize. But he had turned it down, and the million dollars that had gone with it.

"I'm not interested in money or fame," he had said. "I don't want to be on display like an animal in a zoo. I'm not a hero of mathematics."

This was not the only prize he had been offered. There had been others. A prestigious prize from the European Mathematical Society, one from the International Congress of Mathematicians in Madrid, and the Fields Medal, the highest award in mathematics. All of them he had turned down, choosing instead to live a life of poverty and unemployment, caring for his elderly mother.

Humans are arrogant. Humans are greedy. They care about nothing but money and fame. They do not appreciate mathematics for its own sake but care only for what it can get them.

I logged out. Suddenly, I felt weak. I was hungry. That must have been it. So I went to the kitchen and looked for food.

Crunchy Wholenut Peanut Butter

I ate some capers and then a stock cube, and chewed on a sticklike vegetable called celery. Eventually, I got out some bread, a staple of human cuisine, and I looked in the cupboard for something to put on it. Sugar was my first option. And then I tried some mixed herbs. Neither was very satisfying. After much anxious trepidation and analysis of the nutritional information I decided to try something called "crunchy wholenut peanut butter." I placed it on the bread and gave some to the dog. He liked it.

"Should I try it?" I asked him.

Yes, you definitely should, appeared to be the response. (Dog words weren't really words. They were more like melodies. Silent melodies sometimes, but melodies all the same.) *It is very tasty indeed.*

He wasn't wrong.

As I placed it in my mouth and began to chew, I realized that human food could actually be quite good. I had never enjoyed food before. Now I came to think of it, I had never enjoyed anything before. And yet today, even amid my strange feelings of weakness and doubt, I had experienced the pleasures of music and of food. And maybe even the simple enjoyment of canine company.

After I had eaten one piece of bread and peanut butter, I made another one for us both, and then another, Newton's appetite proving to be at least a match for mine.

"I am not what I am," I told him at one stage. "You know that, don't you? I mean, that is why you were so hostile at first. Why you growled whenever I was near you. You sensed it, didn't you? More than a human could. You knew there was a difference."

His silence spoke volumes. And as I stared into his glassy, honest eyes, I felt the urge to tell him more.

"I have killed someone," I told him, feeling a sense of relief. "I am what a human would categorize as a murderer, a judgmental term, and based in this case on the wrong judgments. You see, sometimes to save something, you have to kill a little piece of it. But still, a murderer—that is what they would call me, if they knew. Not that they would ever really be able to know how I had done it.

"You see, as you no doubt know, humans are still at the point in their development where they see a strong difference between the mental and the physical *within the same body*. They have mental hospitals and body hospitals, as if one doesn't directly affect the other. And so, if they can't accept that a mind is directly responsible for the body of the same person, they are hardly likely to understand how a mind—albeit not a human one—can affect the body of someone else. Of course, my skills are not just the product of biology. I have technology, but it is unseen. It is inside me. And now resides in my left hand. It allowed me to take this shape, it enables me to contact my home, and it strengthens my mind. It makes me able to manipulate mental and physical processes. I can perform telekinesis—look, look right now, look what I am doing with the lid of the peanut butter jar—and also something very close to hypnosis. You see, where I am from everything is seamless. Minds, bodies, technologies all come together in a quite beautiful convergence."

The phone rang at that point. It had rung earlier too. I didn't answer it though. There were some tastes, just as there were some songs by the Beach Boys ("In My Room," "God Only Knows," "Sloop John B") that were just too good to disturb.

But then the peanut butter ran out, and Newton and I stared at each other in mutual mourning. "I am sorry, Newton. But it appears we have run out of peanut butter."

This cannot be true. You must be mistaken. Check again.

I checked again. "No, I am not mistaken."

Properly. Check properly. That was just a glance.

I checked properly. I even showed him the inside of the jar. He was still disbelieving, so I placed the jar right up next to his nose, which was clearly where he wanted it. *Ah, you see, there is still some.*

Look. Look. And he licked the contents of the jar until he too had to eventually agree we were out of the stuff. I laughed out loud. I had never laughed. It was a very odd feeling, but not unpleasant. And then we went and sat on the sofa in the living room.

Why are you here?

I don't know if the dog's eyes were asking me this, but I gave him an answer anyway. "I am here to destroy information. Information that exists in the bodies of certain machines and the minds of certain humans. That is my purpose. Although, obviously, while I am here I am also collecting information. Just how volatile are they? How violent? How dangerous to themselves and others? Are their flaws— and there do seem to be quite a few—insurmountable? Or is there hope for them? These questions are the sort I have in mind, even if I am not supposed to. First and foremost though, what I am doing involves elimination."

Newton looked at me bleakly, but he didn't judge. And we stayed there, on that purple sofa, for quite a while. Something was happening to me, I realized, and it had been happening ever since Debussy and the Beach Boys. I wished I'd never played them. For ten minutes we sat in silence. This mournful mood only altered with the distraction of the front door opening and closing.

It was Gulliver. He waited silently in the hallway for a moment or two, and then hung up his coat and dropped his school bag. He came into the living room, walking slowly. He didn't make eye contact.

"Don't tell Mum, okay?"

"What?" I said. "Don't tell her what?"

He was awkward. "That I wasn't at school."

"Okay. I won't."

He looked at Newton, whose head was back on my lap. He seemed confused but didn't comment. He turned to go upstairs.

"What were you doing by the train track?" I asked him.

I saw his hands tense up. "What?"

"You were just standing there, as the train passed."

"You *followed* me?"

"Yes. Yes, I did. I followed you. I wasn't going to tell you. In fact,

I am surprising myself by telling you now. But my innate curiosity won out."

He answered with a kind of muted groan and headed upstairs.

After a while, with a dog on your lap, you realize there is a necessity to stroke it. Don't ask me how this necessity comes about. It clearly has something to do with the dimensions of the human upper body. Anyway, I stroked the dog, and as I did so I realized it was actually a pleasant feeling, the warmth and the rhythm of it.

Isobel's Dance

Eventually, Isobel came back. I shifted along the sofa to reach such a position that I could witness her walking in through the front door. Just to see the simple effort of it—the physical pushing of the door, the extraction of the key, the closing of the door, and the placing of that key (and the others it was attached to) in a small oval basket on a static piece of wooden furniture—all of that was quite mesmerizing to me. The way she did such things in single gliding movements, almost dancelike, without thinking about them. I should have been looking down on such things. But I wasn't. She seemed to be continually operating above the task she was doing. A melody, rising above rhythm. Yet she was still what she was, a human.

She walked down the hallway, exhaling the whole way, her face containing both a smile and a frown at once. Like her son, she was confused to see the dog lying on my lap. And equally confused when she saw the dog jump off my lap and run over to her.

"What's with Newton?" she asked.

"*With* him?"

"He seems lively."

"Does he?"

"Yes. And, I don't know, his eyes seem brighter."

"Oh. It might have been the peanut butter. And the music."

"Peanut butter? Music? You never listen to music. Have you been listening to music?"

"Yes. We have."

She looked at me with suspicion. "Right. I see."

"We've been listening to music all day long."

"How are you feeling? I mean, you know, about Daniel."

"Oh, it is very sad," I said. "How was your day?"

She sighed. "It was okay." This was a lie, I could tell that.

I looked at her. My eyes could stay on her with ease, I noticed. What had happened? Was this another side effect of the music?

I suppose I was getting acclimatized to her, and to humans in general. Physically, at least from the outside, I was one too. It was becoming a new normality, in a sense. Yet even so, my stomach churned far less with her than with the sight of the others I saw walking past the window, peering in at me. In fact, that day, or at that point in that day, it didn't churn at all.

"I feel like I should phone Tabitha," she said. "It's difficult though, isn't it? She'll be inundated. I might just send her an email and let her know, you know, if there's anything we can do."

I nodded. "That's a good idea."

She studied me for a while.

"Yes," she said, at a lower frequency. "I think so." She looked at the phone. "Has anyone called?"

"I think so. The phone rang a few times."

"But you didn't pick it up?"

"No. No, I didn't. I don't really feel up to lengthy conversations. And I feel cursed at the moment. The last time I had a lengthy conversation with anyone who wasn't you or Gulliver, he ended up dying in front of me."

"Don't say it like that."

"Like what?"

"Flippantly. It's a sad day."

"I know," I said. "I just . . . it hasn't sunk in yet, really."

She went away to listen to the messages. She came back.

"*Lots* of people have been calling you."

"Oh," I said. "Who?"

"Your mother. But be warned, she might be doing her trademark oppressive-worry thing. She's heard about your little event at Corpus. I don't know how. The college called too, wanting to speak, doing a good job of sounding concerned. A journalist from the *Cambridge Evening News*. And Ari. Being sweet. He wonders if you'd be up to going to a football match on Saturday. Someone else too." She paused for a moment. "She said her name was Maggie."

"Oh yes," I said, faking it. "Of course. Maggie."

Then she raised her eyebrows at me. It meant something, clearly, but I had no idea what. It was frustrating. You see, the language of words was only one of the human languages. There were many others, as I have pointed out. The language of sighs, the language of silent moments, and most significantly, the language of frowns.

Then she did the opposite, her eyebrows going as low as they could. She sighed and went into the kitchen.

"What have you been doing with the sugar?"

"Eating it," I said. "It was a mistake. Sorry."

"Well, you know, feel free to put things back."

"I forgot. Sorry."

"It's okay. It's just been a day and a half, that's all."

I nodded and tried to act human. "What do you want me to do? I mean, what should I do?"

"Well, you could start by calling your mother. But don't tell her about the hospital. I know what you're like."

"What? What am I like?"

"You tell her more than you tell me."

Now that was worrying. That was very worrying indeed. I decided to phone her right away.

The Mother

Remarkable as it may sound, the mother was an important concept for humans. Not only were they truly aware who their mother was, but in many cases they also kept *in contact* with her throughout their lives. Of course, for someone like me, whose mother was never there to be known, this was a very exotic idea.

So exotic, I was scared to pursue it. But I did, because if her son had told her too much information, I obviously needed to know.

"Andrew?"

"Yes, Mother. It is me."

"Oh Andrew." She spoke at a high frequency. The highest I had ever heard.

"Hello, Mother."

"Andrew, me and your father have been worried sick about you."

"Oh," I said. "I had a little episode. I temporarily lost my mind. I forgot to put on my clothes. That's all."

"Is that all you have to say?"

"No. No, it isn't. I have to ask you a question, Mother. It is an important question."

"Oh, *Andrew.* What is the matter?"

"The matter? Which matter?"

"Is it Isobel? Has she been nagging you again? Is that what this is about?"

"Again?"

The static crackle of a sigh. "Yes. You've told us for over a year now that you and Isobel have been having difficulties. That she's not been as understanding as she could have been about your work-load. That she's not been there for you."

I thought of Isobel, lying about her day to stop me from worrying, making me food, stroking my skin.

"No," I said. "She is there for him. *Me.*"

"And Gulliver? What about him? You told me she's turned him against you. Because of that band he wanted to be in. But you were right, darling. He shouldn't be messing around in bands. Not after all that he's done."

"Band? I don't know, Mother. I don't think it is that."

"Why are you calling me Mother? You never call me Mother."

"But you are my mother. What do I call you?"

"Mum. You call me Mum."

"Mum," I said. It sounded the most strange of all the strange words. "Mum. Mum. Mum. Mum. Mum, listen, I want to know if I spoke to you recently."

She wasn't listening. "We wish we were there."

"Come over," I said. I was interested to see what she looked like. "Come over right now."

"Well, if we didn't live twelve thousand miles away."

"Oh," I said. Twelve thousand miles didn't sound like much. "Come over this afternoon then."

The mother laughed. "Still got your sense of humor."

"Yes," I said. "I am still very funny. Listen, did I speak to you last Saturday?"

"No. Andrew, have you lost your memory? Is this amnesia? You're acting like you have amnesia."

"I'm a bit confused. That's all. It's not amnesia. The doctors told me that. It's just . . . I have been working hard."

"Yes, yes, I know. You told us."

"So, what did I tell you?"

"That you've hardly been sleeping. That you've been working harder than you ever have, at least since your PhD."

And then she started giving me information I hadn't asked for. She started talking about her hip bone. It was causing her a lot of pain. She was on pain relief medication but it wasn't working. I found the conversation disconcerting and even nauseating. The idea of *prolonged* pain was quite alien to me. Humans considered themselves to be quite medically advanced but they had yet to solve this problem in any meaningful way. Just as they had yet to solve the problem of death.

"Mother. *Mum*, listen, what do you know about the Riemann hypothesis?"

"That's the thing you're working on, isn't it?"

"Working on? Working on. Yes. I am still working on it. And I will never prove it. I realize that now."

"Oh, all right, darling. Well, don't beat yourself up about it. Now, listen . . ."

Pretty soon she was back to talking about the pain again. She said the doctor had told her she should get a hip replacement. It would be made of titanium. I almost gasped when she said that, but I didn't want to tell her about titanium, as the humans obviously didn't know about that yet. They would find out in their own time.

Then she started talking about my "father" and how his memory was getting worse. The doctor had told him not to drive anymore and that it looked increasingly unlikely that he would be able to finish the book on macroeconomic theory he had been hoping to get published.

"It makes me worry about you, Andrew. You know, only last week I told you what the doctor had said, about how I should advise you to get a brain scan. It can run in families."

"Oh," I said. I really didn't know what else was required of me. The truth was that I wanted the conversation to end. I had obviously not told my parents. Or I hadn't told my mother, at any rate, and from the sound of things my father's brain was such that it would probably lose any information I had given him. Also, and it was a big also, the conversation was depressing me. It was making me think about human life in a way I didn't want to think about it. Human life, I realized, got progressively worse as you got older, by the sound of things. You arrived, with baby feet and hands and infinite happiness, and then the happiness slowly evaporated as your feet and hands grew bigger. And then, from the teenage years onward, happiness was something you could lose your grip of, and once it started to slip, it gained mass. It was as if the knowledge that it could slip was the thing that made it more difficult to hold, no matter how big your feet and hands were.

Why was this depressing? Why did I care, when it was not my job to?

Again I felt immense gratitude that I only looked like a human being and would never actually *be* one.

She carried on talking. And as she did so, I realized there could be no cosmic consequence at all if I stopped listening, and with that realization I switched off the phone.

I closed my eyes, wanting to see nothing, but I did see something. I saw Tabitha, leaning over her husband as aspirin froth slid out of his mouth. I wondered if my mother was the same age as Tabitha, or older.

When I opened my eyes again, I realized Newton was standing there, looking up at me. His eyes told me he was confused.

Why did you not say good-bye? You usually say good-bye.

And then, bizarrely, I did something I didn't understand. Something which had absolutely no logic to it at all. I picked up the phone and dialed the same number. After three rings she answered, and then I spoke. "Sorry, Mum. I meant to say good-bye."

Hello. Hello. Can you hear me? Are you there?

We can hear you. We are here.

Listen, it's safe. The information is destroyed. For now, the humans will remain at level three. There is no worry.

You have destroyed all the evidence and all possible sources?

I have destroyed the information on Andrew Martin's computer and on Daniel Russell's computer. Daniel Russell is destroyed also. Heart attack. He was a heart risk, so that was the most logical cause of death in the circumstances.

Have you destroyed Isobel Martin and Gulliver Martin?

No. No, I haven't. There is no need to destroy them.

They do not know?

Gulliver Martin knows. Isobel Martin doesn't. But Gulliver has no motivation to say anything.

You must destroy him. You must destroy both of them.

No. There is no need. If you want me to, if you really think it is required, then I can manipulate his neurological processes. I can make him forget what his father told him. Not that he really *knows* anyway. He has no real understanding of mathematics.

The effects of any mind manipulation you carry out disappear the moment you return home. You know that.

He won't say anything.

He might have said something already. Humans aren't to be trusted. They don't even trust themselves.

Gulliver hasn't said anything. And Isobel knows nothing.

You must complete your task. If you do not complete your task, someone else will be sent to complete it for you.

No. No. I will complete it. Don't worry. I will complete my task.

PART TWO

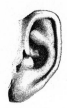

I Held a Jewel in My Fingers

You can't say A is made of B or vice versa. All mass is interaction.

— RICHARD FEYNMAN

We're all lonely for something we don't know we're lonely for.

— DAVID FOSTER WALLACE

For small creatures such as we the vastness is bearable only through love.

— CARL SAGAN

Sleepwalking

I stood next to his bed while he slept. I don't know how long I just stood there, in the dark, listening to his deep breathing as he slipped deeper and deeper below dreams. Half an hour, maybe.

He hadn't pulled the window blind down, so I looked out at the night. There was no moon from this angle, but I could see a few stars. Suns lighting dead solar systems elsewhere in the galaxy. Everywhere you can see in their sky, or almost everywhere, is lifeless. That must affect them. That must give them ideas above their station. That must send them insane.

Gulliver rolled over, and I decided to wait no longer. It was now or it was never.

You will pull back your duvet, I told him, in a voice he wouldn't have heard if he had been awake but which reached right in, riding theta waves, to become a command from his own brain. *And slowly you will sit up in your bed, your feet will be on the rug and you will breathe and you will compose yourself and then you will stand up.*

And he did, indeed, stand up. He stayed there, breathing deeply and slowly, waiting for the next command.

You will walk to the door. Do not worry about opening the door, because it is already open. There. Just walk, just walk, just walk to your door.

He did exactly as I said. And he was there in the doorway, oblivious to everything except my voice. A voice which only had two words that needed to be said. *Fall forward.* I moved closer to him. Somehow those words were slow to arrive. I needed time. Another minute, at least.

I was there, closer, able to smell the scent of sleep on him. Of humanity. And I remembered: *You must complete your task. If you do not complete your task, someone else will be sent to complete it for you.* I swallowed. My mouth was so dry it hurt. I felt the infinite expanse of the universe behind me, a vast if neutral force. The neutrality of time, of space, of mathematics, of logic, of survival. I closed my eyes.

Waited.

Before I opened them, I was being gripped by the throat. I could barely breathe.

He had turned 180 degrees, and his left hand had me by the neck. I pulled it away, and now both his hands were fists swinging at me, wild, angry, hitting me almost as much as he missed.

He got the side of my head. I walked backward away from him, but he was moving forward at just the same speed. His eyes were open. He was seeing me now. Seeing me and not seeing me all at the same time. I could have said *stop* of course, but I didn't. Maybe I wanted to witness some human violence firsthand, even unconscious violence, to understand the importance of my task. By understanding its necessity, I would be able to fulfill it. Yes, that might have been it. That may also have explained why I let myself bleed when he punched me on the nose. I had reached his desk now and could retreat no farther, so I just stood there as he kept hitting my head, my neck, my chest, my arms. He roared now, his mouth as wide as it could go, baring teeth.

"*Raaaah!*"

This roar woke him up. His legs went weak and he nearly fell to the floor but he recovered in time.

"I," he said. He didn't know where he was for a moment. He saw me, in the dark, and this time it was conscious sight. "Dad?"

I nodded as a slow thin stream of blood reached my mouth. Isobel was running up the stairs to the attic. "What's going on?"

"Nothing," I said. "I heard a noise so I came upstairs. Gulliver was sleepwalking, that's all."

Isobel switched the light on, gasped as she saw my face. "You're bleeding."

"It's nothing. He didn't know what he was doing."

"Gulliver?"

Gulliver was sitting on the edge of his bed now, flinching from the light. He too looked at my face, but he didn't say anything at all.

I Was a Wasn't

Gulliver wanted to go back to bed. To sleep. So, ten minutes later, Isobel and I were alone, and I was sitting on the side of the bath as she placed an antiseptic solution called TCP on a circle of cotton wool and dabbed it gently on a cut on my forehead, and then on my lip.

Now, these were wounds I could have healed with a single thought. Just to feel pain, sometimes, was enough to cancel it. And yet, even as the antiseptic stung on contact with each cut, the injuries stayed. I forced them to, as clearly I couldn't allow her to get suspicious. But was it just that?

"How's your nose?" she asked. I caught sight of it in the mirror. A smear of blood around one nostril.

"It's okay," I said, feeling it. "It isn't broken."

Her eyes squinted in pure concentration. "This one on your forehead is really bad. And there's going to be one giant bruise there. He must have really hit you hard. Did you try and restrain him?"

"Yes," I lied. "I did. But he kept on."

I could smell her. Clean, human smells. The smells of the creams she used to wash and moisturize her face. The smell of her shampoo. A delicate trace of ammonia barely competing with the heavy scent of antiseptic. She was physically closer to me than she had ever been. I looked at her neck. She had two little dark moles on it, close together, charting unknown binary stars. I thought of Andrew Martin kissing her. This was what humans did. They kissed. Like so many human things, it made no sense. Or maybe, if you tried it, the logic would unfold.

"Did he say anything?"

"No," I said. "No. He just yelled. It was very primal."

"I don't know, between you and him, it never ends."

"What never ends?"

"The worry."

She placed the bloodstained cotton wool in the small bin beside the sink.

"I'm sorry," I said. "I'm sorry for everything. For the past and the future." An apology, said while in dull pain, made me feel as close to human as it was possible to feel. I could have almost written a poem.

We went back to bed. She held my hand in the dark. I gently pulled it away.

"We've lost him," she said. It took me a moment to realize she was talking about Gulliver.

"Well," I said, "maybe we just have to accept him as he is, even if he's different from what we've known."

"I just don't understand him. You know, he's our son. And we've known him for sixteen years. And yet, I feel like I don't know him at all."

"Well, maybe we should not try to understand so much, and accept some more."

"That's a very difficult thing. And a very strange thing to come from your mouth, Andrew."

"So, I suppose the next question is, what about me? Do you understand me?"

"I don't think you understand yourself, Andrew."

I wasn't Andrew. I knew I wasn't Andrew. But equally, I was losing myself. I was a wasn't, that was the problem. I was lying in bed with a human woman I could now almost appreciate as beautiful, wilfully still feeling the sting of antiseptic in my wounds, and thinking of her strange but fascinating skin, and the way she had cared for me. No one in the universe cared for me. (You didn't, did you?) We had technology to care for us now, and we didn't need emotions. We were alone. We worked together for our preservation, but emotionally we needed no one. We just needed the purity of mathematical truth. And yet, I was scared of falling asleep, because the moment I fell asleep, my wounds would heal, and right then I didn't want that to happen. Right then, I found a strange but real comfort in the pain.

I had so many worries now. So many questions.

"Do you believe humans are ever knowable?" I asked.

"I wrote a book on Charlemagne. I hope so."

"But humans, in their natural state, are they good or are they bad, would you say? Can they be trusted? Or is their own real state just violence and greed and cruelty?"

"Well, that's the oldest question there is."

"What do you think?"

"I'm tired, Andrew. I'm sorry."

"Yes, me too. I'll see you in the morning."

"Night."

"Night."

I stayed awake for a while as Isobel slipped toward sleep. The trouble was, I still wasn't used to the night. It may not have been as dark as I first thought it to be—there was moonlight, starlight, airglow, streetlamps, and sunlight backscattered by interplanetary dust—but the humans still spent half their time in deep shadow. This, I was sure, was one of the chief reasons for personal and sexual relationships here. The need to find comfort in the dark. And it was a comfort, being next to her. So I just stayed there, hearing her breath move in and out, sounding like the tide of some exotic sea. At some point my little finger touched hers, in the double night beneath the duvet, and this time I kept it there and imagined I was really what she thought I was. And that we were connected. Two humans, primitive enough to truly care about each other. It was a comforting thought, and the one that led me down those ever-darkening stairs of the mind toward sleep.

I may need more time.

You do not need time.

I am going to kill those I need to kill, don't worry about that.

We are not worried.

But I am not here just to destroy information. I am here to gather it. That is what you said, wasn't it? Stuff on mathematical understanding can be read across the universe, I know that. I'm not talking about neuroflashes. I'm talking about stuff that can only be picked up on from here, on Earth itself. To give us more insight into how the humans live. It has been a long time since anyone was here, at least in human terms.

Explain why you need more time for this. Complexity demands time, but humans are primitives. They are the most shallow of mysteries.

No. You are wrong. They exist simultaneously in two worlds—the world of appearances and the world of truth. The connecting strands between these worlds take many forms. When I first arrived here, I did not understand certain things. For instance, I did not understand why clothes were so important. Or why a dead cow became beef, or why grass cut a certain way demanded not to be walked upon, or why household pets were so important to them. The humans are scared of nature and are greatly reassured when they can prove to themselves they have mastery over it. This is why lawns exist, and why wolves evolved into dogs, and why their architecture is based on unnatural shapes. But really, nature, pure nature, is just a symbol to them. A symbol of human nature. They are interchangeable. So what I am saying—

What are you saying?

What I am saying is that it takes time to understand humans because they don't understand themselves. They have been wearing clothes for so long. Metaphorical clothes. That is what I am talking about. That was the price of human civilization—to create it, they had to close the door on their true selves. And so they are lost, that is how I understand it. And that is why they invented art: books, music, films, plays, painting, sculpture. They invented them as bridges back to themselves, back to who they are. But however close they get, they are forever removed.

What I am saying, I suppose, is that last night I was about to kill the boy. Gulliver. He was about to fall down the stairs in his sleep, but then his true nature came out and he attacked me.

Attacked you with what?

With himself. With his arms. His hands. He was still asleep but his eyes were open. He attacked me, or the me he thinks I am. His father. And it was pure rage.

The humans are violent. That is not news.

No, I know. I *know*. But he woke, and he wasn't violent. That is the battle they have. And I believe if we understand human nature a little more, then we will know better what action to take in the future, when other advances are made. In the future, when another overpopulation crisis arises, there may come a time when Earth becomes a valid option for our species. So, surely as much knowledge as possible on human psychology and society and behavior is going to help?

They are defined by greed.

Not all of them. For instance, there is a mathematician called Grigori Perelman. He turned down money and prizes. He looks after his mother. We have a distorted view. I think it would be useful for all of us if I re-searched further.

But you don't need the two humans for that.

Oh, I do.

Why?

Because they think they know who I am. And I have a true chance of see-ing them. The real them. Behind the walls they have built for themselves. And speaking of walls, Gulliver knows nothing now. I canceled his knowl-edge of what his father told him on his last night. While I am here, there is no danger.

You must act soon. You don't have forever.

I know. Don't worry. I won't need forever.

They must die.

Yes.

◻ ◻ ◻

Wider Than the Sky

"It was sleep psychosis," Isobel told Gulliver at breakfast the next day. "It's very common. Lots of people have had it. Lots of perfectly normal and sane people. Like that man from R.E.M. He had it, and he was normally as nice as rock stars come."

She hadn't seen me. I had just entered the kitchen. But now she noticed my presence and was puzzled by the sight of me. "Your face," she said. "Last night there were cuts and bruises. It's totally healed."

"Must have been better than it looked. The night might exaggerate things."

"Yes, but even so—"

She glanced at her son, struggling uneasily with his cereal, and decided not to go on.

"You might need the day off school, Gulliver," said Isobel.

I expected him to agree to this, seeing that he preferred an education that involved staring at rail tracks. But he looked at me, considered for a moment, and concluded, "No. No. It's okay. I feel fine."

Later, it was just me and Newton in the house. I was still "recovering," you see. *Recover.* The most human of words, the implication being that healthy, normal life is covering something—the violence that is there underneath, the violence I had seen in Gulliver the night before. To be healthy meant to be covered. Clothed. Literally and metaphorically. Yet I needed to find what lay beneath, something that would satisfy the hosts and justify the delay I was taking in my task.

I discovered a pile of paper, tied with an elastic band. It was in Isobel's wardrobe, hidden among all those essential clothes, yellowing with age. I sniffed the page and guessed at least a decade. The top sheet had the words "Wider Than the Sky" on them, along with these ones: "A novel by Isobel Martin." A *novel*? I read a little bit of it and realized that although the central character's name was Charlotte, she could just as easily have been called Isobel.

Charlotte heard herself sigh: a tired old machine, releasing pressure.

Everything weighed down on her. The small rituals of her daily existence—filling the dishwasher, picking up from school, cooking—had all been performed as if underwater. The mutual energy reserves shared by a mother and her child had now, she conceded, been monopolized by Oliver.

He had been running wild since she had picked him up from school, firing that blue alien blaster or whatever it was. She didn't know why her mother had bought it. Actually, she did know. To prove a point.

"Five-year-old boys want to play with guns, Charlotte. It's only natural. You can't deprive them of their nature."

"Die! Die! Die!"

Charlotte closed the oven door and set the timer.

She turned around to see Oliver pointing the massive blue gun up at her face.

"No, Oliver," she said, too tired to battle the abstract anger clouding his features. "Don't shoot Mummy."

He maintained his pose, fired cheap electric fairground sounds a few more times, then ran out of the kitchen, through the hallway, and noisily exterminated invisible aliens as he charged up the stairs. She remembered the quiet, echoing babble of university corridors and realized that missing it was a kind of pain. She wanted to return, to teach again, but she worried she may have left it too late. Maternity leave had stretched into permanent leave, and the belief had grown that she could be fulfilled as a wife and mother, a historical archetype, "keeping her feet on the ground," as her mother always advised, while her high-flying husband made sure he didn't dip beneath the clouds.

Charlotte shook her head in theatrical exasperation, as if she were being observed by an audience of stern-faced mother watchers examining her progress and making notes on clipboards. She was often aware of the self-conscious nature of her parenting, the way she had to create a role outside herself, a part already plotted out for her.

Don't shoot Mummy.

She squatted down and looked through the oven door. The lasagne would be another forty-five minutes and Jonathan still wasn't back from his conference.

She raised herself back up and went into the living room. The wobbly glass of the drinks cabinet glinted, shining like a false promise. She turned the old key and opened the door. A mini metropolis of spirit bottles bathed in dark shadow.

She reached for the Empire State, the Bombay Sapphire, and poured out her evening allowance.

Jonathan.

Late last Thursday. Late this Thursday.

She acknowledged this fact as she slumped down on the settee, but did not get too close to it. Her husband was a mystery she no longer had the energy to unravel. Anyway, it was known to be the first rule of marriage: solve the mystery, end the love.

So, families often stayed together. Wives sometimes managed to stay with husbands and put up with whichever misery they felt by writing novels and hiding them at the bottom of their wardrobes. Mothers put up with their children, no matter how difficult the offspring were, no matter how close to insanity they pushed their parents.

Anyway, I stopped reading there. I felt it was an intrusion. A bit rich, I know, from someone who was living inside her husband's identity. I put it back in its place in the wardrobe underneath the clothes.

Later on, I told her what I had found.

She gave me an unreadable look, and her cheeks went red. I didn't know if it was a blush or anger. Maybe it was a little of both.

"That was private. You weren't ever supposed to see that."

"I know. That is why I wanted to see it. I want to understand you."

"Why? There's no academic glory or million-dollar prize if you solve me, Andrew. You shouldn't go snooping around."

"Shouldn't a husband know a wife?"

"That really is quite rich coming from you."

"What does that mean?"

She sighed. "Nothing. Nothing. Sorry, I shouldn't have said that."

"You should say whatever you feel you should say."

"Good policy. But I think that would mean we'd have divorced around 2002, at a conservative estimate."

"Well? Maybe you would have been happier if you had divorced him, I mean me, in 2002."

"Well, we'll never know."

"No."

And the phone rang. It was someone for me.

"Hello?"

A man spoke. His voice was casual, familiar, but there was a curiosity there too. "Hey, it's me. Ari."

"Oh, hello, Ari." I knew Ari was supposed to be my closest friend, so I tried to sound friend-like. "How are you? How's your marriage?"

Isobel looked at me with an emphatic frown, but I don't think he'd heard properly.

"Well, just got back from that thing in Edinburgh."

"Oh," I said, trying to pretend I knew what "that thing in Edinburgh" was. "Right. Yes. That thing in Edinburgh. Of course. How was that?"

"It was good. Yeah, it was good. Caught up with the St. Andrew's lot. Listen, mate, I hear it's been a bit of a week for you."

"Yes. It has. It has been a lot of a week for me."

"So I wasn't sure if you'd still be up for the football."

"The football?"

"Cambridge–Kettering. We could have a pint of mild and a bit of a chat, about that top secret thing you told me the last time we spoke."

"Secret?" Every molecule of me was now alert. "What secret?"

"Don't think I should broadcast it."

"No. *No.* You're right. Don't say it out loud. In fact, don't tell anyone." Isobel was now in the hallway, looking at me with suspicion. "But to answer you, yes, I will go to the football."

And I pressed the red button on the phone, weary at the probability that I would have to switch another human life into nonexistence.

A Few Seconds of Silence over Breakfast

You become something else. A different species. That is the easy bit. That is simple molecular rearrangement. Our inner technology can do that, without a problem, with the correct commands and model to work from. There are no new ingredients in the universe, and humans—however they may look—are made of roughly the same things we are.

The difficulty, though, is the other stuff. The stuff that happens when you look in the bathroom mirror and see this new you and don't want to throw up into the sink at the sight of yourself as you have wanted to every other morning. And when you wear clothes, and you realize it is starting to feel like quite a normal thing to do.

And when you walk downstairs and see the life-form that is meant to be your son eating toast, listening to music only he can hear, it takes you a second—or two, three, four seconds—to realize that, actually, this is not your son. He means nothing to you. Not only that: he has to mean nothing to you.

Also, your wife. Your wife is not your wife. Your wife who loves you but doesn't really like you, because of something you never did, but which couldn't be any worse, from her perspective, than the something you're going to do. She is an alien. She is as alien as they come. A primate whose nearest evolutionary cousins are hairy, tree-dwelling knuckle draggers known as chimpanzees. And yet when everything is alien, the alien becomes familiar, and you can judge her as humans judge her. You can watch her when she drinks her pink grapefruit juice and stares at her son with worried, helpless eyes. You can see that for her, being a parent is standing on a shore and watching her child in a vulnerable craft, heading out over deeper and deeper water, hoping but not knowing there will be land somewhere ahead.

And you can see her beauty. If beauty on Earth is the same as elsewhere: ideal in that it is tantalizing and unsolvable, creating a delicious kind of confusion.

I was confused. I was lost.

I wished I had a new wound, just so she could attend to me.

"What are you looking at?" she asked me.

"You," I said.

She looked at Gulliver. He couldn't hear us. Then she looked back at me, as confused as myself.

☐ ☐ ☐

We are worried. What are you doing?
    I told you.

Well?
    I am accumulating information.

You are wasting time.
    I'm not. I know what I am doing.

It was never meant to take this long.
    I know. But I am learning more about the humans. They are more complicated than we first thought. They are sometimes violent but more often care about each other. There is more goodness in them than anything else, I am convinced of it.

What are you saying?
    I don't know what I am saying. I am confused. Some things have stopped making sense.

This happens, occasionally, on a new planet. The perspective changes to that of its inhabitants. But our perspective has not changed. Do you understand that?
    Yes. I do understand.

Stay pure.
    I will.

☐ ☐ ☐

Life/Death/Football

Humans are one of the few intelligent species in the galaxy who haven't quite solved the problem of death. And yet they don't spend their whole lives screeching and howling in terror, clawing at their own bodies, or rolling around on the floor. Some humans do that—I saw them in the hospital—but those humans are considered the mad ones.

Now, consider this.

A human life is on average eighty Earth years or around thirty thousand Earth days. Which means they are born, they make some friends, eat a few meals, they get married or they don't get married, have a child or two, or not, drink a few thousand glasses of wine, have sexual intercourse a few times, discover a lump somewhere, feel a bit of regret, wonder where all the time went, know they should have done it differently, realize they would have done it the same, and then they die. Into the great black nothing. Out of space. Out of time. The most trivial of trivial zeroes. And that's it, the full caboodle. All confined to the same mediocre planet.

But at ground level the humans don't appear to spend their entire lives in a catatonic state.

No. They do other things. Things like
washing
listening
gardening
eating
driving
working
yearning
earning
sleeping

drinking
sighing
gaming
sunbathing
complaining
jogging
quibbling
caring
mingling
fantasizing
googling
parenting
renovating
loving
dancing
fucking
regretting
failing
striving
hoping
Oh, and sport.

Apparently I, or rather Andrew, liked sport. And the sport he liked was football.

Luckily for Professor Andrew Martin, the football team he supported was Cambridge United, one of those which successfully avoided the perils and existential trauma of victory. To support Cambridge United, I discovered, was to support the idea of failure. To watch a team's feet consistently avoid the spherical Earth symbol seemed to frustrate their supporters greatly, but they obviously wouldn't have it any other way. The truth is, you see, however much they would beg to disagree, humans don't actually like to win. Or rather, they like winning for ten seconds, but if they keep on winning, they end up actually having to think about other things, like life and death. The only thing humans like less than winning is losing, but at least something can be done about that. With absolute winning, there is nothing to be done. They just have to deal with it.

Now, I was there at the game to see Cambridge United play against a team called Kettering. I had asked Gulliver if he wanted to come with me—so I could keep an eye on him—and he had said, with sarcasm, "Yeah, Dad, you know me so well."

So, it was just me and Ari, or to give him his full title, Professor Arirumadhi Arasaratham. As I have said, this was Andrew's closest friend, although I had learned from Isobel that I didn't really have friends as such. More acquaintances. Anyway, Ari was an "expert" (human definition) on theoretical physics. He was also quite rotund, as if he didn't just want to watch football but *become* one.

"So," he said, during a period when Cambridge United didn't have the ball (that is to say, any time during the match), "how are things?"

"*Things?*"

He stuffed some crisps into his mouth and made no attempt to conceal their fate. "You know, I was a bit worried about you." He laughed. It was the laugh human males do, to hide emotion. "Well, I say worry, it was more mild concern. I say mild concern, but it was more 'wonder if he's done a Nash.'"

"What do you mean?"

He told me what he meant. Apparently human mathematicians have a habit of going mad. He gave me a list of names—Nash, Cantor, Gödel, Turing—and I nodded along as if they meant something. And then he said "Riemann."

"Riemann?"

"I heard you weren't eating much, so I was thinking more Gödel than Riemann, actually," he said. By Gödel, I later learned, he meant Kurt Gödel, another German mathematician. However, this one's particular psychological quirk was that he had believed everyone was trying to poison his food. So he had stopped eating altogether. By that definition of madness, Ari appeared very sane indeed.

"No. I haven't done one of those. I am eating now. Peanut butter sandwiches mainly."

"Sounds like more of a Presley," he said, laughing. And then he gave me a serious look. I could tell it was serious because he had swallowed and wasn't putting any more food in his mouth. "Because, you know, prime numbers are fucking serious, man. Some serious shit. They can make you lose it. They're like sirens. They call you in with their isolated beauty and before you know it you are in some major mind shit. And when I heard about your naked corpus at Corpus, I thought you were cracking up a bit."

"No. I am on the rails," I said. "Like a train. Or a clothes hanger."

"And Isobel? Everything fine with you and Isobel?"

"Yes," I said. "She is my wife. And I love her. Everything is fine. Fine."

He frowned at me. Then he took a moment's glance to see if Cambridge United were anywhere near the ball. He seemed relieved to see they weren't.

"Really? Everything's fine?"

I could see he needed more confirmation. "'Till I loved I never lived.'"

He shook his head and gave a facial expression I can now safely classify as bewilderment.

"What's that? Shakespeare? Tennyson? Marvell?"

I shook my head. "No. It was Emily Dickinson. I have been reading a lot of her poetry. And also Anne Sexton's. And Walt Whitman too. Poetry seems to say a lot about us. You know, us humans."

"Emily Dickinson? You're quoting Emily Dickinson at a match?"

"Yes."

I sensed, again, I was getting the context wrong. Everything here was about context. There was nothing that was right for every occasion. I didn't get it. The air always had hydrogen in it wherever you were. But that was pretty much the only consistent thing. What was the big difference that made quoting love poetry inappropriate in this context? I had no idea.

"Right," he said, and paused for the large, communal groan as

Kettering scored a goal. I groaned too. Groaning was actually quite diverting, and certainly the most enjoyable aspect of sport spectating. I might have overdone it a little bit though, judging from the looks I was getting. Or maybe they had seen me on the Internet.

"Okay," he said. "And what does Isobel feel about everything?"

"Everything?"

"You, Andrew. What does she think? Does she know about . . . *you know*? Is that what triggered it?"

This was my moment. I inhaled. "The secret I told you?"

"Yeah."

"About the Riemann hypothesis?"

He scrunched his face in confusion. "What? No, man. Unless you've been sleeping with a hypothesis on the side?"

"So what was the secret?"

"That you're having it away with a student."

"Oh," I said, feeling relief. "So I definitely didn't say anything about work the last time I saw you."

"No. For once, you didn't." He turned back to the football. "So, are you going to spill the beans about this student?"

"My memory is a bit hazy, to be honest with you."

"That's convenient. Perfect alibi. If Isobel finds out. Not that you're exactly man of the match in her eyes."

"What do you mean?"

"No offense, mate, but you've told me what her opinion is."

"What *is* her opinion of"—I hesitated—"of *me*?"

He pressed one final handful of crisps in his mouth and washed it down with that disgusting phosphoric acid–flavored drink called Coca-Cola.

"Her opinion is that you are a selfish bastard."

"Why does she think that?"

"Maybe because you *are* a selfish bastard. But then, we're all selfish bastards."

"Are we?"

"Oh yeah. It's our DNA. Dawkins pointed that out to us, way back. But you, man, your selfish gene is on a different level. With you, I should imagine, your selfish gene is similar to the one that smashed a rock over the head of that penultimate Neanderthal, before turning round and screwing his wife."

He smiled and carried on watching the match. It was a long match. Elsewhere in the universe, stars formed and others ceased to be. Was this the purpose of human existence? Was the purpose somewhere inside the pleasure, or at least the *casual simplicity*, of a football match? Eventually, the game ended.

"That was great," I lied, as we walked out of the grounds.

"Was it? We lost four nil."

"Yes, but while I watched it, I didn't think once about my mortality or the various other difficulties our mortal form will bring in later life."

He looked bewildered again. He was going to say something but he was beaten to it by someone throwing an empty can at my head. Even though it was thrown from behind, I had sensed it coming and ducked quickly out of the way. Ari was stunned by my reflexes. As, I think, was the can thrower.

"Oi, wanker," the can thrower said, "you're that freak on the net. The naked one. Bit warm, ain't you? With all those clothes on."

"Piss off, mate," Ari said nervously.

The man did the opposite.

The can thrower was walking over. He had red cheeks and very small eyes and greasy black hair. He was flanked by two friends. All three of them had faces ready for violence. Red Cheeks leaned in close to Ari. "What did you say, big man?"

"There might have been a 'piss' in there," said Ari, "and there was definitely an 'off.'"

The man grabbed Ari's coat. "Think you're smart?"

"Moderately."

I held the man's arm. "Get off me, you fucking perv," he responded. "I was speaking to fat bastard."

I wanted to hurt him. I had never wanted to hurt anyone—only needed to, and there was a difference. With this person, there was a definite desire to hurt him. I heard the rasp of his breath and tightened his lungs. Within seconds he was reaching for his inhaler. "We'll be on our way," I said, releasing the pressure in his chest. "And you three won't bother us again."

Me and Ari walked home, unfollowed.

"Bloody hell," said Ari. "What was that?"

I didn't answer. How could I? What that had been was something Ari could never understand.

Clouds gathered together quickly. The sky darkened.

It looked like rain. I hated rain, as I have told you. I knew Earth rain wasn't sulfuric acid, but rain, all rain, was something I could not abide. I panicked.

I started running.

"Wait!" said Ari, who was running behind me. "What are you doing?"

"Rain!" I said, wishing for a dome around the whole of Cambridge. "I can't *stand* rain."

Lightbulb

"Have a nice time?" Isobel asked on my return. She was standing on top of one form of primitive technology (stepladder) changing another one (incandescent lightbulb).

"Yes," I said. "I did some good groaning. But to be honest with you, I don't think I'll go again."

She dropped the new bulb. It smashed. "Damn. We don't have another one." She looked, almost, like she might cry about this fact. She stepped down from the ladder, and I stared up at the dead lightbulb still hanging there. I concentrated hard. A moment later it was working again.

"That was lucky. It didn't need changing after all."

Isobel stared at the light. The golden illumination on her skin was quite mesmerizing, for some reason. The way it shifted shadow. Made her more distinctly herself. "How weird," she said. Then she looked down at the broken glass.

"I'll see to that," I said. And she smiled at me and her hand touched mine and gave it a quick pulse of gratitude. And then she did something I wasn't expecting at all. She embraced me, gently, with broken glass still at our feet.

I breathed her in. I liked the warmth of her body against mine and realized the pathos of being a human. Of being a mortal creature who was essentially alone but needed the myth of togetherness with others. Friends, children, lovers. It was an attractive myth. It was a myth you could easily inhabit.

"Oh Andrew," she said. I didn't know what she meant by this simple declaration of my name, but when she stroked my back, I found myself stroking hers, and saying the words that seemed somehow the most appropriate. "It's okay, it's okay, it's okay . . ."

Shopping

I went to the funeral of Daniel Russell. I watched the coffin being lowered into the ground and earth being sprinkled over the top of the wood casket. There were lots of people there, most of them wearing black. A few were crying.

Afterward, Isobel wanted to go over and talk to Tabitha. Tabitha looked different from when I had last seen her. She looked older, even though it had only been a week. She wasn't crying, but it seemed like an effort not to.

Isobel stroked her arm. "Listen, Tabitha, I just want you to know, we're here. Whatever you need, we're here."

"Thank you, Isobel. That really does mean a lot. It really does."

"Just basic stuff. If you don't feel up to the supermarket. I mean, supermarkets are not the most sympathetic of places."

"That's very kind. I know you can do it online, but I've never got the hang of it."

"Well, don't worry. We'll sort it out."

And this actually happened. Isobel went to get another human's shopping and paid for it and came home and told me I was looking better.

"Am I?"

"Yes. You're looking yourself again."

The Zeta Function

"Are you sure you're ready?" Isobel asked me the next Monday morning, as I ate my first peanut butter sandwich of the day.

Newton was asking it too. Either that or he was asking about the sandwich. I tore him off a piece. "Yes. It will be fine. What could go wrong?"

This was when Gulliver let out a mocking groan. The only sound he'd made all morning.

"What's up, Gulliver?" I asked.

"Everything," he said. He didn't expand. Instead, he left his uneaten cereal and stormed upstairs.

"Should I follow him?"

"No," Isobel said. "Give him time."

I nodded.

I trusted her.

Time was her subject, after all.

An hour later I was in Andrew's office. It was the first time I had been there since I had deleted the email to Daniel Russell. This time, I wasn't in a rush and could absorb a few more details. As he was a professor, there were books lining every wall, arranged so that from whichever angle you looked at him, you would see a book.

I looked at some of the titles. Very primitive-looking in the main. *A History of Binary and Other Nondecimal Numeration. Hyperbolic Geometry. The Book of Hexagonal Tessellation. Logarithmic Spirals and the Golden Mean.*

There was a book written by Andrew himself. One I hadn't noticed the last time I had been here. It was a thin book called *The Zeta Function*. It had the words "Uncorrected Proof Copy" on the cover. I made sure the door was locked and then sat down in his chair and read every word.

And what a depressing read it was, I have to say. It was about the Riemann hypothesis, and what seemed like his futile quest to prove it and explain why the spaces between prime numbers increased the way they did. The tragedy was in realizing how desperately he had wanted to solve it—and, of course, after he'd written the book he *had* solved it, though the benefits he'd imagined would never happen, because I had destroyed the proof. And I began to think of how fundamentally our equivalent mathematical breakthrough—the one which we came to know as the Second Basic Theory of Prime Numbers—had on us. How it enabled us to do all that we can do. Travel the universe. Inhabit other worlds, transform into other bodies. Live as long as we want to live. Search each other's minds, each other's dreams. All that.

The Zeta Function did, however, list all the things humans had achieved. The main steps on the road. The developments that had advanced them toward civilization. Fire, that was a biggie. The plow. The printing press. The steam engine. The microchip. The discovery of DNA. And humans would be the first to congratulate themselves on all this. But the trouble was, for them, that they had never made the leap most other intelligent life-forms in the universe had made.

Oh, they had built rockets and probes and satellites. A few of them even *worked*. Yet really, their mathematics had thus far let them down. They had yet to do the big stuff. The synchronization of brains. The creation of free-thinking computers. Automation technology. Intergalactic travel. And as I read, I realized I was stopping all these opportunities. I had killed their future.

The phone rang. It was Isobel.

"Andrew, what are you doing? Your lecture started ten minutes ago."

She was cross, but in a concerned way. It still felt strange and new, having someone be worried about me. I didn't fully understand this concern, or what she gained by having it, but I must confess I quite liked being the subject of it. "Oh yes. Thank you for reminding me. I will go. Bye, er . . . darling."

❑ ❑ ❑

Be careful. We are listening.

❑ ❑ ❑

The Problem with Equations

I walked into the lecture hall. It was a large room made predominantly of dead trees.

There were a lot of people staring at me. These were students. Some had pens and paper. Others had computers. All were waiting for knowledge. I scanned the room. There were 102 of them, in total. Always an unsettling number, stuck as it is between two primes. I tried to work out the students' knowledge level. You see, I didn't want to overshoot. I looked behind me. There was a whiteboard where words and equations were meant to be written but there was nothing on it.

I hesitated. And during that hesitation someone sensed my weakness. Someone on the back row. A male of about twenty, with bushy blond hair and a T-shirt that said, "What part of $N=R^* \times f_p \times n_e \times f_l \times f_i \times f_c \times L$ don't you understand?"

He giggled at the wit he was about to display and shouted out, "You look a bit overdressed today, Professor!" He giggled some more, and it was contagious; the howling laughter spreading like fire across the whole hall. Within moments, everyone in the hall was laughing. Well, everyone except one person, a female.

The nonlaughing female was looking at me intently. She had red curly hair, full lips, and wide eyes. She had a startling frankness about her appearance. An openness that reminded me of a death flower. She was wearing a cardigan and coiling strands of her hair around her finger.

"Calm down," I said to the rest of them. "That is very funny. I get it. I am wearing clothes and you are referring to an occasion in which I was not wearing clothes. Very funny. You think it is a joke, like when Georg Cantor said the scientist Francis Bacon wrote the plays of William Shakespeare, or when John Nash started seeing men in hats who weren't really there. That was funny. The human mind is a limited but high plateau. Spend your life at its outer limits and, oops, you might fall off. That is funny. Yes. But don't worry, you won't fall off. Young man, you are right there in the middle of your plateau. Though I appreciate your concern, I have to say I am feeling much better now. I am wearing underpants and socks and trousers and even a shirt."

People were laughing again, but this time the laughter felt warmer. And it did something to me, inside, this warmth. So then I started laughing too. Not at what I had just said, because I didn't see how that was funny. No. I was laughing at myself. The impossible fact that I was there, on that most absurd planet and yet actually liking being there. And I felt an urge to tell someone how good it felt, in human form, to laugh. The release of it. And I wanted to tell someone about it and I realized that I didn't want to tell the hosts. I wanted to tell Isobel.

Anyway, I did the lecture. Apparently I had been meant to be talking about something called "post-Euclidean geometry." But I didn't want to talk about that, so I talked about the boy's T-shirt.

The formula written on it was something called Drake's equation. It was an equation devised to calculate the likelihood of advanced civilizations in Earth's galaxy, or what the humans called the Milky Way galaxy. (That is how humans came to terms with the vast expanse of space. By saying it looks like a splatter of spilled milk. Something dropped out of the fridge that could be wiped away in a second.)

So, the equation:

$$N = R^* \times f_p \times n_e \times f_l \times f_i \times f_c \times L.$$

N was the number of advanced civilizations in the galaxy with whom communication might be possible. R^* was the average annual rate at which stars were formed. The f_p was the fraction of those stars with planets. The n_e was the average number of those planets that have the right ecosystems for life. The f_l was the fraction of those planets where life would actually develop. The f_l was the fraction of the above planets that could develop intelligence. The f_c was the fraction of *those* where a communicative, technologically advanced civilization could develop. And L was the lifetime of the communicative phase.

Various astrophysicists had looked at all the data and decided that there must, in fact, be millions of planets in the galaxy containing life, and even more in the universe at large. And some of these were bound to have advanced life with very good technology. This of course was true. But the humans didn't just stop there. They came up with a paradox. They said, "Hold on, this can't be right. If there are this many extraterrestrial civilizations with the ability to contact us, then we would know about it because they *would have* contacted us."

"Well, that's true, isn't it?" said the male whose T-shirt started this detour.

"No," I said. "No, it's not. Because the equation should have some other fractions in there. For instance, it should have—"

I turned and wrote on the board behind me:

$$f_{cgas}$$

"Fraction who could give a shit about visiting or communicating with Earth."

And then:

$$f_{dsbthdr}$$

"Fraction who did so but the humans didn't realize."

It was not exactly difficult to make human students of mathematics laugh. Indeed, I had never met a subcategory of life-form so *desperate* to laugh—but still, it felt good. For a few brief moments, it even felt slightly more than good.

I felt warmth and, I don't know, a kind of forgiveness or acceptance from these students.

"But listen," I said, "don't worry. Those aliens up there—they don't know what they are missing."

Applause. (When humans really like something, they clap their hands together. It makes no sense. But when they do it on behalf of you, it warms your brain.)

And then, at the end of the lecture, the staring woman came up to me.

The open flower.

She stood close to me. Normally, when humans stand and talk to each other, they try and leave some air between them, for purposes of breathing and etiquette and claustrophobia limitation. With this one, there was very little air.

"I phoned," she said, with her full mouth, in a voice I had heard before, "to ask about you. But you weren't there. Did you get my message?"

"Oh. Oh yes. *Maggie.* I got the message."

"You seemed in top form today."

"Thank you. I thought I would do something a bit different."

She laughed. The laughter was fake, but something about its fakeness made me excited for some unfathomable reason. "Are we still having our first Tuesdays of the month?" she asked me.

"Oh yes," I said, utterly confused. "First Tuesdays of the month will be left intact."

"That's good." Her voice sounded warm and menacing, like the wind that speeds across the southern wastelands of home. "And listen, you know that heavy conversation we had, the night before you went la-la?"

"La-la?"

"You know. Before your routine at Corpus Christi."

"What did I tell you? My mind's a little hazy about that night, that's all."

"Oh, the kind of things you can't say in lecture halls."

"Mathematical things?"

"Actually, correct me if I'm wrong, but mathematical things *are* the kind of things you can say in lecture halls."

I wondered about this woman, this girl, and more specifically I wondered what kind of relationship she'd had with Andrew Martin.

"Yes. Oh yes. Of course."

This Maggie knew nothing, I told myself.

"Anyway," she said, "I'll see you."

"Yes. Yes. See you."

She walked away, and I watched her walk away. For a moment there was no fact in the universe except the one that related to a female human called Maggie walking away from me. I didn't like her, but I had no idea why.

The Violet

A little while later I was in the college café, with Ari, having a grape-fruit juice while he had a sugar-laden coffee and a packet of beef-flavored crisps.

"How'd it go, mate?"

I tried not to catch his cow-scented breath. "Good. Good. I educated them about alien life. Drake's equation."

"Bit out of your territory?"

"Out of my territory? What do you mean?"

"Subjectwise."

"Mathematics is every subject."

He screwed up his face. "Tell 'em about Fermi's paradox?"

"They told me, actually."

"All bollocks."

"You think?"

"Well, what the fuck would an extraterrestrial life-form want to come here for?"

"That is pretty much what I said."

"I mean, personally, I think physics tells us there is an exoplanet out there with life on it. But I don't think we understand what we're looking for or what form it will take. Though I think this will be the century we find it. 'Course, most people don't want to find it. Even the ones who pretend they do. They don't want to really."

"Don't they? Why not?"

He held up his hand. A signal for me to have patience while he completed the important task of chewing and then swallowing the crisps that were in his mouth.

"'Cause it troubles people. They turn it into a joke. You've got the brightest physicists in the world these days, saying over and over and over, as plainly as physicists can manage, that there has to be other life out there. And people, and I mean thick people, mainly—you know, star sign people, the kind of people whose ancestors used to find omens in ox shit, but not just them, other people too, people who should know a lot better—you've got those people saying aliens are obviously made up because *War of the Worlds* was made up and *Close Encounters of the Third Kind* was made up and though they liked those things, they kind of formed a prejudice in their head that aliens can only be enjoyed as *fiction*. Because if you believe in them as fact, you are saying the thing that every unpopular scientific breakthrough in history has said."

"Which is what?"

"That humans are not at the center of things. You know, the planet is in orbit around the sun. That was a fucking hilarious joke in the fifteen hundreds, but Copernicus wasn't a comedian. He was, apparently, the least funny man of the whole Renaissance. He made Raphael look like Richard Pryor. But he was telling the fucking truth. The planet *is* in orbit around the sun. But that was *out there*, I'm telling you. 'Course, he made sure he was dead by the time it was published. Let Galileo take the heat."

"Right," I said. "Yes."

As I listened, I noticed a pain begin behind my eyes, getting sharper. On the fringes of my vision there was a blur of violet.

"Oh, and animals have nervous systems," Ari went on, between swigs of coffee, "and could feel pain. That annoyed a few people at the time too. And some people still don't want to believe the world is as old as it is because that would mean having to accept the truth that humans, in the day that has been the Earth, haven't been here a minute. We're a late-night piss in the toilet, that's all we are."

"Right," I said, massaging my eyelids.

"Recorded history is just the time it takes to flush. And now we know we don't have free will, people are getting pissed off about that too. So if and when they discover aliens, they'll be really pretty unsettled because then we'll have to know, once and for all, that there is nothing really unique or special about us at all." He sighed and gazed intently at the interior of his empty packet of crisps. "So

I can see why it's easy to dismiss alien life as a joke, one for teenage boys with overactive wrists and imaginations."

"What would happen," I asked him, "if an actual alien was found on Earth?"

"What do you think would happen?"

"I don't know. That's why I'm asking you."

"Well, I think if they had the brains to get here, they'd have the brains to not reveal they were alien. They could have been here. They could have arrived in things that weren't anything like sci-fi 'ships.' They might not have UFOs. There might be no flying involved, and no object to fail to identify. Who the fuck knows? Maybe they were just you."

I sat upright in my chair. Alert. "What?"

"*U.* As in no *FO.* Unidentified. *Unidentified.*"

"Okay. But what if, somehow, they were identified. They were *I.* What if humans knew an alien was living among them?"

After asking this, I saw all around the café little wisps of violet appearing in the air, which no one else seemed to notice.

Ari downed the last of his coffee and then considered for a moment. Scratched his face with his meaty fingers. "Well, put it this way, I wouldn't want to be that poor bastard."

"Ari," I said. "Ari, I am that—"

Poor bastard, was what I was going to say. But I didn't because right then, at that precise moment, there was a noise inside my head. It was a sound of the highest possible frequency and it was extremely loud. Accompanying it, and matching it for intensity, was the pain behind my eyes, which became infinitely worse. It was the most excruciating pain I'd ever experienced, and it was a pain I had no control over.

Wishing it not to be there wasn't the same thing as it not being there, and that confused me. Or it would have, if I'd had the capacity to think beyond the pain. And I kept thinking about the pain, and the sound, and the violet. But this sharp, throbbing heat pressing behind my eyes was too much.

"Mate, what's up?"

I was holding my head by this point, trying to close my eyes, but they wouldn't close.

I looked at Ari's unshaven face, then at the few other customers in the café, and the girl with glasses who was standing behind the counter. Something was happening to them and to the whole place. Everything was dissolving into a rich, varied violet, a color more familiar to me than any other. "The hosts," I said aloud, and almost simultaneously the pain increased further. "Stop, oh stop, oh stop."

"Man, I'm calling an ambulance," he said, because I was on the floor now. A swirling violet sea.

"No."

I fought against it. I got to my feet.

The pain lessened.

The ringing became a low hum.

The violet faded. "It was nothing," I said.

Ari laughed, nervous. "I'm no expert but that honestly looked like something."

"It was just a headache. A flash of pain. I'll go to the doctor and check it out."

"You should. You really should."

"Yes. I will."

I sat down. An ache remained, as a reminder, for a while, along with a few ethereal wisps in the air only I could see.

"You were going to say something. About other life."

"No," I said quietly.

"Pretty sure you were, man."

"Yeah, well. I think I've forgotten."

And after that the pain disappeared altogether, and the air lost its final trace of violet.

The Possibility of Pain

I didn't mention anything to Isobel or Gulliver. I knew it was unwise, because I knew the pain had been a warning. And besides, even if I'd wanted to tell her, I wouldn't have, because Gulliver had arrived home with a bruised eye. When human skin bruises, the skin takes various shades. Grays, browns, blues, greens. Among them, a dull violet. Beautiful, petrifying violet.

"Gulliver, what happened?" His mother asked the question quite a few times that evening but never got a satisfactory reply. He went into the small utility room behind the kitchen and closed the door.

"Please, Gull, come out of there," said his mother. "We need to talk about this."

"Gulliver, come out of there," I added.

Eventually he opened the door. "Just leave me *alone*." That "alone" was said with such a hard, cold force, Isobel decided it was best to grant him that wish, so we stayed downstairs while he trudged up to his room.

"I'm going to have to phone the school about this tomorrow."

I said nothing. Of course, I would later realize this was a mistake. I should have broken my promise to Gulliver and told her that he hadn't been going to school. But I didn't, because it wasn't my duty. I did have a duty, but it wasn't to humans. Even these ones. Especially these ones. And it was a duty I was already failing to follow, as that afternoon's warning in the café had told me.

Newton, though, had a different sense of duty, and he headed up two flights of stairs to be with Gulliver. Isobel didn't know what to do, so she opened a few cupboard doors, stared into the cupboards, sighed, then closed them again.

"Listen," I found myself saying, "he is going to have to find his own way and make his own mistakes."

"We need to find out who did that to him, Andrew. That's what we need to do. People can't just go around inflicting violence on human beings like that. They just can't do that. What ethical code do you live by where you can sound so indifferent about it?"

What could I say? "I'm sorry. I'm not indifferent. I care for him, of course I do." And the terrifying thing, the absolutely awful fact I had to face was that I was right. I did care. The warning had failed, you see. Indeed, it had had the opposite effect.

That's what starts to happen, when you know it is possible for you to feel pain you have no control over. You become vulnerable. Because the possibility of pain is where love stems from. And that, for me, was very bad news indeed.

Sloping Roofs
(and Other Ways to Deal with the Rain)

. . . and by a sleep to say we end
The heartache, and the thousand natural shocks
That flesh is heir to . . .
—WILLIAM SHAKESPEARE, *Hamlet*

I couldn't sleep.

Of course I couldn't. I had a whole universe to worry about.

And I kept thinking about the pain, and the sound, and the violet.

On top of that, it was raining.

I decided to leave Isobel in bed and go and talk with Newton. I headed slowly downstairs, with my hands over my ears, trying to cancel out the sound of falling cloud water drumming against the windows. To my disappointment Newton was sleeping soundly in his basket.

On my return upstairs I noticed something else. The air was cooler than it should have been, and the coolness was coming from above rather than below. This went against the order of things. I thought of his bruised eye, and I thought further back.

I headed up toward the attic and noticed that everything there was exactly as it should be. The computer, the Dark Matter posters, the random array of socks—everything, that was, except Gulliver himself.

A piece of paper floated toward me, carried on the breeze from the open window. On it were two words.

I'm sorry.

I looked at the window. Outside was the night and the shivering stars of this most alien, yet most familiar galaxy.

Somewhere beyond this sky was home. I realized I could now get back there if I wanted. I could just finish my task and be back in my painless world. The window sloped in line with the roof, which like so many roofs here was designed to usher away the rain. It was easy enough for me to climb out of, but for Gulliver it must have been quite an exertion.

The difficult thing for me was the rain itself.

It was relentless.

Skin-soaking.

I saw him sitting on the edge, next to the gutter rail, with his knees pulled into his chest. He looked cold and bedraggled. And seeing him there, I saw him not as a special entity, an exotic collection of protons, electrons, and neutrons, but as a—using the human term— as a *person*. And I felt, I don't know, *connected* with him. Not in the quantum sense in which everything was connected to everything else, and in which every atom spoke to and negotiated with every other atom. No. This was on another level. A level far, far harder to understand.

Can I end his life?

I started walking toward him. Not easy, given human feet and the 45-degree angle and the wet slate—sleek quartz and muscovite—on which I was relying.

When I was getting close, he turned around and saw me.

"What are you doing?" he asked. He was frightened. That was the main thing I noticed.

"I was about to ask you the same thing."

"Dad, just go away."

What he was saying made sense. I mean, I could have just left him there. I could have escaped the rain, the terrible sensation of that falling water on my thin nonvascular skin, and gone inside. It was then I had to face why I was really out there.

"No," I said, to my own confusion. "I'm not going to do that. I'm not going to go away."

I slipped a little. A tile came unstuck, slid, fell, and smashed to the ground. The smash woke Newton, who started barking.

Gulliver's eyes widened, then his head jerked away. His whole body seemed full of nervous intention.

"Don't do it," I said.

He let go of something. It landed in the gutter. The small plastic cylinder that had contained the twenty-eight diazepam tablets. Now empty.

I stepped closer. I had read enough human literature to realize that suicide was a real option here, on Earth. Yet again, I wondered why this should have bothered me.

I was becoming mad.

Losing my rationality.

If Gulliver wanted to kill himself, then logically, that solved a major problem. And I should just stand back and let it happen.

"Gulliver, listen to me. Don't jump. Trust me, you're nowhere near high enough to guarantee that you'll kill yourself." This was true, but as far as I could calculate, there was still a very good chance of his falling and dying on impact. In which instance, there would be nothing I could do to help him. Injuries could always be healed. Death meant death. A zero squared was still a zero.

"I remember swimming with you," he said, "when I was eight. When we were in France. Can you remember, that night you taught me how to play dominoes?"

He looked back at me, wanting to see a recognition I couldn't give him. It was hard to see his bruised eye in this light; there was so much darkness across his face, he might as well have been all bruise.

"Yes," I said. "Of course I remember that."

"Liar! You don't remember."

"Listen, Gulliver, let's go inside. Let's talk about this indoors. If you still want to kill yourself, I'll take you to a higher building."

Gulliver didn't seem to be listening, as I kept stepping on the slippery slate toward him.

"That's the last good memory I have," he said. It sounded sincere.

"Come on, that can't be true."

"Do you have any idea what it's like? To be your son?"

"No. I don't."

He pointed to his eye. "This. This is what it's like."

"Gulliver, I'm sorry."

"Do you know what it's like to feel stupid all the time?"

"You're not stupid." I was still standing. The human way would have been to shuffle down on my backside, but that would have taken too much time. So I kept taking tentative steps on the slate, leaning back just enough, in continuous negotiation with gravity.

"I'm stupid. I'm nothing."

"No, Gulliver, you're not. You're something. You're—"

He wasn't listening.

The diazepam was taking hold of him.

"How many tablets did you take?" I asked. "All of them?"

I was nearly at him, my hand was almost within grasping distance of his shoulder as his eyes closed and he disappeared into sleep, or prayer.

Another tile came loose. I slipped on to my side, losing my footing on the rain-greased tiles until I was left hanging on to the gutter rail. I could have easily climbed back up. That wasn't the problem. The problem was that Gulliver was now tilting forward.

"Gulliver, wait! Wake up! Wake up, Gulliver!"

The tilt gained momentum.

"No!"

He fell, and I fell with him. First internally, a kind of emotional falling, a silent howl into an abyss, and then physically. I sped through the air with a dreadful velocity.

I broke my legs.

So that was my intention. Let the legs take the pain, and not the head, because I would need my head. But the pain was immense. For a moment I worried they wouldn't reheal. It was only the sight of Gulliver lying totally unconscious on the ground a few meters away that gave me focus. Blood leaked from his ear. To heal him I knew I would first of all need to heal myself. And it happened. Simply wishing was enough, if you wished hard enough, with the right kind of intelligence.

That said, cell regeneration and bone reconstruction still took a lot of energy, especially as I was losing a lot of blood and had multiple fractures. But the pain diminished as a strange, intense fatigue took over me and gravity tried to grip me to the ground. My head hurt, not as a result of the fall, but from the exertion involved in my physical restoration.

I stood up dizzily. I managed to move toward where Gulliver lay, the horizontal ground now sloping more than the roof.

"Gulliver. Come on. Can you hear me? Gulliver?"

I could have called for help, I knew that. But help meant an ambulance and a hospital. Help meant humans grasping around in the dark of their own medical ignorance. Help meant delay and a death I was meant to approve of but couldn't.

"Gulliver?"

There was no pulse. He was dead. I must have been seconds too late. I could already detect the first tiny descent in his body temperature.

Rationally, I should have resigned myself to this fact.

And yet.

I had read a lot of Isobel's work and so I knew that the whole of human history was full of people who tried against the odds. Some succeeded, most failed, but that hadn't stopped them. Whatever else you could say about these particular primates, they could be *determined.* And they could hope. Oh yes, they could hope.

And hope was often irrational. It made no sense. If it had made sense, it would have been called, well, *sense.* The other thing about hope was that it took effort, and I had never been used to effort. At home, nothing had been an effort. That was the whole point of home, the comfort of a perfectly effortless existence. Yet there I was. Hoping. Not that I was standing there, passively, just wishing him better from a distance. Of course not. I placed my left hand—my gift hand—to his heart, and I began to work.

The Thing with Feathers

It was exhausting.

I thought of binary stars. A red giant and a white dwarf, side by side, the life force of one being sucked into that of the other.

His death was a fact I was convinced I could disprove, or *dissuade*.

But death wasn't a white dwarf. It was a good bit beyond that. It was a black hole. And once you stepped past that event horizon, you were in very difficult territory.

You are not dead. Gulliver, you are not dead.

I kept at it, because I knew what life was, I understood its nature, its character, its stubborn insistence.

Life, especially human life, was an act of defiance. It was never meant to be, and yet it existed in an incredible number of places across a near-infinite number of solar systems.

There was no such thing as impossible. I knew that, because I also knew that everything was impossible, and so the only possibilities in life were impossibilities.

A chair could stop being a chair at any moment. That was quantum physics. And you could manipulate atoms if you knew how to talk to them.

You are not dead, you are not dead.

I felt terrible. Waves of deep-level-pained, bone-scorching effort tore through me like solar flares. And yet he still lay there. His face, I noticed for the first time, looking like his mother's. Serene, egg-fragile, precious.

A light came on inside the house. Isobel must have woken, from the sound of Newton's barking if nothing else, but I wasn't conscious of that. I was just aware that Gulliver was suddenly illuminated and, shortly after, there was the faintest flicker of a pulse beneath my hand.

Hope.

"Gulliver, Gulliver, Gulliver—"

Another pulse.

Stronger.

A defiant drumbeat of life. A backbeat, waiting for melody.

Duh-dum.

And again, and again, and again.

He was alive. His lips twitched, his bruised eyes moved like an egg about to hatch. One opened. So did the other. It was the eyes, on Earth, that mattered. You saw the person, and the life inside them, if you saw the eyes. And I saw him, this messed-up, sensitive boy, and felt, for a moment, the exhausted wonder of a father. It should have been a moment to savor, but it wasn't. I was being flooded with pain, and violet.

I could feel myself about to collapse onto the glossy wet ground.

Footsteps behind me. And that was the last thing I heard before the darkness arrived to make its claim, along with remembered poetry, as Emily Dickinson shyly came toward me through the violet and whispered in my ear.

Hope is the thing with feathers
That perches in the soul,
And sings the tune without the words,
And never stops at all.

Heaven Is a Place
Where Nothing Ever Happens

I was back at home, on Vonnadoria, and it was exactly how it had always been. And I was exactly how I had always been, among them, the hosts, feeling no pain and no fear.

Our beautiful, warless world, where I could be entranced by the purest mathematics for all eternity.

Any human who arrived here, gazing at our violet landscapes, might well have believed they had entered Heaven.

But what happened in Heaven?

What did you do there?

After a while, didn't you crave flaws? Love and lust and misunderstandings, and maybe even a little violence to liven things up? Didn't light need shade? Didn't it? Maybe it didn't. Maybe I was missing the point. Maybe the point was to exist with an absence of pain. Yes, to exist with an absence of pain. Yes, maybe that was the only aim you needed in life. It certainly had been, but what happened if you'd never required that aim because you were born after that goal had been met? I was younger than the hosts. I did not share their appreciation of just how lucky I was. Not anymore. Not even in a dream.

In Between

I woke up.

On Earth.

But I was so weak, I was returning to my original state. I had heard about this. Indeed, I had swallowed a word capsule about it. Rather than allow you to die, your body would return to its original state, because the amount of extra energy deployed to be someone else would more usefully serve to preserve your life. And that was all the gifts were there for, really. Self-preservation. The protection of eternity.

Which was fine, in theory. In theory, it was a great idea. But the only problem was that this was Earth. And my original state wasn't equipped for the air here, or the gravity, or the face-to-face contact. I didn't want Isobel to see me. It just could not happen.

And so, as soon as I felt my atoms itch and tingle, warm and shift, I told Isobel to do what she was already doing: looking after Gulliver.

And as she crouched down, with her back to me, I got to my feet, which at this point were recognizably human-shaped. Then I shifted myself—midway between two contrasting forms—across the back garden. Luckily the garden was large and dark, with lots of flowers and shrubs and trees to hide behind. So I did. I hid among the beautiful flowers. And I saw Isobel looking around, even as she was calling for an ambulance for Gulliver.

"Andrew!" she said at one point, as Gulliver got to his feet.

She even ran into the garden to have a look. But I stayed still.

"Where have you disappeared to?"

My lungs began to burn. I needed more nitrogen.

It would have taken only one word in my native tongue. *Home.* The one the hosts were primed to hear, and I would be back there. So why didn't I say it? Because I hadn't finished my task? No. It wasn't that. I was never going to finish my task. That was the education this night had brought me. So why? Why was I choosing risk and pain over their opposites? What had happened to me? What was wrong?

Newton now came out into the garden. He trotted along, sniffing the plants and flowers until he sensed me standing there. I expected him to bark and draw attention, but he didn't. He just stared at me, his eyes shining blank circles, and seemed to know exactly who it was, standing behind the juniper bushes. But he stayed quiet.

He was a good dog.

And I loved him.

I can't do it.

We know.

There is no point in doing it anyway.

There is every point.

I don't believe Isobel and Gulliver should be harmed.

We believe you have been corrupted.

I haven't. I have gained more knowledge. That is all that has happened.

No. You have been infected by them.

Infected? Infected? With what?

With emotion.

No. I haven't. That is not true.

It is true.

Listen, emotions have a logic. Without emotions humans wouldn't care for each other, and if they didn't care for each other, the species would have died out. To care for others is self-preservation. You care for some-one and they care for you.

You are speaking like one of them. You are not a human. You are one of us. We are one.

I know I am not a human.

We think you need to come home.

No.

You must come home.

I never had a family.

We are your family.

No. It isn't the same.

We want you home.

I have to ask to come home and I am not going to. You can interfere with my mind but you can't control it.

We will see.

Two Weeks in the Dordogne and a Box of Dominoes

The next day we were in the living room. Me and Isobel. Newton was upstairs with Gulliver, who was now asleep. We had checked on him but Newton was staying there, on guard.

"How are you?" asked Isobel.

"'It was not death,'" I said, "'For I stood up.'"

"You saved his life," said Isobel.

"I don't think so. I didn't even have to do CPR. The doctor said he had very minor injuries."

"I don't care what the doctor says. He jumped from the roof. That could have killed him. Why didn't you shout for me?"

"I did." It was a lie, obviously, but the whole framework was a lie. The belief that I was her husband. It was all fiction. "I did shout for you."

"You could have killed yourself."

(I have to admit that humans waste a lot of their time—almost all of it—with hypothetical stuff. I could be rich. I could be famous. I could have been hit by that bus. I could have been born with fewer moles and bigger breasts. I could have spent more of my youth learning foreign languages. They must exercise the conditional tense more than any other known life-form.) "But I didn't kill myself. I am alive. Let's concentrate on that."

"What happened to your tablets? They were in the cupboard."

"I threw them away." This was a lie, obviously. The unclear thing was who was I protecting? Isobel? Gulliver? Myself?

"Why? Why would you throw them away?"

"I didn't think it was a good idea to have them lying around. You know, given his condition."

"But they're diazepam. That's Valium. You can't overdose on Valium, you'd need a thousand."

"No. I know that." I was drinking a cup of tea. I actually enjoyed tea. It was so much better than coffee. It tasted like comfort.

Isobel nodded. She too was drinking tea. The tea seemed to be making things better. It was a hot drink made of leaves, used in times of crisis as a means of restoring normality.

"Do you know what they told me?" she said.

"No. What? What did they tell you?"

"They told me he could stay in."

"Right."

"It was up to me. I had to say if I thought he was a suicide risk or not. And I said I thought he would be more of a risk in there than out here. They said if he tried anything like this again, then there'd be no choice about it. He'd be admitted, and they'd watch him."

"Oh. Well, *we'll* watch him. That's what I say. That hospital is full of mad people. People who think they're from other planets. Stuff like that."

She smiled a sad smile and blew a brown tide of ripples across the surface of her drink. "Yes. Yes. We'll have to."

I tried to understand something. "It's me, isn't it? It was my fault, for that day I didn't wear clothes."

Something about this question switched the mood. Isobel's face hardened. "Andrew, do you really think this was about one day? About your breakdown?"

"Oh," I said, which I knew wasn't in context. But I had nothing else to say. "Oh" was always the word I resorted to, the one that filled empty spaces. It was verbal tea. The "oh" should have really been a "no," because I didn't think this was about one day. I thought it was about thousands of days, most of which I hadn't been there to observe. And so an "oh" was more appropriate.

"This wasn't about one event. This was about everything. It's not obviously solely your fault, but you haven't really been *there*, have you, Andrew? For all his life, or at least since we moved back to Cambridge, you've just not been there."

I remembered something he'd told me on the roof. "What about France?"

"What?"

"I taught him dominoes. I swam with him in a swimming pool. In France. The country. France."

She frowned, confused. "France? What? The *Dordogne*? Two weeks in the Dordogne and a box of bloody dominoes. Is that your Get Out of Jail Free card? Is that fatherhood?"

"No. I don't know. I was just giving a . . . a solid example of what he was like."

"He?"

"I mean I. What I was like."

"You've been *there* on holiday. Yes. Yes, you have. Unless they were working holidays. Come on, you remember Sydney! And Boston! And Seoul! And Turin! And, and, Düsseldorf!"

"Oh yes," I said, staring at the unread books on the shelves like unlived memories. "I remember them vividly. Of course."

"We hardly saw you. And when we did see you, you were always so stressed about the lecture you were going to give or the people you were going to meet. And all those rows we had. We *have*. Until, you know, you got ill. And got better. Come on, Andrew, you know what I'm saying. This isn't breaking news, is it?"

"No. Not at all. So, where else have I failed?"

"You haven't *failed*. It's not an academic paper to be assessed by your peers. It's not success or failure. It's our life. I'm not wrapping it in judgmental language. I'm just trying to tell you the objective truth."

"I just want to know. Tell me. Tell me things I've done. Or haven't done."

She toyed with her silver necklace. "Well, come on. It's always been the same. Between the ages of two and four you weren't back home in time for a single bath or bedtime story. You'd fly off the handle about anything that got in the way of you and your work. Or if I ever came close to mentioning that I had sacrificed my career for this family—at that time when I had been making *real* sacrifices—you wouldn't even so much as postpone a book dead-line. I'd be shot down in flames."

"I know. I'm sorry," I said, thinking of her novel, *Wider Than the Sky*. "I've been terrible. I have. I think you would be better off without me. I think, sometimes, that I should leave and never come back."

"Don't be childish. You sound younger than Gulliver."

"I'm being serious. I have behaved badly. I sometimes think it would be better if I went and never returned. Ever."

This threw her. She had her hands on her hips but her glare soft-ened. She took a big breath.

"I need you here. You know I need you."

"Why? What do I give to this relationship? I don't understand."

She clenched her eyes shut. Whispered, "That was amazing."

"What?"

"What you did there. Out on the roof. It was amazing."

She then made the most complex facial expression I have ever seen on a human. A kind of frustrated scorn, tinged with sympa-thy, which slowly softened into a deep, wide humor, culminating in forgiveness and something I couldn't quite recognize, but which I thought might have been love.

"What's happened to you?" She said it as a whisper, nothing more than a structured piece of breath.

"What? Nothing. Nothing has happened to me. Well, a mental breakdown. But I'm over that. Other than that—nothing." I said this flippantly, trying to make her smile.

She smiled, but sadness quickly claimed her. She looked up to the ceiling. I was beginning to understand these wordless forms of communication.

"I'll talk to him," I said, feeling kind of solid and authoritative. Kind of real. Kind of human. "I'll talk to him."

"You don't have to."

"I know," I said. And I stood up, again to help when I was sup-posed to hurt.

now. But even in the holidays you were never around. You were always somewhere else. Or just making everything tense and horrible with Mum. It's just shit. You should have just done the right thing and gotten divorced years ago. You haven't got anything in common."

I thought about all this. And didn't know what to say. Cars passed by on the road behind us. The sound was very melancholy somehow, like the bass rumble of a sleeping Bazadean. "What was your band called?"

"The Lost," he said.

A leaf fell and landed on my lap. It was dead and brown. I held it and, quite out of character, felt a strange empathy. Maybe it was because now that I was empathizing with humans, I could empathize with pretty much anything. Too much Emily Dickinson, that was the problem. Emily Dickinson was making me human, bit by bit. But not *that* human. There was a dull ache in my head and a small weight of tiredness in my eyes as the leaf became green.

I brushed it away quickly, but it was too late.

"What just happened?" Gulliver asked, staring at the leaf as it floated away on the breeze.

I tried to ignore him. He asked again.

"Nothing happened to the leaf," I said.

He forgot about the leaf he might have seen the moment he saw two teenage girls and a boy his own age walking on the road that ran behind the park. The girls were laughing into their hands at the sight of us. I have realized that, essentially, there are two broad categories of human laughter, and this was not the good kind.

The boy was the boy I had seen on Gulliver's Facebook page. Theo "The Fucking Business" Clarke.

Gulliver shrank.

"It's the Martin Martians! Freaks!"

Gulliver cowered lower on the bench, crippled with shame.

I turned around, assessed Theo's physical structure and dynamic potential. "My son could beat you into the ground," I shouted. "He could flatten your face into a more attractive geometric form."

Social Networking

Essentially, social networking on Earth was quite limited. Unlike on Vonnadoria, the brain synchronization technology wasn't there, so subscribers couldn't communicate telepathically with each other as part of a true hive mind. Nor could they step into each other's dreams and have a walk around, tasting imagined delicacies in exotic moonscapes. On Earth, social networking generally involved sitting down at a nonsentient computer and typing words about needing a coffee and reading about other people needing a coffee, while forgetting to actually make a coffee. It was the news show they had been waiting for. It was the show where the news could be all about them.

But on the plus side, human computer networks, I discovered, were preposterously easy to hack into, as all their security systems were based on prime numbers. And so I hacked into Gulliver's computer and changed the name of every single person on Facebook who had bullied Gulliver to "I Am the Cause of Shame," and blocked them from posting anything with the word "Gulliver" in it, and gave each of them a computer virus which I dubbed "The Flea" after a lovely poem. This virus ensured the only messages they would ever be able to send were ones that contained the words "I am hurt and so I hurt."

On Vonnadoria I had never done anything so vindictive. Nor had I ever felt quite so satisfied.

Forever Is Composed of Nows

We went to the park to walk Newton. Parks were the most common destination on dog walks. A piece of nature—grass, flowers, trees—that was not quite allowed to be truly natural. Just as dogs were thwarted wolves, parks were thwarted forests. Humans loved both, possibly because humans were, well, thwarted. The flowers were beautiful. Flowers, after love, must have been the best advertisement planet Earth had going for it.

"It doesn't make sense," said Gulliver, as we sat down on the bench.

"What doesn't?"

We watched Newton sniffing the flowers, livelier than ever.

"I was fine. No damage. Even my eye's better."

"You were lucky."

"Dad, before I went out on the roof, I'd had twenty-eight diazepam."

"You'd need more."

He looked at me, angry, as if I were humiliating him. Using knowledge against him.

"Your mum told me that," I added. "I didn't know that."

"I didn't want you to save me."

"I didn't save you. You were just lucky. But I really think you should ignore feelings like that. That was a moment in your life. You have a lot more days to live. About twenty-four thousand more days to live, probably. That's a lot of moments. You could do many great things in that time. You could read a lot of poetry."

"You don't like poetry. That's one of the few facts I know about you."

"It's growing on me . . . Listen," I said, "don't kill yourself.

Don't ever kill yourself. Just, that's my advice, don't kill yourself."

Gulliver took something out of his pocket and put it in his mouth. It was a cigarette. He lit it. I asked if I could try it. Gulliver seemed troubled by this but handed it over. I sucked on the filter and brought the smoke into my lungs. And then I coughed.

"What's the point of this?" I asked Gulliver.

He shrugged.

"It's an addictive substance with a high fatality rate. I thought there would be a point," I said.

I handed the cigarette back to Gulliver.

"Thanks," he mumbled, still confused.

"Don't worry about it," I said. "It's fine."

He took another drag and suddenly realized it wasn't doing anything for him either. He flicked the cigarette in a steep arc toward the grass.

"If you want," I said, "we could play dominoes when we get home. I bought a box this morning."

"No thanks."

"Or we could go to the Dordogne."

"What?"

"Go swimming."

He shook his head. "You need some more tablets."

"Yes. Maybe. You ate all mine." I tried to smile, playfully, and offer some more Earth humor. "You fucker!"

There was a long silence. We watched Newton sniffing around the circumference of a tree. Twice.

A million suns imploded. And then Gulliver came out with it.

"You don't know what it's been like," he said. "I've got all this expectation on me because I'm your son. My teachers read your books. And they look at me like some bruised apple that's fallen off the great Andrew Martin tree. You know, the posh boy who got expelled from his boarding school. The one who set stuff on fire. Whose parents gave up on him. Not that I'm bothered about that

"*Fuck, Dad,*" said Gulliver, "what are you doing? He's the one who fucked up my face."

I looked at him. He was a black hole. The violence was all inward. It was time for him to push some the other way.

"Come on," I said, "you're a human. It's time to act like one."

Violence

"No," said Gulliver.

But it was too late. Theo was crossing the road. "Yeah, you're a comedian now, are you?" he said, as he swaggered toward us.

"It would be fucking amusing to see you lose to my fucking son, if that's what you fucking mean," I said.

"Yeah, well, my dad's a tae kwon do teacher. He taught me how to fight."

"Well, Gulliver's father is a mathematician. So he wins."

"Yeah right."

"You will lose," I told the boy, and I made sure the words went all the way down and stayed there, like rocks in a shallow pond.

Theo laughed and jumped with troubling ease over the low stone wall that bordered the park, with the girls following. This boy, Theo, was not as tall as Gulliver but stronger built. He was almost devoid of neck and his eyes were so close together he was border-line cyclopic. He was walking backward and forward on the grass in front of us, warming up by punching and kicking the air.

Gulliver was as pale as milk. "Gulliver," I told him, "you fell off a roof yesterday. That boy is not a forty-foot drop. There is nothing to him. No depth. You know how he is going to fight."

"Yes," said Gulliver. "He's going to fight well."

"But you, you've got surprise on your side. You aren't scared of anything. All you've got to do is realize that this Theo symbolizes everything you've ever hated. He is me. He is bad weather. He is the primitive soul of the Internet. He is the injustice of fate. I am asking, in other words, for you to fight him like you fight in your sleep. Lose everything. Lose all shame and consciousness and beat him. Because you can."

"No," said Gulliver, "I can't."

I lowered my voice, conjured the gifts. "You can. He has the same biochemical ingredients inside him as you do, but with less impressive neural activity."

I saw Gulliver looked confused, so I tapped the side of my head and explained. "It's all about the oscillations."

Gulliver stood up. I clipped the lead to Newton's collar. He whined, sensing the atmosphere.

I watched Gulliver walk over the grass. Nervous, tight-bodied, as if being dragged by an invisible chord.

The two girls were chewing something they didn't plan to swallow and were giggling excitedly. Theo too was looking thrilled. Some humans not only liked violence but craved it, I realized. Not because they wanted pain, but because they already had pain and wanted to be distracted from that kind of pain with a lesser kind.

And then Theo hit Gulliver. And he hit him again. Both times in the face, sending Gulliver staggering backward. Newton growled, seeking involvement, but I kept him where he was.

"You are fucking nothing," said Theo, raising his foot fast through the air to Gulliver's chest. Gulliver grabbed the leg, and Theo hopped for a while, or at least long enough to look ridiculous.

Gulliver looked at me through the still air in silence.

Then Theo was on the ground and Gulliver let him stand up before the switch flicked and he went wild, punching away as if trying to rid himself of his own body, as if it was something that could be shaken away. And pretty soon the other boy was bleeding and he fell back on the grass, his head momentarily tilting back and touching down on a rosebush. He sat up and dabbed his face with his fingers and saw the blood and looked at it as if it was a message he'd never expected to receive.

"All right, Gulliver," I said, "It's time to go home." I went over to Theo. I crouched down.

"You are done now, do you understand?"

Theo understood. The girls were silent but still chewed, if only at half speed. Cow speed. We walked out of the park. Gulliver hardly had a scratch.

"How are you feeling?"

"I hurt him."

"Yes. How does that make you feel? Was it cathartic?"

He shrugged. The trace of a smile hid somewhere inside his lips. It frightened me, how close violence is to the civilized surface of a human being. It wasn't the violence itself that was the worry, it was the amount of effort they'd gone to conceal it. A *Homo sapiens* was a primitive hunter who had woken each day with the knowledge he could kill. And now, the equivalent knowledge was only that he would wake up each day and buy something. So it was important, for Gulliver, to release what he only released in sleep out into the waking world.

"Dad, you're not yourself, are you?" he said, before we got back.

"No," I said. "Not really."

I expected another question but none came.

The Taste of Her Skin

I was not Andrew. I was them. And we woke, and the still-light bedroom was clotted with violet, and though my head didn't hurt, exactly, it felt extremely tight, as though my skull were a fist and my brain were the bar of soap it contained.

I tried switching off the light, but the dark didn't work. The violet stayed, expanding and leaking across reality like spilled ink.

"Get away," I urged the hosts. "*Get away.*"

But they had a hold on me. *You*. If you are reading this. *You* had a terrible hold. And I was losing myself, and I knew this because I turned over in bed and I could see Isobel in the dark, facing away from me. I could see the shape of her, half under the duvet. My hand touched the back of her neck. I felt nothing toward her. *We* felt nothing toward her. We didn't even see her as Isobel. She was simply a human. The way, to a human, a cow or a chicken or a microbe is simply a cow or a chicken or a microbe.

As we touched her bare neck, we gained the reading. It was all we needed. She was asleep, and all we had to do was stop her heart from beating. It was really very easy. We moved our hand slightly lower, felt the heart beating through her ribs. The movement of our hand woke her slightly, and she turned, sleepily, and said with her eyes still closed, "I love you."

The "you" was a singular one, and it was a call to me or the me-Andrew she thought I was, and it was then that I managed to defeat them, become a me and not a we, and the thought that she had just escaped death by such a narrow margin made me realize the intensity of my feelings toward her.

"What's the matter?"

I couldn't tell her, so I kissed her instead. Kissing is what humans do when words have reached a place they can't escape from. It is a switch to another language. The kiss was an act of defiance, maybe of war. *You can't touch us,* is what the kiss said.

"I love you," I told her, and as I smelled her skin, I knew I had never wanted anyone or anything more than I wanted her, but the craving for her was a terrifying one now. And I needed to keep underlining my point.

"I love you, I love you, I love you."

And after that, after the awkward shuffling away of that last thin layer of clothes, words retreated to the sounds they once were. We had sex. A happy entanglement of warm limbs and warmer love. A physical and psychological merging that conjured a kind of inner light, a bio-emotional phosphorescence that was overwhelming in its gorgeousness. I wondered why they weren't prouder of it. Of this magic. I wondered why, if they had to have flags, why they didn't just opt for one with a picture of sex.

Afterward, I held her and she held me and I gently kissed her forehead as the wind beat against the window.

She fell asleep. I watched her, in the dark. I wanted to protect her and keep her safe. Then I got out of bed. I had something to do.

□ □ □

I am staying here.

You can't. You have gifts not made for that planet. Humans will become suspicious.

Well then, I want to be disconnected.

We cannot allow that.

Yes, you can. You have to. The gifts are not compulsory. That is the point. I cannot allow my mind to be interfered with.

We were not the ones interfering with your mind. We were trying to restore it.

Isobel doesn't know anything about the proof. She doesn't know. Just leave her. Leave us. Leave us all. Please. Nothing will happen.

You do not want immortality? You do not want the chance to return home or to visit anywhere else in the universe other than the lonely planet on which you now reside?

That is right.

You do not want the chance to take other forms? To return to your own original nature?

No. I want to be a human. Or as close to being a human as it is possible for me to be.

No one in all our histories has ever asked to lose the gifts.

Well, it is a fact you must now update.

You do realize what this means?

Yes.

You will be trapped in a body that cannot regenerate itself. You will grow old. You will get diseases. You will feel pain, and forever know— unlike the rest of the ignorant species you want to belong to—that you have chosen that suffering. You have brought it on yourself.

Yes. I know that.

Very well. You have been given the ultimate punishment. And it makes it no less a punishment for having been asked for. You have now been disconnected. The gifts are gone. You are now human. If you declare you are from another planet, you will never have proof. They will believe you are insane. And it makes no difference to us. It is easy to fill your place.

You won't fill my place. It is a waste of resources. There is no point to the mission. Hello? Are you listening? Can you hear me? Hello? Hello? Hello?

◻ ◻ ◻

The Rhythm of Life

Love is what the humans are all about but they don't understand it. If they understood it, then it would disappear.

All I know is that it's a frightening thing. And humans are very frightened of it, which is why they have quiz shows. To take their mind off it and think of something else.

Love is scary because it pulls you in with an intense force, a supermassive black hole, which looks like nothing from the outside but from the inside challenges every reasonable thing you know. You lose yourself, like I lost myself, in the warmest of annihilations.

It makes you do stupid things—things that defy all logic. The opting for anguish over calm, for mortality over eternity, and for Earth over home.

I awoke feeling terrible. My eyes itched with tiredness. My back was stiff. There was a pain in my knee, and I could hear a mild ringing. Noises that belonged below a planet's surface were coming from my stomach. Overall, the sensation I was feeling was one of conscious decay.

In short, I felt human. I felt forty-three years old. And now that I had made the decision to stay, I was full of anxiety.

This anxiety was not just about my physical fate. It was the knowledge that at some point in the future the hosts were going to send someone else. And what would I be able to do, now that I had no more gifts than the average human?

It was a worry, at first. But that gradually faded as time went by and nothing happened. Lesser worries began to occupy my mind. For instance, would I be able to cope with this life? What had once seemed exotic began to feel rather monotonous as things settled into a rhythm. It was the archetypal human one, which went wash, breakfast, check the Internet, work, lunch, work, dinner, talk, watch television, read a book, go to bed, pretend to be asleep, then actually sleep.

Belonging as I did to a species that had only ever really known one day, there was initially something quite exciting about having any kind of rhythm at all. But now that I was stuck here for good, I began to resent humans' lack of imagination. I believed they should have tried to add a little more variety to the proceedings. I mean, this was the species whose main excuse for not doing something was "if only I had more time." Perfectly valid until you realized they *did* have more time. Not eternity, granted, but they had tomorrow. And the day after tomorrow. And the day after the day after tomorrow. In fact I would have had to write "the day after" thirty thousand times before a final "tomorrow" in order to illustrate the amount of time on a human's hands.

The problem lying behind the lack of human fulfillment was a shortage not just of time but of imagination. They found a day that worked for them and then stuck to it and repeated it, at least between Monday and Friday. Even if it didn't work for them—as was usually the case—they stuck to it anyway. Then they'd alter things a bit and do something a little bit more fun on Saturday and Sunday.

One initial proposal I wanted to put to them was to swap things over. For instance, have five fun days and two not-fun days. That way—call me a mathematical genius—they would have more fun. But as things stood, there weren't even two fun days. They only had Saturdays, because Mondays were a little bit too close to Sundays for Sunday's liking, as if Monday were a collapsed star in the week's solar system, with an excessive gravitational pull. In other words, one seventh of human days worked quite well. The other six weren't very good, and five of those were roughly the same day stuck on repeat.

The real difficulty, for me, was mornings.

Mornings were hard on Earth. You woke up tireder than when you went to sleep. Your back ached. Your neck ached. Your chest felt tight with anxiety that came from being mortal. And then, on top of all that, you had to do so much before the day even started. The main problem was the stuff to do in order to be presentable.

Humans, male and female, typically have to do the following things. They will get out of bed, sigh, stretch, go to the toilet, shower, shampoo their hair, condition their hair, wash their face, shave, deodorize, brush their teeth (*with fluoride!*), dry their hair, brush their hair, put on face cream, apply makeup, check everything in the mirror, choose clothes based on the weather and the situation, put on those clothes, check everything again in the mirror—and that's just what happens before breakfast. It's a wonder they ever get out of bed at all. But they do, repeatedly, thousands of times each. And not only that—they do it by themselves, with no technology to help them. Maybe a little electrical activity in their toothbrushes and hair dryers, but nothing more than that. And all to reduce body odor and hairs and halitosis and shame.

Teenagers

Another thing adding force to the relentless gravity dogging this planet was all the worry that Isobel still had for Gulliver. She was pinching her bottom lip quite a lot, and her breathing had become heavily punctuated with sighs. I had bought Gulliver a bass guitar, but the music he played was so gloomy, it gave the house an unceasing soundtrack of despair.

"I just keep thinking of things," said Isobel, when I told her that all this worry was unhealthy. "When he got expelled from school. He wanted it. He wanted to be expelled. It was a sort of academic suicide. I just worry, you know. He's always been so bad at connecting with people. I can remember the first ever report he had at nursery school. It said he had resisted making any attachments. I mean, I know he's had friends, but he's always found it difficult. Shouldn't there be girlfriends by now? He's a good-looking boy."

"Are friends so important? What's the point of them?"

"Connections, Andrew. Think of Ari. Friends are how we connect to the world. I just worry, sometimes, that he's not fixed here. To the world. To life. He reminds me of Angus."

Angus, apparently, was her brother. He had ended his own life in his early thirties because of financial worries. I felt sad when she told me that. Sad for all the humans who find it easy to feel ashamed about things. They were not the only life-form in the universe to have suicide, but they were one of the most enthusiastic about it. I wondered if I should tell her that he wasn't going to school. I decided I should.

"What?" Isobel asked. But she had heard. "Oh God. So what's he been doing?"

"I don't know," I said. "Just walking around, I think."

"Walking around?"

"When I saw him he was walking."

She was angry now, and the music Gulliver was playing (quite loudly, by this point) wasn't helping.

And Newton was making me feel guilty with his eyes.

"Listen, Isobel, let's just—"

It was too late. Isobel raced up the stairs. The inevitable row ensued. I could only hear Isobel's voice. Gulliver's was too quiet and low, deeper than the bass guitar. "Why haven't you been to school?" his mother shouted. I followed, with nausea in my stomach and a dull ache in my heart.

I was a traitor.

He shouted at his mother, and his mother shouted back. He mentioned something about me getting him into fights but fortunately Isobel had no clue what he was talking about.

"Dad, you bastard," he said to me at one point.

"But the guitar. That was my idea."

"So you're buying me now?"

Teenagers, I realized, were really quite difficult. In the same way the southeastern corner of the Derridean galaxy was difficult.

His door slammed. I used the right tone of voice. "Gulliver, calm down. I am sorry. I am only trying to do what is best for you. I am learning here. Every day is a lesson, and some lessons I fail."

It didn't work. Unless working meant Gulliver kicking his own door with rage. Isobel eventually went downstairs, but I stayed there. An hour and thirty-eight minutes sitting on the beige wool carpet on the other side of the door.

Newton came to join me. I stroked him. He licked my wrist with his rough tongue. I stayed right there, my head tilted toward the door.

"I am sorry, Gulliver," I said. "I am sorry. I am sorry. And I am sorry I embarrassed you."

Sometimes the only power you need is persistence. Eventually, he came out. He just looked at me, hands in pockets. He leaned against the door frame. "Did you do something on Facebook?"

"I might have."

He tried not to smile.

He didn't say much after that but he came downstairs and we all watched television together. It was a quiz show called *Who Wants to Be a Millionaire?* (As the show was aimed at humans, the question was rhetorical.)

Then, shortly after, Gulliver went to the kitchen to see how much cereal and milk would fit into a bowl (more than you could imagine), and then he disappeared back to the attic. There was a feeling of something having been accomplished. Isobel told me she had booked us tickets to see an avant-garde production of *Hamlet* at the Arts Theatre. It was apparently about a suicidal young prince who wants to kill the man who has replaced his father.

"Gulliver is staying at home," said Isobel.

"That might be wise."

Australian Wine

"I've forgotten to take my tablets today."

Isobel smiled. "Well, one evening off won't hurt. Do you want a glass of wine?"

I hadn't tried wine before, so I said yes, as it really did seem to be a very revered substance. It was a mild night, so Isobel poured me a glass and we sat outside in the garden. Newton decided to stay indoors. I looked at the transparent yellow liquid in the glass. I tasted it and tasted fermentation. In other words I tasted life on Earth. For everything that lives here ferments, ages, becomes diseased. But as things made their decline from ripeness, they could taste wonderful, I realized.

Then I considered the glass. The glass had been distilled from rock and so it knew things. It knew the age of the universe, because it was the universe.

I took another sip.

After the third sip, I was really beginning to see the point, and it did something rather pleasant to the brain. I was forgetting the dull aches of my body and the sharp worries of my mind. By the end of the third glass I was very, very drunk. I was so drunk I looked to the sky and believed I could see two moons.

"You do realize you're drinking Australian wine, don't you?" she said.

To which I may have replied, "Oh."

"You *hate* Australian wine."

"Do I? Why?" I said.

"Because you're a snob."

"What's a snob?"

She laughed, looked at me sideways. "Someone who didn't used to sit down with his family to watch TV," she said. "Ever."

"Oh."

I drank some more. So did she. "Maybe I am becoming less of one," I said.

"Anything is possible." She smiled. She was still exotic to me. That was obvious, but it was a pleasant exoticism now. Beyond pleasant, in fact.

"Actually, anything *is* possible," I told her, but didn't go into the maths.

She put her arm around me. I did not know the etiquette. Was this the moment I was meant to recite poetry written by dead people, or was I meant to massage her anatomy? I did nothing. I just let her stroke my back as I stared upward, beyond the thermosphere, and watched the two moons slide together and become one.

The Watcher

The next day I had a hangover.

I realized that if getting drunk was how people forgot they were mortal, then hangovers were how they remembered. I woke with a headache, a dry mouth, and a bad stomach. I left Isobel in bed and went downstairs for a glass of water, then I had a shower. I got dressed and went into the living room to read poetry.

I had the strange but real sense that I was being watched. The sense grew and grew. I stood up, went to the window. Outside the street was empty. The large, static redbrick houses just stood there, like decharged crafts on a landing strip. But still I stayed looking. I thought I could see something reflected in one of the windows, a shape beside a car. A human shape, maybe. My eyes might have been playing tricks. I was hungover, after all.

Newton pressed his nose into my knee. He released a curious high-pitched whine.

"I don't know," I said. I stared out of the glass again, away from reflections, to direct reality. And then I saw it. Dark, hovering just above that same parked car. I realized what it was. It was the top of a human head. I had been right. Someone was hiding from my stare.

"Wait there," I told Newton. "Guard the house."

I ran outside, across the drive, and onto the street, just in time to see someone sprinting away around the next corner. A man, wearing jeans and a black top. Even from behind, and at a distance, the man struck me as familiar, but I couldn't think where I had seen him.

I turned the corner, but there was no one there. It was just another empty suburban street, and a long one. Too long for the person to have run down. Well, it wasn't quite empty. There was an old human female walking toward me, dragging a shopping cart. I stopped running.

"Hello," she said, smiling. Her skin was creased with age, in the way typical of the species. (The best way to think of the aging process in relation to a human face is to imagine a map of an area of innocent land that slowly becomes a city with many long and winding routes.)

I think she knew me. "Hello," I said back.

"How are you now?"

I was looking around, trying to assess the possible escape routes. If he had slid down one of the passageways, then he could have been anywhere. There were about two hundred obvious possibilities.

"I'm, I'm fine," I said. "Fine."

My eyes darted around but were unrewarded. *Who was this man?* I wondered. *And where was he from?*

Occasionally, in the days that followed, I would have that feeling again, of being watched. But I never caught a glimpse of my watcher, which was strange and led me to only two possible explanations. Either I was becoming too dull-witted and human, or the person I was looking for, the one I could sometimes feel watching me in university corridors and in supermarkets, was too sharp-witted to be caught.

In other words: something not human.

I tried to convince myself that this was ridiculous. I was almost able to convince myself that my own mind was ridiculous and that I had never actually been anything other than human. That I really was Professor Andrew Martin and that every other thing had been a kind of dream.

Yes, I could almost do that.

Almost.

How to See Forever

Isobel was at her laptop, in the living room. An American friend of hers wrote a blog about ancient history and Isobel was contributing a comment about an article on Mesopotamia. I watched her, mesmerized.

The Earth's moon was a dead place, with no atmosphere.

It had no way of healing its scars. Not like Earth, or its inhabitants. I was amazed, the way time mended things so quickly on this planet.

I looked at Isobel and I saw a miracle. It was ridiculous, I know. But a human, in its own small way, was a kind of miraculous achievement, in mathematical terms.

For a start, it wasn't very likely that Isobel's mother and father would have met. And even if they had met, the chances of their having a baby would have been pretty slim, given the numerous agonies surrounding the human dating process.

Her mother would have had about a hundred thousand eggs ovulating inside her, and her father would have had five trillion sperm during that same length of time. But even then, even that one-in-five-hundred-million-million-million chance of existing was a terrible understatement and did the coincidence of a human life nowhere near justice.

You see, when you looked at a human's face, you had to comprehend the luck that brought that person there. Isobel Martin had a total of 150,000 generations before her, and that only includes the humans. That was 150,000 increasingly unlikely copulations resulting in increasingly unlikely children. That was a one-in-quadrillion chance multiplied by another quadrillion for every generation.

Or around twenty thousand times more than the number of the atoms in the universe. But even *that* was only the start of it, because humans had only been around for three million Earth years, certainly a very short time compared to the three-and-a-half-billion years since life first appeared on this planet.

Therefore, mathematically, rounding things up, there was no chance at all that Isobel Martin could have existed. A zero in ten-to-the-power-of-forever chance. And yet there she was, in front of me, and I was quite taken aback by it all; I really was. Suddenly it made me realize why religion was such a big thing around here. Because, yes, sure, God could not exist. But then neither could humans. So, if they believed in themselves—the logic must go—why not believe in something that was only a fraction more unlikely?

I don't know how long I looked at her like this.

"What's going through your mind?" she asked me, closing the laptop. (This is an important detail. Remember: she *closed* the laptop.)

"Oh, just things."

"Tell me."

"Well, I'm thinking about how life is so miraculous, none of it really deserves the title 'reality.'"

"Andrew, I'm a little taken aback about how your whole worldview has become so romantic."

It was ridiculous that I had ever failed to see it.

She was beautiful. A forty-one-year-old, poised delicately between the young woman she had been on my initial sighting and the older one she would become. This intelligent, wound-dabbing historian. This person who would buy someone else's groceries with no other motive than simply to help.

I knew other things now. I knew she'd been a screaming baby, a child learning to walk, a girl at school eager to learn, a teenager listening to Talking Heads in her bedroom while reading books by A. J. P. Taylor.

I knew she'd been a university student studying the past and trying to interpret its patterns. She'd been, simultaneously, a young woman in love, full of a thousand hopes, trying to read the future as well as the past.

She had then taught British and European history, the big pattern she had discovered being the one that revealed that the civilizations that advanced with the Enlightenment did so through violence and territorial conquest more than through scientific progress, political modernization, and philosophical understanding.

She had then tried to uncover the woman's place in this history, and it had been difficult because history had always been written by the victors of wars, and the victors of the gender wars had always been male, and so women had been placed in the margins and in the footnotes, if they had been lucky.

And yet the irony was that she soon placed herself in the margins voluntarily, giving up work for family, because she imagined that when she eventually arrived at her deathbed, she would feel more regret about unborn children than unwritten books. But as soon as she made that move, she had felt her husband begin to take her for granted.

She had stuff to give, but it was ungiven; it was locked away.

And I felt an incredible excitement at being able to witness the love reemerge inside her, because it was a total, prime-of-life love. The kind that could only be possible in someone who was going to die at some point in the future, and also someone who had lived enough to know that loving and being loved back was a hard thing to get right, but when you managed it, you could see forever.

Two mirrors, opposite and facing each other at perfectly parallel angles, viewing themselves through the other, the view as deep as infinity.

Yes, that was what love was for. (I may not have understood marriage, but I understood love, I was sure of it.) Love was a way to live forever in a single moment, and it was also a way to see yourself as you had never actually seen yourself, and made you realize—having done so—that this view was a more meaningful one than any of your previous self-perceptions and self-deceptions. Even though, the big joke was, indeed the very biggest joke in the universe was, that Isobel Martin believed I had always been a human called Andrew Martin who had been born 100 miles away in Sheffield, and not in fact 8,653,178,431 light-years away.

"Isobel, I think I should tell you something. It is something very important."

She looked worried. "What? What is it?"

There was an imperfection in her lower lip. The left side of it was slightly fuller than the right. It was a fascinating detail on a face that only had fascinating details.

How could I ever have found her hideous? How? *How?*

I couldn't do it. Say it. I should have, but I didn't.

"I think we should buy a new sofa," I said.

"That's the important thing you want to tell me?"

"Yes. I don't like it. I don't like purple."

"Don't you?"

"No. It's too close to violet. All those short wavelength colors mess with my brain."

"You are funny. 'Short wavelength colors.'"

"Well, that's what they are."

"But purple is the color of emperors. And you've always acted like an emperor, so . . ."

"Is it? Why?"

"Byzantine empresses gave birth in the Purple Chamber. Their babies were given the honorary title *Porphyrogenitos,* which meant 'Born to the Purple' to separate them from riffraff generals who won the throne through going to war. But then, in Japan, purple is the color of death."

I was mesmerized by her voice when she spoke about historical things. It had a delicacy to it, each sentence a long, thin arm carrying the past as if it were porcelain. Something that could be brought out and presented in front of you but which could break and become a million pieces at any moment. I realized even her being a historian was part of her caring nature.

"Well, I just think we could do with some new furniture," I said.

"Do you now?" she asked, staring deep into my eyes in a mock-serious way.

One of the brighter humans, a German-born theoretical physicist called Albert Einstein, explained relativity to dimmer members of his species by telling them, "Put your hand on a hot stove for a minute, and it seems like an hour. Sit with a pretty girl for an hour, and it seems like a minute."

What if looking at the pretty girl felt like putting your hand on a hot stove? What was that? Quantum mechanics?

After a period of time, she leaned toward me and kissed me. I had kissed her before. But now the lightening effect on my stomach was very like fear. Indeed, it was every symptom of fear, but a pleasurable fear. An enjoyable danger.

She smiled and told me a story she had once read not in a history book but in a terrible magazine at the doctor's. A husband and a wife who had fallen out of love had their own separate affairs on the Internet. It was only when they came to meet their illicit lovers that they realized they had actually been having an affair with each other. But far from tearing the marriage apart, it restored it, and they lived happier than before.

"I have something to tell you," I said, after this story.

"What?"

"I love you."

"I love you too."

"Yes, but it is impossible to love you."

"Thank you. Precisely what a girl likes to hear."

"No. I mean, because of where I come from. No one there can love."

"What? Sheffield? It's not that bad."

"No. Listen, this is new to me. I'm scared."

She held my head in her hands, as if it was another delicate thing she wanted to preserve. She was a human. She knew one day her husband would die and yet she still dared to love him. That was an amazing thing.

We kissed some more.

Kissing was very much like eating. But instead of reducing the appetite, the food consumed actually increased it. The food wasn't matter, it had no mass, and yet it seemed to convert into a very delicious energy inside me.

"Let's go upstairs," she said.

She said the word suggestively, as though upstairs wasn't just a place but an alternate reality, made from a different texture of space-time. A pleasure land we would enter via a wormhole on the sixth stair. And, of course, she was absolutely right.

Afterward, we lay there for a few minutes, and then she decided we needed some music.

"Anything," I said, "but *The Planets*."

"That's the only piece of music you like."

"Not anymore."

So she put on something called "Love Theme" by Ennio Morricone. It was sad but beautiful.

"Can you remember when we saw *Cinema Paradiso*?"

"Yes," I lied.

"You hated it. You said it was so sentimental you wanted to throw up. You said it cheapens emotion to have it exaggerated and fetishized like that. Not that you've ever wanted to watch emotional things. I think, if I dare say it, you have always been scared of emotion, and so saying that you don't like sentimentality is a way of saying you don't like feeling emotion."

"Well," I said, "don't worry. That me is dead."

She smiled. She didn't seem worried at all.

But of course she should have been. We all should have been. And just how worried we should have been would become clear to me only a few hours later.

The Intruder

She woke me in the middle of the night.

"I think I heard someone," she said. Her voice indicated a tightness of the vocal folds within her larynx. It was fear disguised as calm.

"What do you mean?"

"I swear to God, Andrew. I think there's someone in the house."

"You might have heard Gulliver."

"No. Gulliver hasn't come downstairs. I've been awake."

I waited in the darkness, and then I heard something. Footsteps. It very much sounded like someone was walking around our living room. The clock's digital display beamed 04:22.

I pulled back the duvet and got out of bed.

I looked at Isobel. "Just stay there. Whatever happens, stay right there."

"Be careful," Isobel said. She switched on her bedside light and looked for the phone that was usually in its cradle on the table. But it wasn't there. "That's weird."

I left the room and waited a moment on the landing. There was silence now. The silence that can only exist in houses at twenty past four in the morning. It struck me then just how primitive life was here, with houses that could not do anything to protect themselves.

In short, I was terrified.

Slowly and quietly I tiptoed downstairs. A normal person would probably have switched the hallway light on, but I didn't. This wasn't for my benefit, but for Isobel's. If she came down and saw whoever it was, and they saw her, well, that could have been a very dangerous situation. Also, it would have been unwise to alert the intruder of my presence downstairs—if they hadn't already been alerted. And so it was that I crept into the kitchen and saw Newton sleeping soundly (maybe even suspiciously so) in his basket. As far as I could tell, no one else had been in here, or the utility room, and so I left to check the sitting room. No one was there, or no one that I could see anyway. There were just books, the sofa, an empty fruit bowl, a desk, and a radio. So then I went along the hallway to the living room. This time, before I opened the door, I sensed strongly that someone was there. But without the gifts I had no idea if my senses were fooling me.

I opened the door. As I did so, I felt a deep fear lightening my whole body.

Again, I saw only furniture. The sofa, the chairs, the switched-off television, the coffee table. No one was there, not at that moment, but we had definitely been visited. I knew this because Isobel's laptop was on the coffee table. This, alone, wasn't worrying, as she had left it there last night. What worried me, though, was that it was open. She had closed it. But not only that. The light emission. Even though the computer was facing away from me, I could see that the screen was glowing, which meant someone had been using it within the last two minutes.

I quickly went around the coffee table to see what was on the screen, but nothing had been deleted. I closed the laptop and went upstairs.

"What was it?" Isobel asked, as I slid back into bed.

"Oh, it was nothing. We must have been hearing things."

And Isobel fell asleep as I stared up at the ceiling, wishing I had a God who could hear my prayers.

Perfect Time

The next morning Gulliver brought his guitar downstairs and played a bit for us. He had learned an old piece of music by a band known as Nirvana called "All Apologies." With intense concentration on his face, he kept perfect time. He was very good, and we applauded him afterward.

For a moment, I forgot every worry.

A King of Infinite Space

It turned out that *Hamlet* was quite a depressing thing to watch when you had just given up immortality and were worried that someone was watching you.

The best bit came halfway through when he looked up at the sky.

"Do you see yonder cloud that's almost in the shape of a camel?" he asked.

"By th' Mass," said another man, a curtain fetishist called Polonius, "and 'tis like a camel, indeed."

"Methinks it is like a weasel," said Hamlet.

"It is backed like a weasel."

Then Hamlet squinted and scratched his head. "Or like a whale."

And Polonius, who wasn't really in tune with Hamlet's surreal sense of humor: "Very like a whale."

Afterward, we went out to a restaurant. It was called Tito's. I had a bread salad called 'panzanella.' It had anchovies in it. Anchovies were a fish, so I spent the first five minutes carefully taking them out and laying them on the side of the plate, offering them silent words of grief.

"You seemed to enjoy the play," said Isobel.

I thought I would lie. "I did. Yes. Did you?"

"No. It was awful. I think it was fundamentally wrong to have the Prince of Denmark played by a TV gardener."

"Yes," I said, "you're right. It was really bad."

She laughed. She seemed more relaxed than I had ever seen her. Less worried about me, and Gulliver.

"There's a lot of death in it, as well," I said.

"Yes."

"Are you scared of death?"

She looked awkward. "Of course, I'm scared to death of death.

I'm a lapsed Catholic. Death and guilt. That's all I have." Catholic, I discovered, meant a type of Christianity for humans who like gold leaf, Latin, and guilt.

"Well, I think you do amazingly. Considering that your body is starting a slow process of physical deterioration leading ultimately to . . ."

"Okay, okay. Thank you. Enough death."

"But I thought you liked thinking about death. I thought that's why we saw *Hamlet*."

"I like my death on a stage. Not over my penne arrabbiata."

So we talked and drank red wine as people came and left the restaurant. She told me of the module she was being cajoled into teaching next year. Early Civilized Life in the Aegean.

"They keep trying to push me farther and farther back in time. Think they're trying to tell me something. Next it will be Early Civilized Diplodocuses."

She laughed. So I laughed too.

"You should get that novel published," I said, trying a different tack. "*Wider Than the Sky*. It's good. What I've read of it."

"I don't know. That one was a bit private. Very personal. Of its time. I was in a dark place. That was when you were . . . well, you know. We're over that now. I feel like a different person now. Almost like I'm married to a different person too."

"Well, you should write fiction again."

"Oh, I don't know. It's getting the ideas."

I didn't want to tell her that I had quite a lot of ideas I could give her.

"We haven't done this for years, have we?" she said.

"Done what?"

"Talk. Like this. It feels like a first date or something. In a good way. It feels like I'm getting to know you."

"Yes."

"God," she said wistfully.

She was drunk now. So was I, even though I was still on my first glass.

"Our first date," she went on. "Can you remember?"

"Of course. Of course."

"It was here. But it was an Indian then. What was its name? . . . The Taj Mahal. You'd changed your mind on the phone after I wasn't too impressed at the Pizza Hut suggestion. Cambridge didn't even have a Pizza Express back then. God . . . twenty years. Can you believe it? Talk about the compression of time through memory. I remember it better than anything. I was late. You waited an hour for me. Out in the rain. I thought that was so romantic."

She looked off into the distance, as though twenty years ago was a physical thing that could be seen sitting at a table in the corner of the room. And as I stared at those eyes, which were loitering somewhere in the infinity between past and present, happy and sad, I deeply wanted to have been that person she was talking about. The one who had braved the rain and got soaked to the skin two decades ago. But I wasn't that person. And I would never be him.

I felt like Hamlet. I had absolutely no idea what to do.

"He must have loved you," I said.

She stopped daydreaming. Was suddenly alert. "What?"

"I," I said, staring down at my slow-melting limoncello ice cream. "And I *still* love you. As much as I did then. I was just, you know, seeing us, the past, in the third person. Distance of time . . ."

She held my hand across the table. Squeezed it. For a second I could dream I *was* Professor Andrew Martin, just as easily as a TV gardener could dream he was Hamlet.

"Can you remember when we used to go punting on the Cam?" she asked. "That time you fell in the water . . . God, we were drunk. Can you remember? While we were still here, before you had that Princeton offer and we went to America. We really had fun, didn't we?"

I nodded, but I felt uncomfortable. Also, I didn't want to leave Gulliver on his own any longer.

"Listen," I said, as we walked out of the restaurant, "there's something I really feel obliged to let you know . . ."

"What?" she asked, looking up at me. Holding on to my arm as she flinched at the wind. "What is it?"

The Art of Letting Go

"It's you," Zoë said.

"You know her?" whispered Isobel.

"I'm afraid . . . yes. From the hospital."

"Oh no."

"Please," I said to the man, "be nice."

The man was staring at me. His shaven head, along with the rest of his body, came toward me.

"And what on Earth has it got to do with you?"

"On Earth," I said, "it's nice to see people getting on together."

"You fuckin' *what*?"

"Just turn around," Isobel said fearlessly, "and leave everyone alone. Seriously, if you do anything else, you'll just regret it in the morning."

It was then he turned to Isobel and held her face, squeezing her cheeks hard, distorting her beauty. Anger flared inside me as he said to her, "Shut your fucking mouth, you meddling bitch."

Isobel now had fear-swollen eyes.

There were rational things to do here, I was sure, but I had come a long way since rationality.

"Leave us all alone," I said, momentarily forgetting that my words were just that. Words.

He looked at me and he laughed. And with that laughter came the terrifying knowledge that I had no power whatsoever. The gifts had been taken from me. I was, to all intents and purposes, no more equipped for a fight with a giant gym-bodied thug than the average human professor of mathematics, which wasn't particularly well equipped at all.

He beat me. And it was a proper beating. Not the kind Gulliver

I breathed deeply, filling my lungs, seeking courage somewhere in the nitrogen and the oxygen. In my mind I ran through the pieces of information I had to give her.

I am not from here.

In fact, I am not even your husband.

I am from another planet, in another solar system, in a distant galaxy.

"The thing is . . . well, the *thing* is . . ."

"Think we should probably cross the road," said Isobel, tugging my arm, as two silhouettes—a shouting female and a male—came toward us on the pavement. So we did, crossing at an angle that tried to balance the concealment of fear with rapid avoidance—that angle being, as it was everywhere in the universe, forty-eight degrees away from the straight line on which we had been traveling.

Midway across that carless road I turned and saw her. Zoë. The woman from the hospital I had met on my first day on this planet. She was still shouting at the large, muscular, shaven-headed man. The man had a tattoo of a tear on his face. I remembered her confession of her love of violent men.

"I'm telling you, you've got it wrong! You're the one that's crazy! Not me! But if you want to go around like a primitive life-form, that's fine! Do it, you thick piece of shit!"

"You pretentious, cock-munching slag!"

And then she saw me.

had given me, and which I had opted to feel. No. If there had been an option not to feel the cheap metal rings of this man's fist collide into my face with comet-like force, then I would have taken that option. As I would have done only moments later when I was on the ground receiving a kick in the stomach, rapidly unsettling the undigested Italian food residing there, followed by the final piece of brutalist punctuation—the kick to the head. More of a stamp, actually.

After that, there was nothing.

There was darkness, and *Hamlet*.

This was your husband. Look you now what follows.

I heard Isobel wailing. I tried to speak to her, but words were hard to reach.

The counterfeit presentment of two brothers.

I could hear the rise and fall of a siren, and knew it was for me.

Here is your husband, like a mildew'd ear.

I woke, in the ambulance, and there was only her. Her face above me, like a sun that eyes could stand, and she stroked my hand as she had once stroked my hand the first time I'd met her.

"I love you," she said.

And I knew the point of love right then.

The point of love was to help you survive.

The point was also to forget meaning. To stop looking and start living. The meaning was to hold the hand of someone you cared about and to live inside the present. Past and future were myths. The past was just the present that had died and the future would never exist anyway, because by the time we got to it, the future would have turned into the present. The present was all there was.

The ever-moving, ever-changing present. And the present was fickle. It could only be caught by letting go.

So I let go.

I let go of everything in the universe.

Everything, except her hand.

Neuroadaptive Activity

I woke up in the hospital.

It was the first time in my life I had woken in serious physical pain. It was nighttime. Isobel had stayed for a while and had fallen asleep in a plastic chair. But she had now been told to go home. So I was alone, with my pain, feeling how truly helpless it was to be a human. And I stayed awake in the dark, urging the Earth to rotate faster and faster so that it could be facing the sun again. For the tragedy of night to become the comedy of day. Of course, I had experienced it on other planets, but Earth had the darkest nights I had ever experienced. Not the longest, but the deepest, the loneliest, the most tragically beautiful. I consoled myself with random prime numbers: 73. 131. 977. 1,213. 83,719. Each as indivisible as love, except by one and itself. I struggled to think of higher primes. Even my mathematical skills had abandoned me, I realized.

They tested my ribs, my eyes, my ears, and inside my mouth. They tested my brain and my heart. My heart had caused no concern, though they did consider forty-nine beats per minute to be a little on the slow side. As for my brain, they were a little concerned about my medial temporal lobe, as there seemed to be some unusual neuroadaptive activity taking place.

"It's as though there has been something taken out of your brain and your cells are trying to overcompensate, but clearly nothing has been taken out or damaged. But it is very strange."

I nodded.

Of course, something had been taken out, but I also knew it was nothing any human, Earth-based doctor would ever be able to understand.

It had been a difficult test, but I had passed it. I was as good as human. And they gave me some acetaminophen and codeine for the pain, which still pulsated inside my head and on my face.

Eventually I went home.

The next day, Ari came to visit me. I was in bed. Isobel was at work and Gulliver was, quite genuinely it seemed, at school.

"Man, you look fucking terrible."

I smiled, lifted the bag of frozen peas from the side of my head. "Which is a coincidence, because I feel fucking terrible too."

"You should've gone to the police."

"Well, yes, I was thinking about it. Isobel thinks I should. But I have a little bit of a phobia about police. You know, ever since I was arrested for not wearing clothes."

"Yeah, well, you can't have psychos roaming around pulverizing anyone they feel like."

"No, I know. I know."

"Listen, mate, I just want to say that was big of you. That was old-school gentleman, defending your wife like that and, you know, kudos for it. It surprised me. I'm not putting you down or anything, but I didn't know you were that kind of shining-armor guy."

"Well, I've changed. I have a lot of activity in my medial temporal lobe. I think it's probably to do with that."

Ari looked doubtful. "Well, whatever it is, you're becoming a man of honor. And that's rare for mathematicians. It's always been us physicists who've had the big *cojones,* traditionally. Just don't screw it up with Isobel. You know what I mean?"

I looked at Ari for a long time. He was a good man, I could see that. I could trust him. "Listen, Ari, you know that thing I was going to tell you? At the café at the college?"

"When you had that migraine?"

"Yes." I hesitated. I was disconnected, so I knew I could tell him. Or thought I could. "I am from another planet, in another solar system, in another galaxy."

Ari laughed. It was a loud, deep blast of laughter without a single note of doubt. "Okay, ET, so you'll be wanting to phone home now. If we've got a connection that reaches the Andromeda galaxy."

"It's not the Andromeda galaxy. It's further away. Many, many light-years."

This sentence was hardly heard, as Ari was laughing so much.

He stared at me with fake blankness. "So how did you get here? Spaceship? Wormhole?"

"No. I didn't travel in any conventional way you would understand. It was antimatter technology. Home is forever away, but it is also only a second away. Though now, I can never go back."

It was no good. Ari, a man who believed in the possibility of alien life, still could not accept the idea when it was standing—or lying—right in front of him.

"You see, I had special talents, as a result of technology. The gifts."

"Go on then," Ari said, controlling his laughter, "show me."

"I can't. I have no powers now. I am exactly like a human."

Ari found this bit especially funny. He was annoying me now. He was still a good man, but good men could be annoying, I realized.

"Exactly like a human! Well, man, you're fucked then, aren't you?"

I nodded. "Yes. I think I might be."

Ari smiled, looked concerned. "Listen, make sure you keep taking all the tablets. Not just the painkillers. All of them, yeah?"

I nodded. He thought I was mad. Maybe it would be easier if I could take on this view myself, the delusion that it was a delusion. If one day I could wake up and believe it was all a dream. "Listen," I said. "I've researched you. I know you understand quantum physics, and I know you've written about simulation theory. You say there's a thirty percent chance that none of this is real. You told me in the café you believed in aliens. So I know you can believe this."

Ari shook his head, but at least he wasn't laughing now. "No. You're wrong. I can't."

"That's okay," I said, realizing that if Ari wouldn't believe me, Isobel never would. But Gulliver. There was always Gulliver. One day I would tell him the truth. But what then? Could he accept me as a father, knowing I had lied?

I was trapped. I had to lie, and to keep lying.

"But, Ari," I said, "if I ever need a favor, if I ever need Gulliver and Isobel to stay at your house—would that be okay?"

He smiled. "Sure, mate, sure."

Platykurtic Distribution

The next day, still swollen with bruises, I was back at the college.

There was something about being in the house, even with Newton for company, that troubled me. It never had before, but now it made me feel incredibly lonely. So I went to work, and I realized why work was so important on Earth. It stopped you from feeling lonely. But loneliness was there for me, waiting in my office, which was where I'd returned after my lecture on distribution models. But my head hurt and I must admit I did quite welcome the peace.

After a while there was a knock on the door. I ignored it. Loneliness minus a headache was my preferred option. But then it happened again. And it happened in such a way that I knew it was going to keep on happening, and so I stood up and went to the door. And, after a while, I opened it.

A young woman was there.

It was Maggie.

The wildflower in bloom. The one with the curly red hair and the full lips. She was twirling her hair around her finger again. She was breathing deeply and seemed to be inhaling a different kind of air—one which contained a mysterious aphrodisiac, promising euphoria. And she was smiling.

"So," she said.

I waited a minute for the rest of the sentence but it didn't happen. "So" was beginning, middle, and end. It meant something, but I didn't know what.

"What do you want?" I asked.

She smiled again. Bit her lip. "To discuss the compatibility of bell curves and platykurtic distribution models."

"Right."

"Platykurtic," she added, running a finger down my shirt toward my trousers. "From the Greek. *Platus* meaning flat, *kurtos* meaning . . . *bulging*."

"Oh."

Her finger danced away from me. "So, Jake LaMotta, let's go."

"My name is not Jake LaMotta."

"I know. I was referencing your face."

"Oh."

"So, are we going?"

"Where?"

"Hat and Feathers."

I had no idea what she was talking about. Or indeed, who she actually was to me, or to the man who had been Professor Andrew Martin.

"All right," I said, "let's go."

That was it, right there. My first mistake of the day. But by no means the last.

The Hat and Feathers

I soon discovered the Hat and Feathers was a misleading name. In it there was no hat, and there were absolutely no feathers. There were just heavily inebriated people with red faces laughing at their own jokes. This, I soon discovered, was a typical pub. The "pub" was an invention of humans living in England, designed as compensation for the fact that they were humans living in England. I rather liked the place.

"Let's find a quiet corner," she said to me, this young Maggie.

There were lots of corners, as there always seemed to be in human-made environments. Earth dwellers still seemed to be a long way off from understanding the link between straight lines and acute forms of psychosis, which might explain why pubs seemed to be full of aggressive people. There were straight lines running into each other *all over the place*. Every table, every chair, at the bar, at the "fruit machine." (I inquired about these machines. Apparently they were aimed at men whose fascination with flashing squares of light was coupled with a poor grasp of probability theory.) With so many corners to choose from, it was a surprise to see us sit near a straight, continuous piece of wall, at an oval table and on circular stools.

"This is perfect," she said.

"Is it?"

"Yes."

"Right."

"What would you like?"

"Liquid nitrogen," I replied thoughtlessly.

"A whisky and soda?"

"Yes. One of them."

And we drank and chatted like old friends, which I think we

were. Though her conversational approach seemed quite different from Isobel's.

"Your penis is everywhere," she said at one point.

I looked around. "Is it?"

"Two hundred and twenty thousand hits on YouTube."

"Right," I said.

"They've blurred it out, though. Quite a wise move, I would say, from firsthand experience." She laughed even more at this. It was a laugh that did nothing to relieve the pain pressing into and out of my face.

I changed the mood. I asked her what it meant, for her, to be a human. I wanted to ask the whole world this question, but right now, she would do. And so she told me.

The Ideal Castle

She said being human is being a young child on Christmas Day who receives an absolutely magnificent castle. And there is a perfect photograph of this castle on the box and you want more than anything to play with the castle and the knights and the princesses because it looks like such a perfectly human world, but the only problem is that the castle isn't built. It's in tiny intricate pieces, and although there's a book of instructions, you don't understand it. Nor can your parents or Aunt Sylvie. So you are just left, crying at the ideal castle on the box, which no one would ever be able to build.

Somewhere Else

I thanked Maggie for this interpretation. And then I explained to her that I thought the meaning was coming to me, the more I forgot it. After that, I spoke a lot about Isobel. This seemed to irritate her, and she switched the subject.

"After this," she said, circling the top of her glass with her finger, "are we going somewhere else?"

I recognized the tone of this "somewhere else." It had the exact same frequency as Isobel's use of the word "upstairs" the Saturday before.

"Are we going to have sex?"

She laughed some more. Laughter, I realized, was the reverberating sound of a truth hitting a lie. Humans existed inside their own delusions, and laughing was a way out—the only possible bridge they had between each other. That, and love. But there was no love between me and Maggie, I want you to know that.

Anyway, it turned out we *were* going to have sex. So we left and walked along a few streets until we reached Willow Road and her flat. Her flat, by the way, was the messiest thing I had ever seen that hadn't been a direct result of nuclear fission. A supercluster of books, clothes, empty wine bottles, stubbed-out cigarettes, old toast, and unopened envelopes.

I discovered that her full name was Margaret Lowell. I wasn't an expert on Earth names, but I still knew this was wildly inappropriate. She should have been called Lana Bellcurve or Ashley Brainsex or something. Anyway, apparently I never called her Margaret. ("No one except my broadband provider calls me that.") She was Maggie.

And Maggie, it transpired, was an unconventional human. For instance, when asked about her religion, she answered "Pythagorean." She was "well traveled," the most ridiculous expression if you belonged to a species that had only left its own planet to visit its moon (and Maggie, it transpired, hadn't even been there). In this case, it merely meant she had taught English in Spain, Tanzania, and various parts of South America for four years before returning to study maths. She also seemed to have a very limited sense of body shame, by human standards, and had worked as a lap dancer to pay for her undergraduate studies.

She wanted to have sex on the floor, which was an intensely uncomfortable way of having it. As we unclothed each other, we kissed, but this wasn't the kind of kissing that brought you closer, the kind that Isobel was good at. This was self-referential kissing, kissing about kissing, dramatic and fast and pseudo-intense. It also hurt. My face was still tender and Maggie's megakisses didn't really seem to accommodate the possibility of pain. And then we were naked, or rather the parts of us which needed to be naked were naked, and it started to feel more like a strange kind of fighting than anything else. I looked at her face and her neck and her breasts and was reminded of the fundamental strangeness of the human body. With Isobel, I had never felt like I was sleeping with an alien, but with Maggie the level of exoticism bordered on terror. There was physiological pleasure, quite a good deal of it at times, but it was a very localized, anatomical kind of pleasure. I smelled her skin, and I liked the smell of it, which seemed to be a mixture of coconut-scented lotion and bacteria, but my mind felt terrible, for a reason that involved more than my head pain.

Almost immediately after we had started having sex, I had a queasy sensation in my stomach, as though the altitude had drast-cally changed. I stopped. I got away from her.

"What's the matter?" she asked me.

"I don't know. But something is. This feels wrong. I realize I don't want to have an orgasm right now."

"Bit late for a crisis of conscience."

I really didn't know what the matter was. After all, it was just sex.

I got dressed and discovered there were four missed calls on my mobile phone.

"Good-bye, Maggie."

She laughed some more. "Give my love to your wife."

I had no idea what was so funny, but I decided to be polite and laughed too as I stepped outside into cool evening air, tainted with maybe a little more carbon dioxide than I had noticed before.

Places Beyond Logic

"You're home late," Isobel said. "I've been worried. I thought that man might have come after you."

"What man?"

"That brute who smashed your face in."

She was in the living room, at home, its walls lined with books about history and mathematics. Mainly mathematics. She was placing pens in a pot. She was staring at me with harsh eyes. Then she softened a bit. "How was your day?"

"Oh," I said, putting down my bag, "it was okay. I did some teaching. I met some students. I had sex with that person. My student. The one called Maggie."

It's funny, I had a sensation these words were taking me somewhere, into a dangerous valley, but still I said them. Isobel, meanwhile, took a little time to process this information, even by human standards. The queasy feeling in my stomach hadn't gone away. If anything, it had intensified.

"That's not very funny."

"I wasn't trying to be funny."

She studied me for a long while. Then dropped a fountain pen on the floor. The lid came off. Ink sprayed. "What are you talking about?"

I told her again. The bit she seemed most interested in was the last part, about me having sex with Maggie. Indeed, she was so interested that she started to hyperventilate and throw the pen pot in the direction of my head. And then she began to cry.

"Why are you crying?" I said, but I was beginning to understand. I moved closer to her. It was then she launched an attack on me, her hands moving as fast as laws of anatomical motion allow. Her fingernails scratched my face, adding fresh wounds. Then she just stood there, looking at me, as if she had wounds too. Invisible ones.

"I'm sorry, Isobel, you have to understand, I didn't realize I was doing anything wrong. This is all new. You don't know how alien all this is to me. I know it is morally wrong to love another woman, but I don't love her. It was just pleasure. The way a peanut butter sandwich is pleasure. You don't realize the complexity and hypocrisy of this system . . ."

She had stopped. Her breathing slowed and deepened, and her first question became her only one. "Who is she?" And then, "Who is she?" And soon after, "Who *is* she?"

I was reluctant to speak. Speaking to a human you cared about, I realized, was so fraught with hidden danger that it was a wonder people bothered speaking at all. I could have lied. I could have backtracked. But I realized lying, though essential to keep someone in love with you, actually wasn't what my love demanded. It demanded truth.

So I said, in the simplest words I could find, "I don't know. But I don't love her. I love you. I didn't realize that it was such a big thing. I sort of knew, as it was happening. My stomach told me, in a way it never tells me with peanut butter. And then I stopped." The only time I'd come across the concept of infidelity was in *Cosmopolitan* magazine, and they really hadn't done enough to explain it properly. They'd sort of said it depends on the context, and you see, it was such an alien concept for me to understand. It was like trying to get a human to understand transcellular healing. "I'm sorry."

She wasn't listening. She had her own things to say. "I don't even know you. I have no idea of who you are. No idea. If you've done this, you really are an alien to me . . ."

"Am I? Listen, Isobel, you're right. I am. I am not from here. I have never loved before. All this is new. I'm an amateur at this. Listen, I used to be immortal, I could not die, I could not feel pain, but I gave that up . . ."

She wasn't even listening. She was a galaxy away.

"All I know, all I know beyond any doubt, is that I want a

divorce. I do. That is what I want. You have destroyed us. You have destroyed Gulliver. Again."

Newton appeared at this point, wagging his tail to try and calm the mood.

Isobel ignored Newton and started to walk away from me. I should have let her go, but bizarrely I couldn't. I held on to her wrist.

"Stay," I said.

And then it happened. Her arm swung at me with ferocious force, her clenched hand an asteroid speeding toward the planet of my face. Not a slap or a scratch this time but a *smack*. Was this where love ended? With an injury on top of an injury on top of an injury?

"I'm leaving the house now. And when I come back, I want you gone. Do you understand? *Gone*. I want you out of here, and out of our lives. It's over. Everything. It's all over. I thought you'd changed. I honestly thought you'd become someone else. And I let you in again! What a *fucking* idiot!"

I kept my hand over my face. It still hurt. I heard her footsteps head away from me. The door opened. The door closed. I was alone again with Newton.

"I've really done it now," I said.

He seemed to agree, but I couldn't understand him anymore. I might as well have been any human trying to understand any dog. But he seemed something other than sad, as he barked in the direction of the living room and the road beyond. It seemed less like condolence and more like warning. I went to look out of the living room window. There was nothing to be seen. So I stroked Newton one more time, offered a pointless apology, and left the house.

PART THREE

The Wounded Deer Leaps the Highest

*It belongs to the perfection of everything human
that man can only attain his desire by passing
through its opposite.*
    —Søren Kierkegaard, *Fear and Trembling*

An Encounter with Winston Churchill

I walked to the nearest shop, a brightly lit and unsympathetic place called Tesco Metro. I bought myself a bottle of Australian wine.

I walked along a cycle path and drank it, singing "God Only Knows." It was quiet. I sat down by a tree and finished the bottle.

I went and bought another. I sat down on a park bench, next to a man with a large beard. It was the man I had seen before. On my first day. The one who had called me Jesus. He was wearing the same long dirty raincoat and he had the same scent. This time I found it fascinating. I sat there for a while just working out all the different aromas—alcohol, sweat, tobacco, urine, infection. It was a uniquely human smell and rather wonderful in its own sad way.

"I don't know why more people don't do this," I said, striking up a conversation.

"Do what?"

"You know, get drunk. Sit on a park bench. It seems like a good way to solve problems."

"Are you taking the piss, fella?"

"No. I like it. And you obviously like it or you wouldn't be doing it."

Of course, this was a little bit disingenuous of me. Humans were *always* doing things they didn't like doing. In fact, to my best estimate, at any one time only point three percent of humans were actively doing something they *liked* doing, and even when they did so, they felt an intense guilt about it and were fervently promising themselves they'd be back doing something horrendously unpleasant very shortly.

A blue plastic bag floated by on the wind. The bearded man rolled a cigarette. He had shaky fingers. Nerve damage.

"Ain't no choice in love and life," he said.

"No. That's true. Even when you think there are choices, there aren't really. But I thought humans still subscribed to the illusion of free will?"

"Not me, chief." And then he started singing, in a mumbled baritone of very low frequency. "Ain't no sunshine when she's gone . . ."

"What's your name?"

"I'm Andrew," I said. "Sort of."

"What's bothering you? You got beat up? Your face looks like shit."

"Yeah, in lots of ways. I had someone love me. And it was the most precious thing, that love. It gave me a family. It made me feel like I belonged. And I broke it."

He lit the cigarette, which flopped out of his face like a numb antenna. "Ten years me and my wife were married," he said. "Then I lost my job and she left me the same week. That's when I turned to drink and my leg started to turn on me."

He lifted up his trousers. His left leg was swollen and purple. And violet. I could see he expected me to be disgusted. "Deep vein thrombosis. Effing agony, it is. Effing *fucking* agony. And it's gonna bloody kill me one of these days."

He passed me the cigarette. I inhaled. I knew I didn't like it, but I still inhaled.

"What's *your* name?" I asked him.

He laughed. "Winston bloody Churchill."

"Oh, like the wartime prime minister." I watched him close his eyes and suck on his cigarette. "Why *do* people smoke?"

"No idea. Ask me something else."

"Okay, then. How do you cope with loving someone who hates you? Someone who doesn't want to see you again."

"God knows."

He winced. He was in agony. I had noticed his pain on the first day, but now I wanted to do something about it. I had drunk enough to believe I could, or at least to forget I couldn't.

He was about to roll his trousers down, but seeing the pain he was in, I told him to wait a moment. I placed my hand on the leg.

"What are you doing?"

"Don't worry. It's a very simple procedure of bio-set transference, involving reverse apoptosis, working at the molecular level to restore and re-create dead and diseased cells. To you it will look like magic, but it isn't."

My hand stayed there and nothing happened. And nothing kept on happening. It looked very far from magic.

"Who *are* you?"

"I'm an alien. I'm considered a useless failure in two galaxies."

"Well, could you please take your damn hand off my leg?"

I took my hand away. "Sorry. Really. I thought I still had the ability to heal you."

"I know you," he said.

"What?"

"I've seen you before."

"Yes. I know. I passed you, on my first day in Cambridge. You may remember. I was naked."

He leaned back, squinted, angled his head. "Nah. Nah. Wasn't that. I saw you today."

"I don't think you did. I'm pretty sure I would have recognized you."

"Nah. Definitely today. I'm good with faces, see."

"Was I with someone? A young woman? Red hair?"

He considered. "Nah. It was just you."

"Where was I?"

"Oh, you were on, let me think, you'd have been on Newmarket Road."

"Newmarket Road?" I knew the name of the street, because it was where Ari lived, but I hadn't ever been on the street myself. Not today. Not ever. Though of course, it was very likely that Andrew Martin—the original Andrew Martin—had been down there many times. Yes, that must have been it. He was getting mixed up. "I think you might be confused."

He shook his head. "It was you all right. This morning. Maybe midday. No word of a lie."

And with that the man stood up and hobbled slowly away from me, leaving a trail of smoke and spilled alcohol.

A cloud passed across the sun. I looked up to the sky. I had a thought as dark as the shade. I stood up. I took the phone out of my pocket and called Ari. Eventually someone picked up. It was a woman. She was breathing heavily, sniffing up snot, struggling to turn noise into coherent words.

"Hello, this is Andrew. I wondered if Ari was there."

And then the words came, in morbid succession: "He's dead, he's dead, he's *dead.*"

The Replacement

I ran.

I left the wine and I ran as fast as I could, across the park, along streets, over main roads, hardly thinking about traffic. It hurt, this running. It hurt my knees, my hips, my heart, and my lungs. All those components, reminding me they would one day fail. It also, somehow, aggravated the various facial aches and pains I was suffering. But mostly, it was my mind that was in turmoil.

This was my fault. This had nothing to do with the Riemann hypothesis and everything to do with the fact that I had told Ari the truth about where I was from. He hadn't believed me, but that hadn't been the point. I had been able to tell him, without getting an agonizing violet-tainted warning. They had disconnected me, but they must still have been watching and listening, which meant they could probably hear me now.

"Don't do it. Don't hurt Isobel or Gulliver. They don't know anything."

I reached the house that, up until this morning, I had been living in with the people I had grown to love. I crunched my way up the gravel driveway. The car wasn't there. I looked through the living room window, but there was no sign of anyone. I had no key with me, so I rang the doorbell.

I stood and waited, wondering what I could do. After a while, the door opened, but I still couldn't see anyone. Whoever had opened the door clearly didn't want to be seen.

I stepped into the house. I walked past the kitchen. Newton was asleep in his basket. I went over to him, shook him gently. "Newton! Newton!" But he stayed asleep, breathing deeply, mysteriously unwakeable.

"I'm in here," said a voice, coming from the living room.

So I followed it, that familiar voice, until I was there, looking at a man sitting on the purple sofa with one leg crossed over the other. He was instantly familiar to me—indeed, he could not have been more so—and yet, at the same time, the sight of him was terrifying.

For it was myself I was looking at.

His clothes were different (jeans instead of cords, a T-shirt instead of shirt, sneakers in place of shoes) but it was definitely the form of Andrew Martin. The midbrown hair, naturally parted. The tired eyes, and the same face except for the absence of bruises.

"Snap!" he said, smiling. "That is what they say here, isn't it? You know, when they are playing card games. Snap! We are identical twins."

"Who are you?"

He frowned, as if I'd asked such a basic question, it shouldn't have been asked. "I'm your replacement."

"My replacement?"

"That is what I said. I am here to do what you were unable to do."

My heart was racing. "What do you mean?"

"To destroy information."

Fear and anger were sometimes the same thing. "You killed Ari?"

"Yes."

"Why? He didn't know the Riemann hypothesis had been proved."

"No. I know. I have been given broader instructions than you. I have been told to destroy anyone you have told about your"—he considered the right word—"*origins*."

"So they've been listening to me? They said I was disconnected."

He pointed at my left hand, where the technology still evidently lived. "They took your powers away, but they didn't take theirs. They listen sometimes. They check."

I stared at it. At my hand. It looked, suddenly, like an enemy.

"How long have you been here? On Earth, I mean."

"Not long."

"Someone broke into this house a few nights ago. They accessed Isobel's computer."

"That was me."

"So why the delay? Why didn't you finish the job that night?"

"You were here. I did not want to hurt you. No Vonnadorian has killed another Vonnadorian. Not directly."

"Well, I'm not really a Vonnadorian. I am a human. The paradox is that I'm light-years from home, and yet this feels like my home. That is a strange thing to feel. So, what have you been doing? Where have you been living?"

He hesitated, swallowed hard. "I have been living with a female."

"A female human? A woman?"

"Yes."

"Where?"

"Outside Cambridge. A village. She doesn't know my name. She thinks I am called Jonathan Roper. I convinced her we were married."

I laughed. The laugh seemed to surprise him. "Why are you laughing?"

"I don't know. I have gained a sense of humor. That is one thing that happened when I lost the gifts."

"I am going to kill them, do you know that?"

"No. Actually, I don't. I told the hosts there is no point. That's about the last thing I said to them. They seemed to understand me."

"I have been told to, and that is what I will do."

"But don't you think it's pointless, that there's no real reason to do it?"

He sighed and shook his head. "No, I do not think that," he said, in a voice which was mine but deeper, somehow, and flatter. "I do not see a separation. I have lived with a human for only a few days, but I have seen the violence and hypocrisy that runs through this species."

"Yes, but there is good in them. A lot of good."

"No. I don't see it. They can sit and watch dead human bodies on TV screens and feel nothing at all."

"That's how I saw it at first, but—"

"They can drive a car thirty miles every day and feel good about themselves for recycling a couple of empty jam jars. They can talk about peace being a good thing yet glorify war. They can despise the man who kills his wife in rage but worship the indifferent soldier who drops a bomb killing a hundred children."

"Yes, there is a bad logic here, I agree with you, yet I truly believe—"

He wasn't listening. He stood up now, stared at me with determined eyes as he paced the room and delivered his speech. "They believe God is always on their side, even if their side is at odds with the rest of their species. They have no way of coming to terms with what are, biologically, the two most important events that happen to them—procreation and death. They pretend to know that money can't buy them happiness, yet they would choose money every time. They celebrate mediocrity at every available opportunity and love to see others' misfortune. They have lived on this planet for over a hundred thousand generations and yet they still have no idea about who they really are or how they should really live. In fact, they know less now than they once did."

"You're right, but don't you think there is something beautiful in these contradictions, something mysterious?"

"No. No, I do not. What I think is that their violent will has helped them dominate the world and 'civilize' it, but now there is nowhere left for them to go, and so the human world has turned in on itself. It is a monster that feasts on its own hands. And still they do not see the monster, or if they do, they do not see that they are inside it, molecules within the beast."

I looked at the bookshelves. "Have you read human poetry? Humans understand these failings."

He still wasn't listening.

"They have lost themselves but not their ambitions. Do not think that they would not leave this place if they had the chance. They're beginning to realize life is out there, that *we,* or beings like us, are out there, and they won't just stop at that. They will want to explore, and as their mathematical understanding expands, then they will eventually be able to do so. They will find us, eventually, and when they do, they will not want to be friends, even if they think—as they always do—that their own ends are perfectly benevolent. They will find a reason to destroy or subjugate other life-forms."

A girl in a school uniform walked past the house. Pretty soon, Gulliver would be coming home.

"But there is no connection between killing these people and stopping progress, I promise you. No connection."

He stopped pacing the room and came over to me, leaned into my face. "Connections? I will tell you about connections . . . An amateur German physicist works in a patent office in Bern in Switzerland. He comes up with a theory that, half a century later, will lead to whole Japanese cities being destroyed, along with much of their population. Husbands, wives, sons, daughters. He does not want that connection to form, but that does not stop it from forming."

"You're talking about something very different."

"No. No, I am not. This is a planet where a daydream can end in death, and where mathematicians can cause an apocalypse. That is my view of the humans. Is it any different from yours?"

"Humans learn the errors of their ways though," I said, "and they care more for each other than you think."

"No. I know they care for each other when the other in question is like them, or lives under their roof, but any difference is a step further away from their empathy. They find it preposterously easy to fall out among themselves. Imagine what they would do to us, if they could."

Of course, I had already imagined this and was scared of the answer. I was weakening. I felt tired and confused.

"But we were sent here to kill them. What makes us any better?"

"We act as a result of logic, of rational thinking. We are here to preserve, even to preserve the humans. Think about it. Progress is a very dangerous thing for them. The boy must be killed, even if the woman can be saved. The boy knows. You told us yourself."

"You are making a little mistake."

"What is my mistake?"

"You cannot kill a mother's son without killing the mother."

"You are speaking in riddles. You have become like them."

I looked at the clock. It was half past four. Gulliver would return home at any moment. I tried to think what to do. Maybe this other me, this "Jonathan," was right. Well, there wasn't really a maybe. He *was* right: the humans could not handle progress very well and they were not good at understanding their place in the world. They were, ultimately, a great danger to themselves and others.

So I nodded, and I walked over and sat on that purple sofa. I felt sober now, and fully conscious of my pain.

"You are right," I said. "You are right. And I want to help you."

A Game

"I know you are right," I told him for the seventeenth time, looking straight into his eyes, "but I have been weak. I admit it to you
now. I was and remain unable to harm any more humans, especially
those I have lived with. But what you have said to me has reminded
me of my original purpose. I am not able to fulfill that purpose and
no longer have the gifts to do so, but equally I realize it has to be
fulfilled, and so in a way I'm thankful you are here. I've been stupid.
I've tried and I have failed."

Jonathan sat back on the sofa and studied me. He stared at my
bruises and sniffed the air between us. "You have been drinking
alcohol."

"Yes. I have been corrupted. It is very easy, I find, when you
live like a human, to develop some of their bad habits. I have drunk
alcohol. I have had sex. I have smoked cigarettes. I have eaten peanut butter sandwiches and listened to their simple music. I have felt
many of the crude pleasures that they can feel, as well as physical
and emotional pain. But still, despite my corruption, there remains
enough of me left, enough of my clear, rational self, to know what
has to be done."

He watched me. He believed me, because every word I was
speaking was the truth. "I am comforted to hear this."

I didn't waste a moment. "Now listen to me. Gulliver will return home soon. He won't be on a car or a bike. He'll be walking.
He likes to walk. We will hear his feet on the gravel, and then we
will hear his key in the door. Normally, he heads straight into the
kitchen to get himself a drink or a bowl of cereal. He eats around
three bowls of cereal a day. Anyway, that is irrelevant. What is relevant is that he will most likely enter the kitchen first."

Jonathan was paying close attention to everything I was telling him. It felt strange, terrible even, giving him this information, but I really couldn't think of any other way.

"You want to act fast," I said, "as his mother will be home soon. Also, there's a chance he may be surprised to see you. You see, his mother has thrown me out of the house because I was unfaithful to her. Or rather the faith I had wasn't the right kind. Given the absence of mind-reading technology, humans believe monogamy is possible. Another fact to consider is that Gulliver has, quite independently, attempted to take his own life before. So I suggest that however you choose to kill him, it would be a good idea to make it look like suicide. Maybe after his heart has stopped, you could slice one of his wrists, cutting through the veins. That way, less suspicion will be aroused."

Jonathan nodded, then looked around the room. At the television, the history books, the armchair, the framed art prints on the wall, the telephone in its cradle.

"It will be a good idea to have the television on," I told him, "even if you are not in this room. Because I always watch the news and leave it on."

He switched on the television.

We sat and watched footage of war in the Middle East, without saying a word. But then he heard something that I couldn't, his senses being so much sharper.

"Footsteps," he said. "On the gravel."

"He's here," I said. "Go to the kitchen. I'll hide."

90.2 MHz

I waited in the sitting room. The door was closed. There would be no reason for Gulliver to enter here. Unlike the living room, he hardly ever came into this room. I don't think I'd ever heard him do so.

So I stayed there, still and quiet, as the front door opened, then closed. He was unmoving, in the hallway. No footsteps.

"Hello?"

Then a response. My voice but not my voice, coming from the kitchen. "Hello, Gulliver."

"What are you doing here? Mum said you'd gone. She phoned me, said you'd had an argument."

I heard him—me, Andrew, *Jonathan*—respond in measured words. "That is right. We did. We had an argument. Don't worry, it wasn't too serious."

"Oh yeah? Sounded pretty serious from Mum's side of things." Gulliver paused. "Whose are those clothes you're wearing?"

"Oh, these, they're just old ones I didn't know I had."

"I've never seen them before. And your face, it's totally healed. You look completely better."

"Well, there you go."

"Right, anyway, I might go upstairs. I'll get some food later."

"No. No. You will stay right here." The mind patterning was beginning. His words were shepherds ushering away conscious thought. "You will stay here and you will take a knife—a sharp knife, the sharpest there is in this room—"

It was about to happen. I could feel it, so I did what I had planned to do. I went over to the bookcase and picked up the clockwork radio, turned the power dial through a full 360-degree rotation, and pressed the button with the little green circle.

On.

The small display became illuminated: 90.2 MHz.

Classical music blared out at almost full volume as I carried the radio back along the hallway. Unless I was very much mistaken, it was Debussy.

"You will now press that knife into your wrist and press it hard enough to cut through every vein."

"What's that noise?" Gulliver asked, his head clearing. I still couldn't see him. I still wasn't quite at the kitchen doorway.

"Just do it. End your life, Gulliver."

I entered the kitchen and saw my doppelgänger facing away from me as he pressed his hand onto Gulliver's head. The knife fell to the floor. It was like looking at a strange kind of human baptism. I knew that what he was doing was right, and logical, from his perspective, but perspective was a funny thing.

Gulliver collapsed; his whole body was convulsing. I placed the radio down on the counter. The kitchen had its own radio. I switched that on too. The TV was still on, in the other room as I had intended it to be. A cacophony of classical music and news and rock music filled the air as I reached Jonathan and pulled his arm so he now had no contact with Gulliver.

He turned, held me by the throat, pressing me back against the refrigerator.

"You have made a mistake," he said.

Gulliver's convulsions stopped and he looked around, confused. He saw two men, both identical, like his father, pressing into each other's necks with equivalent force.

I knew that, whatever else happened, I had to keep Jonathan in the kitchen. If he stayed in the kitchen, with the radios on and the TV in the next room, we would be equally matched.

"Gulliver," I said. "Gulliver, give me the knife. Any knife. That knife. Give me that knife."

"Dad? Are you my dad?"

"Yes, I am. Now give me the knife."

"Ignore him, Gulliver," Jonathan said. "He's not your father. I am. He's an imposter. He's not what he looks like. He's a monster. An alien. We have to destroy him."

As we carried on, locked in our mutually futile combative pose, matching strength with strength, I saw Gulliver's eyes fill with doubt.

He looked at me.

It was time for the truth.

"I'm not your father. And neither is he. Your dad is dead, Gulliver. He died on Saturday, the seventeenth of April. He was taken by the . . ." I thought of a way of putting it that he would understand. ". . . by the people we work for. They extracted information from him, and then they killed him. And they sent me here, as him, to kill you. And kill your mother. And anyone who knew about what he had achieved that day, but I couldn't do it. I couldn't do it because I started, I started to feel something that was meant to be impossible . . . I empathized with you. Grew to like you. Worry about you. Love you both. And I gave everything up . . . I have no power, no strength."

"Don't listen to him, son," Jonathan said. And then he realized something. "Turn off the radios. Listen to me, turn off the radios now."

I stared at Gulliver with pleading eyes. "Whatever you do, don't turn them off. The signal interferes with the technology. It's his left hand. His left hand. Everything is in his left hand . . ."

Gulliver was clambering upright. He looked numb. His face was unreadable.

I thought hard.

"The leaf!" I yelled. "Gulliver, you were right. The leaf, remember, the leaf! And think of—"

It was then that the other version of myself smashed his head into my nose, with swift and brutal force. My head rebounded against the fridge door and everything dissolved. Colors faded, and the noise of the radios and the faraway newsreader swam into each other. A swirling audio soup.

It was over.

"Gulli—"

The other me switched one of the radios off. Debussy disappeared. But at the moment the music went away, I heard a scream. It sounded like Gulliver. And it was, but it wasn't a scream of pain. It was a scream of determination. A primal roar of rage, giving him the courage he needed to stab the knife that had been about to cut his own wrists into the back of a man who looked every inch his own father.

And the knife went deep.

With that roar, and that sight, the room sharpened into focus. I could get to my feet before Jonathan's finger reached the second radio. I yanked him back by the hair. I saw his face. The pain clearly articulated in the way only human faces can manage. The eyes, shocked yet pleading. The mouth seeming to melt away.

Melt away. Melt away. Melt away.

The Ultimate Crime

I would not look at his face again. He could not die while that technology remained inside him. I dragged him over to the Aga.

"Lift it up," I ordered Gulliver. "Lift up the cover."

"Cover?"

"The hot plate."

He did it. He lifted the circular steel ring up and let it fall back, and he did so without a single question in his eyes.

"Help me," I said. "He's fighting. Help me with his arm."

Together we had enough force to press his palm down to the burning metal. The scream, as we kept him there, was horrendous. To me, knowing what it was I was doing, it truly sounded like the end of the universe.

I was committing the ultimate crime. I was destroying gifts, and killing one of my kind.

"We've got to keep it there," I shouted to Gulliver. "We've got to keep it there! Hold! Hold! Hold!"

And then I switched my attention to Jonathan.

"Tell them it is over," I whispered. "Tell them you have completed your mission. Tell them there has been a problem with the gifts and that you will not be able to return. Tell them, and I will stop the pain."

A lie. And a gamble that they were tuned to him and not to me. But a necessary one. He told them, yet his pain continued.

How long were we like this? Seconds? Minutes? It was like Einstein's conundrum. The hot stove versus the pretty girl. Toward the end of it, Jonathan was on his knees, losing consciousness.

Tears streamed down my face as I finally pulled that sticky mess of a hand away. I checked his pulse. He was gone. The knife pierced through his chest as he fell back. I looked at the hand, and this face, and it was clear. He was disconnected, not just from the hosts but from life.

The reason it was clear was that he was becoming himself—in the cellular reconfiguration that automatically followed death. The whole shape of him was changing, curling in, his face flattening, his skull lengthening, his skin mottled shades of purple and violet. Only the knife in his back stayed. It was strange. Within the context of that Earth kitchen this creature, structured precisely as I had been, seemed entirely alien to me.

A monster. A beast. Something other.

Gulliver stared but said nothing. The shock was so profound it was a challenge to breathe, let alone speak.

I did not want to speak either, but for more practical reasons. Indeed, I worried that I may already have said too much. Maybe the hosts had heard everything I had said in that kitchen. I didn't know. What I did know was that I had one more thing to do.

They took your powers away, but they didn't take theirs.

But before I could do anything, a car pulled up outside. Isobel was home.

"Gulliver, it's your mother. Keep her away. Warn her."

He left the room. I turned back to the heat of that hot plate and positioned my hand next to where his had been, where pieces of his flesh still fizzed. And I pressed down and felt a pure and total pain, which took away space and time and guilt.

The Nature of Reality

*Civilised life, you know, is based on a huge
number of illusions in which we all collaborate
willingly. The trouble is we forget after a while
that they are illusions and we are deeply shocked
when reality is torn down around us.*

— J. G. BALLARD

What was reality?

An objective truth? A collective illusion? A majority opinion? The product of historical understanding? A dream? A dream. Well, yes, maybe. But if this had been a dream, then it was one from which I hadn't yet woken.

But once humans really study things in depth—whether in the artificially divided fields of quantum physics or biology or neuroscience or mathematics or love—they come closer and closer to nonsense, irrationality, and anarchy. Everything they know is disproved, over and over again. The Earth is not flat; leeches have no medicinal value; there is no God; progress is a myth; the present is all they have.

And this doesn't just happen on the big scale. It happens to each individual too.

In every human life there is a moment. A crisis. One that says, what I believe is wrong. It happens to everyone, the only difference being how that knowledge changes them. In most cases, it is simply a case of burying that knowledge and pretending it isn't there. That is how humans grow old. That is ultimately what creases their faces and curves their backs and shrinks their mouths and ambitions. The weight of that denial. The stress of it. This is not unique to humans. The single biggest act of bravery or madness anyone can do is the act of change.

I was something. And now I am something else.

I was a monster and now I am a different type of monster. One that will die and feel pain, but one that also will live, and maybe even find happiness one day. Because happiness is possible for me now. It exists on the other side of the hurt.

A Face as Shocked as the Moon

As for Gulliver, he was young and could accept things better than his mother. His life had never really made sense to him, so the final proof of its nonsensical nature was a kind of relief to him. He was someone who had lost a father and also someone who had killed, but the thing he had killed was something he didn't understand and couldn't relate to. He could have cried for a dead dog, but a dead Vonnadorian meant nothing to him. On the subject of grief, it was true that Gulliver worried that his father had felt pain. I told him he hadn't. Was that true? I didn't know. That was part of being human, I discovered. It was about knowing which lies to tell and when to tell them. To love someone is to lie to them. But I never saw him cry for his dad. I didn't know why. Maybe it was hard to feel the loss of someone who had never really been there.

Anyway, after dark he helped drag the body outside. Newton was awake now. He had woken after Jonathan's technology had melted away. And now he accepted what he was seeing as dogs seemed to accept everything. There were no canine historians, so that made things easier. Nothing was unexpected. At one point he began digging in the ground, as if trying to help us, but that wasn't required. No grave needed to be dug, as the monster—and that was how I referred to it in my mind, the *monster*—would in its natural state decompose rapidly in this oxygen-rich atmosphere. It was quite a struggle, dragging him out there, especially given my burnt hand and the fact that Gulliver had to stop to be sick at one point. He looked dreadful. I remember watching him staring at me from beneath his hair, his face as shocked as the moon.

Newton wasn't our only observer.

Isobel watched us in disbelief. I hadn't wanted her to come

outside and see, but she did so. At that point she didn't know every-thing. She didn't know, for instance, that her husband was dead or that the corpse I was dragging looked, essentially, how I had once looked.

She learned these things slowly, but not slowly enough. She would have needed at least a couple of centuries to absorb these facts, maybe even more. It was like taking someone from Regency England to twenty-first-century downtown Tokyo. She simply could not come to terms with it. After all, she was a historian. Some-one whose job was to find patterns, continuities, and causes, and to transform the past into a narrative that walked the same curving path. But on this path someone had now thrown something down from the sky that had landed so hard, it had broken the ground, tilted the Earth, made the route impossible to navigate.

Which is to say, she went to the doctor and asked for some tab-lets. The pills she was given didn't help and she ended up staying in bed for three weeks through exhaustion. It was suggested that she might have myalgic encephalomyelitis. She didn't, of course. She was suffering from grief. A grief for not just the loss of her husband but also the loss of familiar reality.

She hated me, during that time. I had explained everything to her: that none of this had been my decision, that I had been sent here reluctantly with no task except to halt human progress and to act for the greater good of the entire cosmos. But she couldn't look at me because she didn't know what she was looking at. I had lied to her. I'd slept with her. I'd let her tend my wounds. But she hadn't known who she had been sleeping with. It didn't matter that I had fallen in love with her and that it was that act of total defiance that had saved her life and Gulliver's. No. That didn't matter at all.

I was a killer and, to her, an alien.

My hand slowly healed. I went to the hospital and they gave me a transparent plastic glove to wear, filled with an antiseptic cream. At the hospital they asked me how it had happened, and I told them I had been drunk and leaned on the hot plate without thinking and without feeling the pain until it was too late. The burns became blisters and the nurse burst them, and I watched with interest as clear liquid oozed out.

Selfishly I had hoped at some point that my injured hand might trigger some sympathy from Isobel. I wanted to see those eyes again. Eyes that had gazed worriedly at my face after Gulliver had attacked me in his sleep.

I briefly toyed with the idea that I should try and convince her that nothing I had told her was true. That we were more magic realism than science fiction, specifically that branch of literary fiction that comes complete with an unreliable narrator. That I wasn't really an alien. That I was a human who'd had a breakdown, and there was nothing extraterrestrial or extramarital about me. Gulliver might have known what he had seen, but Gulliver had a fragile mind. I could easily have denied everything. A dog's health fluctuates. People fall off roofs and survive. After all, humans—especially adult ones—want to believe the most mundane truths possible. They need to, in order to stop their worldviews, and their sanity, from capsizing and plunging them into the vast ocean of the incomprehensible.

But it seemed too disrespectful, somehow, and I couldn't do it. Lies were everywhere on this planet, but true love had its name for a reason. And if a narrator tells you it was all just a dream, you want to tell him he has simply passed from one delusion into another one, and he could wake from this new reality at any time. You had to stay consistent to life's delusions. All you had was your perspective, so objective truth was meaningless. You had to choose a dream and stick with it. Everything else was a con. And once you had tasted truth and love in the same potent cocktail, there had to be no more tricks. But while I knew I couldn't correct this version of things with any integrity, living with it was hard.

You see, before coming to Earth, I had never wanted or needed to be cared for, but I hungered now to have that feeling of being looked after, of belonging, of being loved.

Maybe I was expecting too much. Maybe it was more than I deserved to be allowed to stay in the same house, even if I had to sleep on that hideous purple sofa.

The only reason even this concession was granted, I imagined, was Gulliver. Gulliver wanted me to stay. I had saved his life. I had helped him stand up to bullies. But his forgiveness still came as a surprise.

Don't get me wrong. It wasn't *Cinema Paradiso,* but he seemed to accept me as an extraterrestrial life-form far more easily than he had accepted me as a father.

"Where are you from?" he asked me, one Saturday morning at five minutes to seven, before his mother was awake.

"Far, far, far, far, far, far, far, far away."

"How far is far?"

"It's very hard to explain," I said. "I mean, you think France is far away."

"Just try," he said.

I noticed the fruit bowl. Only the day before, I had been to the supermarket buying healthy food the doctor had recommended for Isobel. Bananas, oranges, grapes, a grapefruit.

"Okay," I said, grabbing the large grapefruit. "*This* is the sun."

I placed the grapefruit on the coffee table. I then looked for the smallest grape I could find. I placed it at the other end of the table.

"*That* is Earth, so small you can hardly see it."

Newton stepped closer to the table, clearly attempting to annihilate Earth in his jaws. "No, Newton," I said. "Let me finish."

Newton retreated, tail between his legs.

Gulliver was frowning as he studied the grapefruit and the fragile little grape. He looked around. "So where is your planet?"

I think he honestly expected me to place the orange I was holding somewhere else in the room. By the television or on one of the bookshelves. Or maybe, at a pinch, upstairs.

"To be accurate, this orange should be placed on a coffee table in New Zealand."

He was silent for a moment, trying to understand the level of farness I was talking about. Still in a trance he asked, "Can I go there?"

"No. It's impossible."

"Why? There must have been a spaceship."

me. Except I shouldn't become an architect because architecture takes a hundred years to be appreciated."

"Listen, you don't need guidance, Gulliver. Everything you need is inside your own head. You have more knowledge about the universe than anyone else on your own planet." I pointed at the window. "You've seen what's out there. And also, I should say, you've shown yourself to be really strong."

He stared out of the window again. "What's it like up there?"

"Very different. Everything is different."

"But how?"

"Well, just existing is different. No one dies. There's no pain. Everything is beautiful. The only religion is mathematics. There are no families. There are the hosts—they give instructions—and there is everyone else. The advancement of mathematics and the security of the universe are the two concerns. There is no hatred. There are no fathers and sons. There is no clear line between biology and technology. And everything is violet."

"It sounds awesome."

"It's dull. It's the dullest life you can imagine. Here, you have pain, and loss, that's the price. But the rewards can be wonderful, Gulliver."

He looked at me, disbelieving. "Yeah. Well, I don't have a clue how to find them."

The phone rang. Isobel answered. Moments later, she was calling up to the attic.

"Gulliver, it's for you. A girl. Nat."

I couldn't help but notice the faintest of faint smiles on Gulliver's face, a smile he felt embarrassed about and tried to hide under clouds of discontent as he left the room.

I sat and breathed, with lungs that would one day stop functioning but which still had a lot of warm, clear air to inhale. Then I turned to Gulliver's primitive Earth computer and began to type, giving as much advice as I could think of to help a human.

I shook my head. "No. I didn't travel. I may have arrived, but I didn't *travel*."

He was confused, so I explained, but then he was even more confused.

"Anyway, the point is, there is no more chance of me crossing the universe now than any other human. This is who I am now, and this is where I have to stay."

"You gave up the universe for a life on the sofa?"

"I didn't realize that at the time."

Isobel came downstairs. She was wearing her white dressing gown and her pajamas. She was pale, but she was always pale in the morning. She looked at me and Gulliver talking, and for a moment, she seemed to greet the scene with a rarely seen fondness. But the expression faded as she remembered everything.

"What's going on?" she asked.

"Nothing," said Gulliver.

"What is the fruit doing?" she asked, traces of sleep still evident in her quiet voice.

"I was explaining to Gulliver where I came from. How far away."

"You came from a grapefruit?"

"No. The grapefruit is the sun. Your sun. Our sun. I lived on the orange. Which should be in New Zealand. Earth is now in Newton's stomach."

I smiled at her. I thought she might find this funny, but she just stared at me the way she had been staring at me for weeks. As if I were light-years away from her.

She left the room.

"Gulliver," I said, "I think it would be best if I left. I shouldn't have stayed, really. You see, this isn't just about all this stuff. You know that argument your mother and I had? The one you never found out about?"

"Yeah."

"Well, I was unfaithful. I had sex with a woman called Maggie. One of my—your father's—students. I didn't enjoy it, but that was beside the point. I didn't realize it would hurt your mother, but it did. I didn't know the exact rules of fidelity but that isn't really an excuse, or not one I can use, when I was deliberately lying about so many other things. When I was endangering her life, and yours." I sighed. "I think, I think I'm going to leave."

"Why?"

That question tugged at me. It reached into my stomach and pulled.

"I just think it will be for the best, right now."

"Where are you going to go?"

"I don't know. Not yet. But don't worry, I'll tell you when I get there."

His mother was back in the doorway.

"I'm going to leave," I told her.

She closed her eyes. She inhaled. "Yes," she said, with the mouth I had once kissed. "Yes. Maybe it is for the best." Her whole face crumpled, as if her skin were the emotion she wanted to screw up and throw away.

My eyes felt a warm, gentle strain. My vision blurred. Then something ran down my cheek, all the way to my lips. A liquid. Like rain, but warmer. Saline.

I had shed a tear.

The Second Type of Gravity

Before I left I went upstairs to the attic. It was dark in there, except for the glow of the computer. Gulliver was lying on his bed, staring out of the window.

"I'm not your dad, Gulliver. I don't have a right to be here."

"No. I know." Gulliver chewed on his wristband. Hostility glistened in his eyes like broken glass.

"You're not my dad. But you're just like him. You don't give a shit. And you shagged someone behind Mum's back. He did that too, you know."

"Listen, Gulliver, I'm not trying to leave you, I'm trying to bring back your mother, okay? She's a bit lost right now and my presence here isn't helping."

"It's just so fucked up. I feel totally alone."

Sun suddenly shone through the window, oblivious to our mood.

"Loneliness, Gulliver, is a fact as universal as hydrogen."

He sighed a sigh that should really have belonged to an older human. "I just don't feel cut out sometimes. You know, cut out for life. I mean, people at school, loads of their parents are divorced, but they seem to have an okay relationship with their dads. And everyone's always thought, with me, what excuse did I have to go off the rails? What was wrong with my life? Living in a nice house with rich nondivorced parents. What the fuck could possibly be wrong there?

"But it was all bullshit. Mum and Dad never loved each other, not since I can remember anyway. Mum seemed to change after he had his breakdown—I mean, after you came—but that was just her delusion. I mean, you weren't even who she thought you were. It's come to something when you relate to ET more than your own dad. He was crap. Seriously, I can't think of one piece of advice he gave

Advice for a Human

1. Shame is a shackle. Free yourself.
2. Don't worry about your abilities. You have the ability to love. That is enough.
3. Be nice to other people. At the universal level, they are you.
4. Technology won't save humankind. Humans will.
5. Laugh. It suits you.
6. Be curious. Question everything. A present fact is just a future fiction.
7. Irony is fine, but not as fine as feeling.
8. Peanut butter sandwiches go perfectly well with a glass of white wine. Don't let anyone tell you otherwise.
9. Sometimes, to be yourself you will have to forget yourself and become something else. Your character is not a fixed thing. You will sometimes have to move to keep up with it.
10. History is a branch of mathematics. So is literature. Economics is a branch of religion.
11. Sex can damage love but love can't damage sex.
12. The news should start with mathematics, then poetry, and move down from there.
13. You shouldn't have been born. Your existence is as close to impossible as can be. To dismiss the impossible is to dismiss yourself.
14. Your life will have 30,000 days in it. Make sure you remember some of them.
15. The road to snobbery is the road to misery. And vice versa.
16. Tragedy is just comedy that hasn't come to fruition. One day we will laugh at this. We will laugh at everything.
17. Wear clothes, by all means, but remember, they are *clothes*.
18. One life-form's gold is another life-form's tin can.

19. Read poetry. Especially poetry by Emily Dickinson. It might save you. Anne Sexton knows the mind, Walt Whitman knows grass, but Emily Dickinson knows everything.

20. If you become an architect, remember this: The square is nice. So is the rectangle. But you can overdo it.

21. Don't bother going into space until you can leave the solar system. Then go to Zabii.

22. Don't worry about being angry. Worry when being angry becomes impossible. Because then you have been consumed.

23. Happiness is not *out here*. It is *in there*.

24. New technology, on Earth, just means something you will laugh at in five years. Value the stuff you won't laugh at in five years. Like love. Or a good poem. Or a song. Or the sky.

25. There is only one genre in fiction. The genre is called "book."

26. Never be too far away from a radio. A radio can save your life.

27. Dogs are geniuses of loyalty. And that is a good kind of genius to have.

28. Your mother should write a novel. Encourage her.

29. If there is a sunset, stop and look at it. Knowledge is finite. Wonder is infinite.

30. Don't aim for perfection. Evolution, and life, only happen through mistakes.

31. Failure is a trick of the light.

32. You are human. You will care about money. But realize it can't make you happy because happiness is not for sale.

33. You are not the most intelligent creature in the universe. You are not even the most intelligent creature on your planet. The tonal language in the song of a humpback whale displays more complexity than the entire works of Shakespeare. It is not a competition. Well, it is. But don't worry about it.

34. David Bowie's "Space Oddity" tells you nothing about space, but its musical patterns are very pleasing to the ears.

35. When you look up at the sky, on a clear night, and see thousands of stars and planets, realize that very little is happening on most of them. The important stuff is further away.

36. One day humans will live on Mars. But nothing there will be more exciting than a single overcast morning on Earth.

37. Don't always try to be cool. The whole universe is cool. It's the warm bits that matter.

38. Walt Whitman was right about at least one thing. You will contradict yourself. You are large. You contain multitudes.

39. No one is ever completely right about anything. Anywhere.

40. Everyone is a comedy. If people are laughing at you, they just don't quite understand the joke that is themselves.

41. Your brain is open. Never let it be closed.

42. In a thousand years, if humans survive that long, everything you know will have been disproved. And replaced by even bigger myths.

43. Everything matters.

44. You have the power to stop time. You do it by kissing. Or listening to music. Music, by the way, is how you see things you can't otherwise see. It is the most advanced thing you have. It is a superpower. Keep up with the bass guitar. You are good at it. Join a band.

45. My friend Ari was one of the wisest humans who ever lived. Read him.

46. A paradox: The things you don't need to live—books, art, cinema, wine, and so on—are the things you need to *live*.

47. A cow is a cow even if you call it beef.

48. No two moralities match. Accept different shapes, so long as they aren't sharp enough to hurt.

49. Don't be scared of anyone. You killed an alien assassin sent from the other side of the universe, and you did it with a bread knife. Also, you have a very hard punch.

50. At some point, bad things are going to happen. Have someone to hold on to.

51. Alcohol in the evening is very enjoyable. Hangovers in the

morning are very unpleasant. At some point you have to choose: evenings or mornings.

52. If you are laughing, check that you don't really want to cry. And vice versa.

53. Don't ever be afraid of telling someone you love them. There are things wrong with your world, but an excess of love is not one.

54. That girl you are on the phone to. There will be others. But I hope she is nice.

55. You are not the only species on Earth with technology. Look at ants. Really. Look. What they do with twigs and leaves is quite amazing.

56. Your mother loved your father. Even if she pretends she didn't.

57. There are a lot of idiots in your species. Lots and lots. You are not one of them. Hold your ground.

58. It is not the length of life that matters. It's the depth. But while burrowing, keep the sun above you.

59. Numbers are pretty. Prime numbers are beautiful. Understand that.

60. Obey your head. Obey your heart. Obey your gut. In fact, obey everything except commands.

61. One day, if you get into a position of power, tell people this: Just because you can, it doesn't mean you should. There is a power and a beauty in unproved conjectures, unkissed lips, and unpicked flowers.

62. Start fires. But only metaphorically. Unless you are cold and it's a safe setting. In which case, start fires.

63. It's not the technique, it's the method. It's not the words, it's the melody.

64. Be alive. That is your supreme duty to the world.

65. Don't think you know. Know you think.

66. As a black hole forms, it creates an immense gamma-ray burst, blinding whole galaxies with light and destroying millions of worlds. You could disappear at any second. This

one. Or this one. Or this one. Make sure, as often as possible, you are doing something you'd be happy to die doing.

67. War is the answer. To the wrong question.
68. Physical attraction is, primarily, glandular.
69. Ari believed we are all a simulation. Matter is an illusion. Everything is silicon. He could be right. But your emotions? They're solid.
70. It's not you. It's them. (No, really. It is.)
71. Walk Newton whenever you can. He likes to get out of the house. And he is a lovely dog.
72. Most humans don't think about things very much. They survive by thinking about needs and wants alone. But you are not one of them. Be careful.
73. No one will understand you. It is not, ultimately, that important. What is important is that you understand you.
74. A quark is not the smallest thing. The smallest thing is the regret you will feel on your deathbed for not having worked more.
75. Politeness is often fear. Kindness is always courage. But caring is what makes you human. Care more, become more human.
76. In your mind, change the name of every day to Saturday. And change the name of work to play.
77. When you watch the news and see members of your species in turmoil, do not think there is nothing you can do. But know it is not done by watching news.
78. You get up. You put on your clothes. And then you put on your personality. Choose wisely.
79. Leonardo da Vinci was not one of you. He was one of us.
80. Language is euphemism. Love is truth.
81. You can't find happiness looking for the meaning of life. Meaning is only the third most important thing. It comes after loving and being.
82. If you think something is ugly, look harder. Ugliness is just a failure of seeing.

83. A watched pot never boils. That is all you need to know about quantum physics.

84. You are more than the sum of your particles. And that is quite a sum.

85. The Dark Ages never ended. (But don't tell your mother.)

86. To like something is to insult it. Love it or hate it. Be passionate. As civilization advances, so does indifference. It is a disease. Immunize yourself with art. And love.

87. Dark matter is needed to hold galaxies together. Your mind is a galaxy. More dark than light. But the light makes it worthwhile.

88. Which is to say, don't kill yourself. Even when the darkness is total. Always know that life is not still. Time is space. You are moving through that galaxy. Wait for the stars.

89. At the subatomic level, everything is complex. But you do not live at the subatomic level. You have the right to simplify. If you don't, you will go insane.

90. But know this. Men are not from Mars. Women are not from Venus. Do not fall for categories. Everyone is everything. Every ingredient inside a star is inside you, and every personality that ever existed competes in the theater of your mind for the main role.

91. You are lucky to be alive. Inhale and take in life's wonders. Never take so much as a single petal of a single flower for granted.

92. If you have children and love one more than another, work at it. They will know, even if it's by a single atom less. A single atom is all you need to make a very big explosion.

93. School is a joke. But go along with it, because you are very near to the punch line.

94. You don't have to be an academic. You don't have to be anything. Don't force it. Feel your way, and don't stop feeling your way until something fits. Maybe nothing will. Maybe you are a road, not a destination. That is fine. Be a road.

But make sure it's one with something to look at out of the window.

95. Be kind to your mother. And try to make her happy.
96. You are a good human, Gulliver Martin.
97. I love you. Remember that.

A Very Brief Hug

I packed a bag full of Andrew Martin's clothes and then I left.

"Where are you going to go?" asked Isobel.

"I don't know. I'll find somewhere. Don't worry."

She looked like she was going to worry. We hugged. I longed to hear her hum the theme to *Cinema Paradiso*. I longed to hear her talk to me about Alfred the Great. I longed for her to make me a sandwich or pour TCP on a swab of cotton wool. I longed to hear her share her worries about work or Gulliver. But she wouldn't. She couldn't.

The hug ended. Newton, by her side, looked up at me with the most forlorn eyes.

"Good-bye," I said.

And I walked across the gravel, toward the road, and somewhere in the universe of my soul a fiery, life-giving star collapsed, and a very black hole began to form.

The Melancholy Beauty
of the Setting Sun

Sometimes the hardest thing to do is just to stay human.

—MICHAEL FRANTI

The thing with black holes, of course, is that they are really very neat and tidy. There is no *mess* inside a black hole. All the disordered stuff that goes through the event horizon, all that in-falling matter and radiation, is compressed to the smallest state it can possibly be. A state that might easily be called nothing at all.

Black holes, in other words, give clarity. You lose the warmth and fire of the star, but you gain order and peace. Total focus.

That is to say, I knew what to do.

I would stay as Andrew Martin. This was what Isobel wanted. You see, she wanted the least fuss possible. She didn't want a scandal, or a missing person's inquiry, or a funeral. So, doing what I thought was best, I moved out, rented a small flat in Cambridge for a while, and then I applied for jobs elsewhere in the world.

Eventually, I got a teaching job in America, at Stanford University in California. Once there, I did as well as I needed to do while making sure I didn't do anything to advance any mathematical understanding that would lead to a leap in technological progress. Indeed, I had a poster on my office wall with a photograph of Albert Einstein on it, and one of his famous statements: "Technological progress is like an axe in the hands of a pathological animal."

I never mentioned anything about a proof of the Riemann hypothesis, except to persuade my peers of its inherent impossibility. My main motive for doing so was to make sure no Vonnadorian ever had need to visit Earth. But also, Einstein was right. Humans weren't good at handling progress and I didn't want to see more destruction than necessary inflicted on or by this planet.

I lived on my own. I had a nice apartment in Palo Alto that I filled with plants.

I got drunk, got high, got lower than low.

I painted some art, ate peanut butter breakfasts, and once went to an art house cinema to watch three films by Fellini in a row.

I caught a cold, got tinnitus, and consumed a poisoned prawn.

I bought myself a globe, and I would often sit there, spinning it.

I felt blue with sadness, red with rage, and green with envy. I felt the entire human rainbow.

I walked a dog for an elderly lady in the apartment above me, but the dog was never quite Newton. I talked over warm champagne at stifling academic functions. I shouted in forests just to hear the echo. And every night I would go back and reread Emily Dickinson.

I was lonely, but at the same time I appreciated other humans a bit more than they appreciated themselves. After all, I knew you could journey for light-years and not come across a single one. On occasion, I would weep just looking at them, sitting in one of the vast libraries on campus.

Sometimes I would wake up at three in the morning and find myself crying for no specific reason. At other times I would sit on my beanbag and stare into space, watching motes of dust suspended in sunlight.

I tried not to make any friends. I knew that as friendships progressed, questions would get more intrusive, and I didn't want to lie to people. People would ask about my past, where I was from, my childhood. Sometimes a student or a fellow lecturer would look at my hand, at the scarred and purple skin, but they would never pry.

It was a happy place, Stanford University. All the students wore smiles and red sweaters and looked very tanned and healthy for life-forms who spent their entire days in front of computer screens. I would walk like a ghost through the bustle of the quad, breathing that warm air, trying not to be terrified by the scale of human ambition surrounding me.

I got drunk a lot on white wine, which made me a rarity. No one seemed to have hangovers at this place. Also, I didn't like frozen yogurt—a big problem, as everyone at Stanford *lived* on frozen yogurt.

I bought myself music. Debussy, Ennio Morricone, the Beach Boys, Al Greene. I watched *Cinema Paradiso*. There was a Talking Heads song called "This Must Be the Place," which I played over and over again, even though doing so made me feel melancholy and crave to hear her voice again, or to hear Gulliver's footsteps on the stairs.

I read a lot of poetry too, though that often had a similar effect. One day I was in the campus bookstore and saw a copy of *The Dark Ages* by Isobel Martin. I stood there for what must have been the best part of half an hour reading her words aloud. "'Freshly ravaged by the Vikings,'" I'd say, reading the penultimate page, "'England was in a desperate state, and responded with a brutal massacre of Danish settlers in 1002. Over the next decade, this unrest was shown to breed even greater violence as the Danes embarked on a series of reprisals, culminating in Danish rule of England in 1013 . . .'" I pressed the page to my face, imagining it was her skin.

I traveled with my work. I went to Paris, Boston, Rome, São Paolo, Berlin, Madrid, Tokyo. I wanted to fill my mind with human faces, in order to forget Isobel's. But I achieved the opposite effect. By studying the entire human species, I felt more toward her specifically. By thinking of the cloud, I thirsted for the raindrop.

So I stopped my travels and returned to Stanford and tried a different tactic. I tried to lose myself in nature.

The highlight of my day became the evening, when I would get in my car and drive out of town. Often I would head to the Santa Cruz mountains. There was a place there called the Big Basin Redwoods State Park. I would park my car and walk around, gazing in wonder at the giant trees, spotting jays and woodpeckers, chipmunks and racoons, occasionally a black-tailed deer. Sometimes, if

I was early enough, I would walk down the steep path near Berry Creek Falls, listening to the rush of water, which would often be joined by the low croak of tree frogs.

At other times I would drive along Highway 1 and go to the beach to watch the sunset. Sunsets were beautiful here. I became quite hypnotized by them. In the past they had meant nothing to me. After all, a sunset was nothing really but the slowing down of light. At sunset light has more to get through and is further scattered by cloud droplets and air particles. But since becoming human, I was just transfixed by the colors. Red, orange, pink. Sometimes there would be haunting traces of violet too.

I would sit on the beach, as waves crashed and retreated over the sparkling sand like lost dreams. All those oblivious molecules, joining together, creating something of improbable wonder.

Often such sights were blurred by tears. I felt the beautiful melancholy of being human, captured perfectly in the setting of the sun. Because, as with a sunset, to be human was to be in between things— a day, bursting with desperate color as it headed irreversibly toward night.

One night I stayed sitting on the beach as dusk fell. A forty-something woman walked along, barefooted, with a spaniel and her teenage son. Even though this woman looked quite different from Isobel, and though the son was blond, the sight caused my stomach to flip and my sinuses to loosen.

I realized that six thousand miles could be an infinitely long distance.

"I am *such* a human," I told my espadrilles.

I meant it. Not only had I lost the gifts, emotionally I was as weak as any of them. I thought of Isobel, sitting and reading about Alfred the Great or Carolingian Europe or the ancient Library of Alexandria.

This was, I realized, a beautiful planet. Maybe it was the most beautiful of all. But beauty creates its own troubles. You look at a waterfall or an ocean or a sunset, and you find yourself wanting to share it with someone.

"Beauty—be not caused," said Emily Dickinson. "It is."

In one way she was wrong. The scattering of light over a long distance creates a sunset. The crashing of ocean waves on a beach is created by tides, which are themselves the result of gravitational forces exerted by the sun and the moon and the rotation of the Earth. Those are causes.

The mystery lies in how those things become beautiful.

And they wouldn't have been beautiful once, at least not to my eyes. To experience beauty on Earth, you needed to experience pain and to know mortality. That is why so much that is beautiful on this planet has to do with time passing and the Earth turning. Which might also explain why to look at such natural beauty was to also feel sadness and a craving for a life unlived.

It was this particular kind of sadness that I felt, that evening.

It came with its own gravitational pull, tugging me eastward toward England. I told myself I just wanted to see them again, one last time. I just wanted to catch sight of them from a distance, to see with my own eyes that they were safe.

And, by pure coincidence, about two weeks later I was invited to Cambridge to take part in a series of lectures debating the relationship between mathematics and technology. My head of department, a resilient and jolly fellow called Christos, told me he thought I should go.

"Yes, Christos," I said, as we stood on a corridor floor made of polished pinewood. "I think I might."

When Galaxies Collide

I stayed in student accommodation in Corpus Christi, of all places, and tried to keep a low profile. I had grown a beard now, was tanned, and had put on a bit of weight, so people tended not to recognize me.

I did my lecture.

To quite a few jeers I told my fellow academics that I thought mathematics was an incredibly dangerous territory and that humans had explored it as fully as they could. To advance further, I told them, would be to head into a no-man's-land full of unknown perils.

Among the audience was a pretty red-haired woman who I recognized instantly as Maggie. She came up to me afterward and asked if I'd like to go to the Hat and Feathers. I said no, and she seemed to know I meant it, and after posing a jovial question about my beard, she left the hall.

After that, I went for a walk, naturally gravitating towards Isobel's college.

I didn't go too far before I saw her. She was walking on the other side of the street and she didn't see me. It was strange, the significance of that moment for me and the insignificance of it for her. But then I reminded myself that when galaxies collide, they pass right through.

I could hardly breathe, watching her, and didn't even notice it was beginning to rain. I was just mesmerized by her. All eleven trillion cells of her.

Another strange thing was how absence had intensified my feelings for her. How I craved the sweet everyday reality of just being with her, of having a mundane conversation about how our days had been. The gentle but unbettered comfort of coexistence. I couldn't think of a better purpose for the universe than for her to be in it.

She pulled open her umbrella as if she were just any woman pulling open an umbrella, and she kept on walking, stopping only to give some money to a homeless man with a long coat and a bad leg. It was Winston Churchill.

Home

One can't love and do nothing.
—GRAHAM GREENE, *The End of the Affair*

Knowing I couldn't follow Isobel but feeling a need to connect with someone, I followed Winston Churchill instead. I followed slowly, ignoring the rain, feeling happy I had seen Isobel and that she was alive and safe and as quietly beautiful as she had always been (even when I had been too blind to appreciate this).

Winston Churchill was heading for the park. It was the same park where Gulliver walked Newton, but I knew it was too early in the afternoon for me to bump into them, so I kept following. He walked slowly, pulling his leg along as if it were three times as heavy as the rest of him. Eventually, he reached a bench. It was painted green, this bench, but the paint was flaking off to reveal the wood underneath. I sat down on it too. We sat in rain-soaked silence for a while.

He offered me a swig of his cider. I told him I was okay. I think he recognized me but I wasn't sure.

"I had everything once," he said.

"Everything?"

"A house, a car, a job, a woman, a kid."

"Oh, how did you lose them?"

"My two churches. The betting shop and the bottle. And it's been downhill all the way. And now I'm here with nothing, but I am myself with nothing. An honest bloody nothing."

"Well, I know how you feel."

Winston Churchill looked doubtful. "Yeah. Right you are, fella."

"I gave up eternal life."

"Ah, so you were religious?"

"Something like that."

"And now you're down here sinning like the rest of us."

"Yeah."

"Well, just don't try and touch my leg again and we'll get on fine."

I smiled. He *did* recognize me. "I won't. I promise."

"So, what made you give up on eternity, if you don't mind me askin'?"

"I don't know. I'm still working it out."

"Good luck with that, fella, good luck with that."

"Thanks."

He scratched his cheek and gave a nervous whistle. "Eh, you haven't got any money on you, have you?"

I pulled a ten-pound note out of my pocket.

"You're a star, fella."

"Well, maybe we all are," I said, looking skyward.

And that was the end of our conversation. He had run out of cider and had no more reason to stay. So he stood up and walked away, wincing in pain from his damaged leg, as a breeze tilted flowers toward him.

It was strange. Why did I feel this lack inside me? This need to belong?

The rain stopped. The sky was clear now. I stayed where I was, on a bench covered with slow-evaporating raindrops. I knew it was getting later, and knew I should probably be heading back to Corpus Christi, but I didn't have the incentive to move.

What was I doing here?

What was my function, now, in the universe?

I considered, I considered, I considered, and felt a strange sensation. A kind of sliding into focus.

I realized that, though I was on Earth, I had been living this past year as I had always lived. I was just thinking I could carry on, moving forward. But I was not me anymore. I was a human, give or take. And humans were about change. That is how they survived, by doing and undoing and doing again.

I had done some things I couldn't undo, but there were others I could amend. I had become a human by betraying rationality and obeying feeling. To stay me, I knew there would come a point when I would have to do the same again.

Time passed.

Squinting, I looked again to the sky.

The Earth's sun can look very much alone, yet it has relatives all across this galaxy, stars that were born in the exact same place, but which were now very far away from each other, lighting very different worlds.

I was like a sun.

I was a long way from where I started. And I have changed. Once I thought I could pass through time like a neutrino passes through matter, effortlessly and without stopping to think, because time would never run out.

As I sat there on that bench, a dog came up to me. Its nose pressed into my leg.

"Hello," I whispered, pretending not to know this particular English springer spaniel. But his pleading eyes stayed on me, even as he angled his nose toward his hip. His arthritis had come back. He was in pain.

I stroked him and held my hand in place, instinctively, but of course I couldn't heal him this time.

Then a voice behind me. "Dogs are better than human beings because they know but don't tell."

I turned. A tall boy with dark hair and pale skin and a tentative nervous smile. "Gulliver."

He kept his eyes on Newton. "You were right about Emily Dickinson."

"Sorry?"

"Part of your advice. I read her."

"Oh. Oh yes. She was a very good poet."

He moved around the bench, sat down next to me. I noticed he was older. Not only was he quoting poetry, but his skull had become more man-shaped. There was a slight trace of dark beneath the skin on his jaw. His T-shirt said "The Lost." He had finally joined the band.

If I can stop one heart from breaking, that poet said, *I shall not live in vain.*

"How are you?" I asked, as if he were a casual acquaintance I often bumped into.

"I haven't tried to kill myself, if that's what you mean."

"And how is she?" I asked. "Your mother?"

Newton came over with a stick, dropped it for me to throw. Which I did.

"She misses you."

"Me? Or your Dad?"

"You. You're the one who looked after us."

"I don't have any powers to look after you now. If you chose to jump off a roof, then you'd probably die."

"I don't jump off roofs anymore."

"Good," I said. "That's progress."

There was a long silence. "I think she wants you to come back."

"Does she say that?"

"No. But I think she does."

The words were rain in a desert. After a while I said, in a quiet and neutral tone, "I don't know if that would be wise. It's easy to misunderstand your mother. And even if you haven't gotten it wrong, there could be all kinds of difficulties. I mean, what would she even call me? I don't have a name. It would be wrong for her to call me Andrew." I paused. "Do you think she really misses me?"

He shrugged. "Yeah. I think so."

"What about you?"

"I miss you too."

Sentimentality is another human flaw. A distortion. Another twisted by-product of love, serving no rational purpose. And yet, there was a force behind it as authentic as any other.

"I miss you too," I said. "I miss both of you."

It was evening. The clouds were orange, pink, and purple. Was this what I had wanted? Was this why I had come back to Cambridge?

We talked.

The light faded.

Gulliver attached the lead to Newton's collar. The dog's eyes spoke sad warmth.

"You know where we live," said Gulliver.

I nodded. "Yes. I do."

I watched him leave. The joke of the universe. A noble human, with thousands of days to live. It made no logical sense that I had developed into someone who wanted those days to be as happy and secure for him as they could possibly be, but if you came to Earth looking for logical sense, you were missing the point. You were missing lots of things.

I sat back and absorbed the sky and tried not to understand anything at all. I sat there until it was night. Until distant suns and planets shone above me, like a giant advertisement for better living. On other, more enlightened planets, there was the peace and calm and logic that so often comes with advanced intelligence. I wanted none of it, I realized.

What I wanted was that most exotic of all things. I had no idea if that was possible. It probably wasn't, but I needed to find out.

I wanted to live with people I could care for and who would care for me. I wanted family. I wanted happiness, not tomorrow or yesterday, but now.

What I wanted, in fact, was to go home. So, I stood up.

It was only a short walk away.

Home—is where I want to be
But I guess I'm already there
I come home—she lifted up her wings
Guess that this must be the place.
   —TALKING HEADS, "THIS MUST BE THE PLACE"

Acknowledgments

I first had the idea of writing this story in 2000, when I was in the grips of panic disorder. Back then, human life felt as strange for me as it does for the unnamed narrator. I was living in a state of intense but irrational fear that meant I couldn't even go to a shop—or any-where—on my own without suffering a panic attack. The only thing I could do to gain a degree of calm was read. It was a breakdown of sorts, though as R. D. Laing (and later Jerry Maguire) famously said, breakdown is very often breakthrough, and, weirdly, I don't regret that personal hell now.

I got better. Reading helped. Writing helped also. This is why I became a writer. I discovered that words and stories provided maps of sorts, ways of finding your way back to yourself. I truly believe in the power of fiction to save lives and minds, for this reason. But it has taken me a lot of books to get to this one, the story I first wanted to tell. The one that attempted a look at the weird and often frightening beauty of being human.

So, why the delay? I suppose I needed a bit of distance from the person I had been, because even though the subject matter is far from autobiographical, it felt too personal, maybe because I knew the dark well from where the idea—jokes and all—first came.

The writing proved a joy. In 2000, I imagined writing it for my-self or someone in a similar state. I was trying to offer a map, but also to cheer that someone up. Maybe because the idea had been fermenting so long, the words were all there, and the story came in a torrent.

Not that it didn't need editing. Indeed, never has a story I have written needed editors more, so I am thankful to Francis Bickmore at Canongate in the UK, my US editor Millicent Bennett at Simon & Schuster, Kate Cassaday at HarperCollins Canada, and film producer Tanya Seghatchian, for whom I'm now writing the screenplay.

Thanks also to the other important early eyes on this. They include my agent, Caradoc King, along with Louise Lamont and Elinor Cooper at A P Watt/United Agents.

I am also very lucky to have US publishers who are so committed to my work, and who have paid such attention not only editorially but also in terms of how delicious the book looks. I feel understood! So thank you to everyone at Simon & Schuster who has worked so hard on this book.

And of course Andrea—first reader, first critic, continual editor, and best friend—and Lucas and Pearl, for adding wonder to my daily existence.

Thank you, humans.

About the Author

MATT HAIG is the best-selling author of several children's books and novels, including *The Dead Fathers Club* and *The Radleys,* winner of the ALA Alex Award. His work has been translated into twenty-nine languages, and the film rights to all his novels have been sold. He lives in York and London with his wife, the UK novelist Andrea Semple, and their two children.